Living Right On Wrong Street

Living Right On Wrong Street

Tilus Pollard

www.urbanchristianonline.net

Urban Books
1199 Straight Path
West Babylon, NY 11704

ISBN-13: 978-1-60162-969-2
ISBN-10: 1-60162-969-9

First Printing September 2008
Printed in the United States of America

10 9 8 7 6 5 4 3 2 1

Distributed by Kensington Corp.
Submit Wholesale Orders to:
Kensington Publishing Corp.
C/O Penguin Group (USA) Inc.
Attention: Order Processing
405 Murray Hill Parkway
East Rutherford, NJ 07073-2316
Phone: 1-800-526-0275
Fax: 1-800-227-9604

I'm Taking This Time To Recognize . . .

God, whose son is my Lord and Savior, Jesus the Christ. His life is the perfect story.

My wife and friend, Melissa. You've had to pray and wait while I struggle in spiritual and artistic endeavors. I truly love you.

To my son, Quincy. Never allow anyone or anything hold back your success.

My brothers, Daniel and Joseph, and my sister, Lily. My mother-in-law, Nell, my sisters-in-law, Sundae and Sandy. My nieces and nephews: Tamiko, Akima, Adrian, Janell, Jeremy, Dominique, Christian, and Marcello. Joe's friend, Sabrina. I love each of you.

A very special dedication to both of my parents and father-in-law, all who have gone on to be with the Lord, Fletcher and Arlivia Pollard, and Gene Huntspon.

My agent, Kim Matthews. Thanks for keepin' it real. Your techniques must work, because I'm published!

My editor, Joylynn Jossel. I'm already looking forward to the next novel under your direction.

My mentor, Jacquelin Thomas. Your prayers and push have added the title "Author" to my resume.

The New Vision Writer's group. Remember to plan your work, work your plan.

Four women who are my 'sisters,' friends, and readers: Linda, Tara, Terrance, and Toya. Thanks for your encouragement and assistance in helping me understand the meaning of a good story.

My pastor, Daniel Sanders, and Springfield Baptist

Church in Raleigh. I know that nothing in life works without true spiritual guidance.

To anyone who knows they're important to me, but I left you out: I love you. Charge it to my head and not to my heart! TP

My Story before the Story

Job here. I'm trying to tell you a few things for your own good, so you need to give a listen.

I've had setbacks before, but nothing compared to the time that I moved my family to Phoenix, Arizona's Resi'Stanz Subdivision; 2333 Rong Street. Mercy, Jesus. If only I had the power to delete portions of my life.

I can tell that you're anxious to see how my story played out. And to tell the truth, I'm just as anxious for you. But I'm not givin' out any secrets. You have to read and experience it for yourself.

After you've finished reading, crying, laughing, or whatever you do when you put yourself in someone else's shoes, remember that the same life situations can very well happen to you if you get stubborn, you fail in listening to God, or you operate under the belief that, no matter how you live, it will have a positive outcome.

Oh well. Consider yourself warned.

God Bless.

Rewind.

Chapter 1

Ye shall not steal, neither deal falsely, neither lie one to another. Leviticus 19:11 KJV

Have you ever been convicted of a crime, whether misdemeanor or felony, other than speeding tickets or minor traffic violations? Job read. He sighed, realizing that his soul had brought the truth of the question to light.

Desperation overwhelmed better judgment. He clicked his mechanical pencil a couple times and then checked the box labeled 'No.' He blinked, hoping to clear the guilt from his mind and the fatigue from his eyes.

"Joseph Bertram Wright, lunch is almost ready, so you need to start making your way downstairs now! If you don't, everything's going in the fridge—after I fix my plate," Monica shouted from the kitchen.

"Be down in a minute, honey," Job sounded back.

Monica was the only person who would call him by his full name. His wife would spill out his first, middle, and last names when she was in certain moods. It wasn't a good thing.

To Job, a shortened name was much easier to say, more succinct. He didn't want to be called Joe. That sounded thuggish, and he wasn't the type. Bertram had Old-

English flair, and he was far removed from any semblance of British aristocracy. Monica had told him on more occasions than he could count that a Biblical character named Job was described as a good man with enough earthly possessions to take care of his family. He believed that Job was the appellation that best fit his persona.

"How long do you think you'll be?" Monica asked her husband.

Job didn't answer back. Reason one was that she had startled him. Reason two: well, he just knew there had to be another reason.

He wasn't intentionally delaying his trek to dinner. An aromatic combination of Chipotle, fresh salsa, ground chuck, paprika, and Monterey Jack teased his nostrils. He recognized Tex-Mex, his favorite cuisine: that flavorful combo whose name was derived from the second largest state in the union and the country just south of its border.

But at that moment, Job didn't need to divert his attention from the task at hand. Monica's impatience and lunch would just have to wait.

Time worked against him with every pass of the second hand. He glimpsed at the wall calendar, compliments of Kenyon's Auto Body Shop. May 17, 2000. Paradise Public Schools of suburban Phoenix had supplied the employment documents over three weeks ago. Job needed to have them postmarked for that day, because the cover letter stated there would be no exceptions. He shook his head and breathed, feeling that he was always being overwhelmed with dates. He had put off completing the forms until there was no more time to waste. He had taken pains to have, if he were ever asked, an excellent explanation for such procrastination: recent life-altering episodes.

They spawned from his dissolved realty partnership, Wright & Storm of Louisville. The firm was born in 1995 as a result of Job's lifelong dream of bearing his personal imprint on the heading of a corporate paycheck. The business struggled along until 1998, when they had more than twenty-five million in residential and commercial sales. In that same year, he and his partner graced the covers of the *National Association of Realtors* and *Black Enterprise* magazines. He accepted invitations from all over the country for speaking engagements, radio and television appearances, establishing himself as a renowned personality in the financial world.

He'd done pretty well, he thought, for a poor kid from Country Music Town, USA. He purchased 4213 Lakespur Drive, more than 4,900 opulent square feet on the city's northwest side, as his personal residence. Against his tax consultant's advice, he made a 60% down payment on the million dollar property and financed the remainder. He purchased cars with cash. Every fiscal quarter for a year and a half, he spent his income amassing more than a reasonable portion of assets, believing that the "money well" ran deep and had no bottom.

Then, as his coming-into-the-new-millennium gift, or someone's idea of a bad joke, he became a tail on the spin. Life events unfurled in rapid speed. And all over, at least Job figured, some unnecessary mess.

On the morning of January 6, 2000, Job sat in his office sipping a frappuccino and sharing future ideas with Delvin Storm, his partner in the firm and a classmate from Syracuse University where they had both majored in business administration. Upon Job's insistence, Delvin, a New York native, moved to Louisville, attended real estate school and added his name to the firm in early 1996.

They were busy enjoying a joke one of their clients had emailed them, when the Kentucky Real Estate Commission knocked on their door.

"We can't let them in," Delvin replied nervously.

"Why not?"

"It's no telling what they want."

"Be for real," Job said. He had a fleeting thought that some jealous broker from a competing agency was trying to thrust the firm out of business. But it was a fleeting thought, nothing more. Believing that the company's finances were in order, Job invited the commission into their offices with confidence.

Much to his chagrin, when the investigators audited the trust bank account files, they found evidence that their books had been cooked.

Job wondered how that could've happened. He was the broker-in-charge, debiting and crediting the account in earnest, to the best of his ability. When the commission questioned if anyone other than himself had access to that particular set of funds, he responded, "No. Well, actually, my partner makes deposits on my behalf sometimes."

Delvin Storm was behind it all? Job was aware that his partner engaged in questionable financial tactics, to which he chose not to be privy or, even to present-day, inform a soul that he knew. But he had trouble believing that his partner had robbed funds from accounts that rightfully belonged to the firm once a pending realty transaction was consummated.

The realty commission staked their reputations on relentlessness when they suspected trust funds had been mishandled. It was just a matter of nailing the culprit.

And it was Delvin who became the main specimen under their examination. They questioned, cajoled, and then accused. They locked down the business, revoking its license and both Job's and Delvin's individual broker licenses. They detained files. They halted personal, trust, and operating bank account activities until further notice. Ninety days later, the verdict was rendered.

Guilty.

Delvin had fraudulently misrepresented trust account monies for his personal use to the tune of $1,237,980.00. Racketeering charges were added to that, and he was sentenced to ten years in a correctional institution, with parole eligibility in three.

On the day before he was to report to prison, Delvin requested a meeting with Job.

Job was reluctant to have a one-on-one, fearing that harm may come his way. Delvin had demonstrated an uncharacteristic hostility throughout the trial, and his refusal to disclose the subject of the upcoming meeting fueled Job's suspicion that if Delvin would steal, he was also capable of killing.

Despite Monica's insistence that he should decline, Job consented to a public meeting with his defunct partner at The Oakroom, an exclusive Louisville restaurant.

Job's remembrance of that dismal meeting was as vivid as a sunny day was clear. He surveyed the room, mapping out an escape route just in case—

They sat among the customers who had come for fun and upscale cuisine. They didn't eat a meal. The tab for the overpriced water, of which Delvin drank bottle after bottle, was dependent upon Job's wallet.

Delvin didn't shift sitting positions by a single degree during the entire ninety minute meeting. He started the conversation with, "I get the shaft and you, you . . . get away a free man, huh?"

The shadow of the room was yet an illumination compared to Delvin's haunting form. It was a struggle for Job to keep his composure. He did not, in their last face to face meeting for a long time, want to appear to Delvin as clay—malleable against a criminal's evocative persona.

Delvin told Job, "Nobody gets rich by being honest."

"Maybe."

"And getting rich is something you wanted as badly as I did. You can't deny it."

Job ran the fine hem of the tablecloth between his fingers. "I still want wealth, but I'm not willing to do something illegal to get it."

Delvin was annoyed by Job's comment. "You're a real piece of work, a very real piece of work," Delvin said. He cut his eyes toward a corner of the room, and then he brought them back around to Job. "Who's guiltier? The man who dips in the cookie jar or the man that the cookie is shared with?"

Job wasn't answering the trick question.

Delvin said, "When that automated truck wash facility sold with that big shot Oklahoma realtor as the exclusive, we took a fifty percent share of the nearly quarter million in commission."

Job didn't know where the explanation was leading. "So?"

"Humph." Delvin paused and lit a cigarette. "So, Oklahoma and Kentucky have no reciprocity agreement among their realtors. After the sale, to keep from complicating things, I requested our cut of the commission in cash. That money never passed through our trust account, only into the operating funds. And you knew how it was going to go down the whole time."

"Not from the beginning, I didn't." Job fumed in embarrassment. His probe into the lawfulness of that transaction had been sloppy. He had taken Delvin's word and work at face value. But even that money had been confiscated, along with countless dollars from countless transactions.

"I can go on with another story. If you want me to, if you really need to hear some more examples . . ." Delvin's vile soliloquy seemed to fade on Job's ears, but not in his mind.

Delvin was right. Every occurrence happened right under Job's watch. Although he didn't receive prison time for any criminal act, he had turned a blind eye and benefited financially. His punishment, in addition to the liquidation of his personal and business assets, was a permanent loss of his Kentucky brokerage license, a suspended three year sentence for negligence, and a twenty-five thousand dollar fine.

It had now been one month since Job's most dreaded day. Three weeks, four days, and nine hours ago, the final gavel had dropped. Though the realty commission's and criminal court's pronouncement didn't put him behind bars, Job had a feeling he had not yet realized the fullness of what had actually occurred.

Job decided that another career, another location, and new people were needed to regain order in his and Monica's lives.

He picked up a pen and placed it between his teeth as he examined the last document. Depending on the question, Job marked *Yay*, *Nay*, or *N/A*, scrawled his signature on the documents and shoved them into the SASE provided.

"What's taking so long? I hope you're packing that office," Monica shouted.

He looked around and said nothing.

Two rooms needed major attention: the kitchen and his office. When they first put the house on the market, Monica told him that she would take care of the kitchen. It was one of the last areas that needed to be packed. They did, after all, have to eat.

The office, though, was her worry and his responsibility.

Would the packing ever get done? His eyes danced across the rows and columns of books still sitting on the shelves. Self-help and how-to, novels, African-American diaspora, Bible commentaries. A stack of U-haul boxes were over in a remote corner, yet to be put together. Packing tape was lying dormant on the desk. "Oh my God," Job said when he spotted the paperwork for the yet-unfiled '99 taxes. Thank goodness he had been granted an extension. There was too much work to do.

He jumped up, bumping his knee against the edge of the Riverside desk. "Mercy," he scolded himself. The resulting twinge reminded him of a previous high school football injury. "I'm coming down right now," Job called out to Monica as he hobbled down the stairs with the Paradise School's employment package in hand. He ambled into the kitchen doorway, his bones and muscles protesting against the sudden movement.

"It's about time. Are you ready for dinner?" Monica asked.

"Hurt my leg. Not watching what I was doin.' "

"Um hm." Monica curled her mouth, which reflected an abnormality in her thoughts.

Now Monica was 'The Package,' but the reverse of how Job thought most packages he'd met were wrapped. Most men, even the Christian ones, began their love pursuits based on an outside-in process—what they saw, how she looked. To Job, Monica's attractiveness was inside-out; she was most powerful by what she thought and how she spoke. Her words could chain him, break him at the knees. Then, when she finally allowed his mouth to pucker, his glands to drench, and his loins to strengthen, he wasted no time getting her to the altar for a ring presentation.

Job took a spoon, dipped it in the refried beans, blew on them, and tasted. "This is great."

Monica moved the pan out of his reach. "You need to hold off putting that in your mouth until we've prayed."

Job ignored Monica's reprimand. "This food is reminding me of Phoenix."

"Everything reminds you of Phoenix. Food doesn't make me act all crazy like that."

"Well, it's better than the tastes of Louisville."

"What do you mean?"

"Living here. Can't you smell it?" Job whiffed. "Horse manure mixed with Mint Juleps." He grinned at Monica in hopes that she would make a comment about his stale joke. He placed the employment package on the kitchen counter and then looked at Monica, who was busy stirring pots. "You were calling me like the food was ready."

Monica looked over her shoulder. "I thought you were upstairs packing. What were you working on?"

Job held up the envelope. "Some last minute changes."

"Changes?" she paused. "I thought you had sent that off a couple weeks ago."

"Calm down. It's going in today's mail. Now c'mon," he said.

Monica's face changed in a way that struck fear. "Today's mail, huh?" she asked.

"Um hm."

"How is that going to happen? Job, the mail has already run, hours ago. Please take care of business, please. I don't want you to lose the job before you even get it."

Her statement resounded in his head. The court sentencing and loss of the business were the start of his trouble, and he needed the new career for more than a self-esteem boost. Paradise Schools just *had* to grant him this job.

They were living on one income and couldn't afford the mortgage, so they had to sell the house well below market value. Fortunately, their cars were paid off and saved from repossession. Friends and business associates purchased most of their extensive art collection, giving them necessary emergency funds. He had been so pre-occupied with nurturing a lifestyle that he had failed to save any money, even though Monica had urged him to slow the spending.

"I'm not going to let you down," Job told her.

Monica had finished preparing two plates of food and filled a couple of glasses with iced tea.

"I believe you'll do your best." She grabbed his hand. "But right now we need to pray for our meal, and ask God to continue to guide our future." Monica closed her eyes.

Job shut his eyes, but he didn't feel like offering any words up to the Lord. As far as he was concerned, Monica was only half right. His actions alone would deter-mine their future. God was a figure-head for Sunday worship, not an immortal to lean on for life direction.

Monica opened her eyes. "I'm searching in Phoenix for a job myself. Just a back-up, you know what I mean?" She sounded almost apologetic.

Job would've felt better had he been able to tell Monica that her job searching wouldn't be necessary and that his income would be sufficient. But he had been forced from a six-figure range down to—if the teaching position was given to him—the middle five figures. He pulled at the edges of the postal package. "Hey, honey," he said, "let me ask you something . . ."

Monica paused and turned to him. "Hmm?"

"Are you happy with our move?" he asked.

"I love the west and Phoenix is beautiful. It's an excel-lent opportunity for both of us." She sighed and looked Job square in the eyes. "If we don't foul it up."

His thoughts lingered on the falsified employment ap-plication. He wondered just how Monica would react if she had all the facts about what had caused the realty firm's dissolve. He had to keep certain details buried from then to eternity. "I just want to know how you feel, that's all."

Monica squinted, as though she was assessing Job from head to toe. "Stop racking your brain over how I feel," she told him. "I'm okay."

Monica would, after all, be closer to her roots with the move. She was born in Nevada as part Lovelock Paiute, part Italian, and part African-American. He had landed himself a multi-cultural woman. But at a quick glimpse, most would simply say, *Black*. He glanced at his plate, noticing that it was paper.

"So I guess you've packed the real stuff," he said as he gathered the last bites of food.

"If it makes you feel any better," she tapped an empty dish, "know that it's Chinet, not just any paper plate. I've packed most of the real china, which is more than I can say for you. You do understand that the closing, c-l-o-s-i-n-g, is in two weeks?"

"Please don't remind me. I know we've really gotta step up and find a house."

"I'm waiting on your lead."

Job assured Monica that he had talked to a relocation specialist about certain subdivisions inside and outside of Phoenix's city limits, and a list of potential houses would be emailed to them in a couple of days. "Remember, this is my expertise."

After silence thickened the air for a moment's time, Monica said, "I don't want God taking His hand off us like He did a few months ago."

Job stopped eating and glared. "God has nothing to do with any of the things that happened, good or bad. If we do what we're supposed to do, we'll be able to see our way again. Clearly."

* * *

It was on the following day that Job packed and emptied the home office. Monica rewarded him that evening with hours of physical love that had been withheld until he had done what she had been begging him to do.

The master suite was bare except for their makeshift bed of a bedspring with a mattress. A bowl of leftover kiwi was at her feet with lavender scented candles marking the four corners of the room. Remnants of his Fahrenheit cologne adorned her nostrils. The last track of Grover Washington's *Winelight* CD reminded her that the portable player was still on.

Job was the first to rise out of bed about 6:00 A.M., Wednesday. Monica's eyes traced up his spine to the neck and head she had rubbed just hours earlier, so smooth from his fresh, bald-fade cut. Monica weakened at the sight of his glistening black physique.

When Job had retreated into the bathroom and closed the door, she buried her head into the pillow, wishing and praying to God that their family would someday increase by at least one. They had been married for seven years, and it was time.

She had done all the proper things. She had checked the calendar against her rhythm, her ovulation phase. On occasion, she fed Job appetizers of oysters on the half shell. She had taken the physician prescribed vitamins. A child would make her feel complete.

Job returned to the bedroom, settled himself onto the mattress, and started nibbling on Monica's ear.

She whiffed his citrus fresh breath. "What do you call yourself doing? You know I've got to get ready for work." She backed her body into his, enveloping herself against his contours, but they were interrupted by the phone.

Job reached over and answered the phone. Monica

was glad. If she had answered, whoever was on the other end would have heard the irritation in her voice.

His phone responses were a vague series of *Umm hmms, uh huhs, oh, okay, yes I can do that*. The first coherent sentence from his mouth was, "Thanks so much, Mr. Mc-Manus. We'll see you next week."

Job made some notes on a pad by the bedside stand. Then he got off the bed, walked over to the bathroom doorway, and reached inside. He wrapped himself in a towel and leaned against the wall. "That was Paradise Valley Schools. They received my application and want to interview me for a high school teaching position. I have an appointment with the assistant superintendent next Friday. Let's fly out next Thursday evening."

Monica felt a glint of relief. The sale of their Louisville home on June 9 coupled with the fact that neither she nor Job had secured a job in Arizona made her uncomfortable with their plans. The forced liquidation of the firm followed by the fire sale of their residence netted them about ninety thousand to live off of as they made their transition out west. Job's assurance of, "Don't worry, I'll find a new niche," had her confident when he first said it a couple months ago, but she had an honesty meeting with herself since then, and her poise had begun to wane.

"Do you think it's possible for us to fly out next Wednesday evening?" Monica asked.

"What for, honey?"

"While we're there, we can spend time looking at houses." Monica sat up. "I have a job prospect. There's one particular position available in Scottsdale that I think I qualify for. They want me to interview, so it's perfect timing. I can do it next week."

"So you've done a little more than a brief search." Job was far from jubilant. Yesterday, he figured that if he ignored the subject of house searching, that it would roll over and die.

"Even if we had a million dollars I'd still work, if nothing else but for sanity's sake. The position's at Nine Iron Resorts as a reservations manager. I didn't commit to an interview until we had concrete dates for flying out there."

Job's lips pursed and there was a nerve-curdling look on his face. "It would be better to know you didn't have to work, but I guess we need it. Anyhow, I wasn't really sure my initial application would go through. Their routine background check had me concerned."

Monica was already panicky with Job's apathy about the postal deadline for his employment documents. He never failed to drop bad news on her after lovemaking. Despite her reluctance, she asked, "Why?"

In fractions of a second, Job's skin went from a parched to a drenched canvas. "I, I told them I didn't h-have a criminal record."

Monica wasn't sure which of her emotions was sprouting. There wasn't an adequate response to what she'd just been told.

"Technically, I don't have a record," Job said with a hailstorm of defensiveness in his voice. "I didn't steal the money. I wasn't the one who went to prison. Baby, you've got to trust me on this. Not bringing it up was the better thing to do."

The more Job spoke, the more Monica's neck tightened and her sight fogged. She jerked the top sheet up above her shoulders as she sat upright on the mattress. "So you made up something and lied? Joseph Bertram Wright. We won't make it through life in any kind of decent shape like this. Trust you? You should have trusted God and told the truth."

"If I'd done it your way, there's a great chance I wouldn't

have gotten the job." He moved over to her and sat on the bed. "Monica, it's not doing anybody any harm. Leave it alone, please."

She felt dizzy, hoping that he was about to admit the joke, but his punch line never came. "How in the world did they do a background check and nothing came up?" she asked.

Job shook his head. "I don't know. And don't you go stirring up anything," he said.

"I'll be sure to keep some boxes packed when we get to Phoenix because the tables are sure to turn on us." She felt tears surfacing. "Now I know I need to keep a job."

Job sucked his teeth. "Whatever."

"Shake me off if you want to, man. Things won't be right until you show some honesty. Mark my word."

Job rose off the mattress and checked his towel. "I didn't lie. I just didn't tell them everything."

"Character's a big part of this new career you call yourself pursuing," she said. "I wonder if you'll want your business students to be truthful."

"This has nothing to do with my effectiveness as a teacher." Job stomped off to the bathroom. He might as well have. Anything else that morning would've been wasted words.

Monica made it to her Louisville job, the marketing firm of Cavin & Kross, later that morning. She had hoped that her day would be filled with tearful good-byes, well wishes, going away gifts and such. Instead, she went on a quest for answers. She phoned their family attorney, Wendy Axford, and left a message. Wendy returned the call after lunch, around 1:30. Their schedules prevented them from meeting, so Monica had to be satisfied with stating her concerns via telephone.

"All he had to do was mark 'Yes' on the form and say

that the culprit was behind bars," she told Wendy. "He could've given a written explanation of his negligence on the application. I thought he understood that when you counseled him after the trial."

Wendy confirmed her belief. "The main reason schools have criminal background checks is to weed out violent felons, child molesters, DUI, and drug offenders."

"But how is it that the conviction didn't show up in their check? At least, I don't guess it did. Come to think of it, Job didn't mention it, so, I'm assuming."

"I'm stabbing in the dark, because I don't know Arizona's procedures and statutes. It differs from state to state."

"What's your best guess?" Monica asked.

"The case results apparently haven't been entered into the database. It's only been thirty days since the judgment was rendered. His timing was lucky."

"Or blessed," Monica said. "I imagine if I convince Job to call Paradise Schools and ask to correct his app, they would do it."

"I wouldn't make a call. I wouldn't try to make things right with the district. Monica, I wouldn't do a thing."

"Why not?"

"If he's already lied on the application and they're considering him for the job, I wouldn't try to undo it. That's definite grounds to take back their job offer. My advice is that you leave it alone in hopes that this school district never finds out the truth, and that when they do, it's so far into his career that they won't care."

"You're telling me that in the future this can come back to haunt us?" Monica asked.

"Truthfully? It could haunt you in the worst way."

Chapter 2

And they shall be gathered together as prisoners are gathered in the pit. Isaiah 24:22a

Delvin Storm was in a tight spot. He had never been to a place like this before. The guards had locked the prison doors behind him, but he wasn't thinking about literal, geographical, touch the ground with your fingers kind of places.

His surroundings had already formed a print in his mind. Oil slick, gun-barrel gray walls. Heavy-gauge metal furniture, bolted down with screws larger than those found in the average toolbox. Yellow lines were painted on the floors of hallways. Ammonia mixed with urine, marijuana, and blood. What he could touch, see, taste, and smell was the dream. His mental picture gave him a reality.

He was fresh felon fodder; he was in Ashland Minimum Security Facility looking like an international playboy. He was in that spot for a dime, receiving day-to-day schoolings on his new life from strange acquaintances. He saw a lot of people around, but nobody he felt he could trust. A decade—thirty-six months with an early parole—was a long time for everyone to be his enemy.

"Get used to the grub, 'cause it ain't getting no better," a booming voice declared with uncanny mysticism.

"Humph," Delvin grunted, refusing to look up to see who had made the statement. He focused on his meal. Quick-fix potatoes right out of the cardboard packaging, pork and beans with that recognizable generic aftertaste and cold, processed chicken dogs in discount bakery buns. For dessert, he had fruit cocktail with too many peaches and not enough cherries. He yearned for deliverance from the worst food he had ever tasted.

"You hard o' hearing?" asked another voice.

Delvin nodded up and down and side to side. He figured all it would take is one faulty verbal move, and an exploding light bulb or a shank in the back could be his fate. A nod in no particular direction was safe for the moment.

"I guess the cat's got his tongue, huh fellas?" asked the booming voice whose resonance cut far above the others in the eating hall.

His eyes shifted to the loudmouth, Caucasian, gargantuan figure with the cropped haircut and sleeveless shirt. He had the guy—he silently nicknamed him Pectorals—figured out from jump street. Pectorals was trying to be the don of FCI-Ashland. Delvin wasn't afraid of the guy, and no one else seemed to be either.

"Whatcha in for, huh?" Pectorals boomed.

Delvin brushed his fingertips across his forehead, remaining speechless. *Good question. Not a hard one, but good.*

"Man, you don't say a word, do ya?" The guy continued to chide.

Delvin heard talking, but he interpreted it as reverberations, not real words. There was too much on his mind to entertain needless conversation. Since Pectorals couldn't help him get paroled, they had nothing to discuss.

"Hey," he said, spitting as he spoke, "I guess you're deaf."

"Naw, man, that ain't it," another man spoke up. "Looks to me like he just don't talk to nobody."

Delvin took a peripheral look at this man, named him Saks, as in Fifth Avenue. The guy was as white as a sheet, with a contrasting mop of red hair, neatly placed. He had sleeves on his shirt, but had chosen to roll and crease them as a personal fashion statement.

Pectorals said, "I guess he's our new Mr. Uppity."

"Leave him alone," Saks said. "We were all uppity at one time or another. We all wore Hickey Freeman's with custom-made tab collars, barrel cuffs starched n' pressed by the locals. That's why they call us white-collar cons."

Sporadic laughter consumed the mess hall. Delvin searched and found no humor.

He had the criminal and personality profiles of specific men fixed into his mental Rolodex. He glanced at the securities fraud expert sitting next to the European portrait fencer. The U.S. Treasury counterfeiter stood against the west wall chatting with the mass copyright infringement specialist; big-time, money-making criminals, and he was among them. He could have, at any moment, opened his mouth and told his life history, but he figured that the less known, the better shown.

"I can't figure you out. I ain't trying to make you my ace-duce; just letting you know that prison time is a mutha, and I'm hear to listen, 'n case you need an ear," Pectorals continued.

"Get off him, Stinson. You see he's on the new and doesn't wanna talk," Saks insisted.

Delvin locked in on what Saks had just said; Pectorals's real name was Stinson.

"Shucks, he can't keep silent the whole time in here. He'll talk . . . eventually," Stinson said.

Delvin reasoned that truer words couldn't have been spoken, but the when, where, and how to his bio would have his seal of approval before it was disseminated.

"Prison life makes you do and think funny things. You're right, dude, I know he'll talk. Maybe sooner, maybe later."

Delvin determined he would make it later. He traced the cuticles of his manicured hand, thinking how quickly he had learned to improvise a nail tech's instrument from a plastic knife and paper clips, and the damage it could do to a loudmouth instigator.

"Gotta name?" Stinson asked.

Delvin hung on to his lip.

"Hey, man," Stinson said. "Givin' your name ain't gon' kill you."

Delvin gripped his plastic spoon as a weapon, but it gave way as he attacked a dig of pork and beans. He imagined his less than fourth class rations as Hollandaise sauce, filet mignon, or chicken cordon bleu, but his taste buds wouldn't cooperate. He gulped his Kool-Aid, the air from his nostrils fogging his plastic cup.

Stinson moved closer, narrowing Delvin's personal space. "That's right. Getting to ya, ain't it? Got some freedom—but you ain't really got none. Maybe now and then you get some homemade mash or a bale from the commissary. Spa membership gone, but at least you're here with us at the Cross-bar Hilton." He nodded and laughed with the slickness of a bull. "Like I said a while ago, get used to it."

Delvin felt turbulence in the declaration. *Show nothing, say nothing*, he reminded himself.

"I know some things, many things," a slim, slew-footed, asphalt-black inmate spouted off in a low tone, through-the-teeth. "Information, that's what's up. Dangerous thing, information. Can be used for a multiplicity of ideas, theories, end-results and goals. Power's in the hands and minds of those who have it. It's suicide for those who don't."

Delvin felt a chill of exposure from the hand of an inmate with whom he had not made acquaintance. That non-entity was preparing to dispel his name, his being. He struggled to hinder the inmate from speaking any further, but nothing came to mind that wouldn't yield a regrettable consequence.

"Storm," spoke the nameless voice.

"Huh?" asked Saks.

"Storm," he repeated. "Still working on the first name, but Storm is his last." He turned to Delvin. "Isn't that your label, your given, the tag below the family crest?"

Delvin's heartbeat raced, and his temples throbbed. Determined not to let any other information leak, he lunged forward and gripped his shirt. "You got any other information you want to share about me?"

"Storm," another inmate acknowledged, "What's he in for, Murphy?"

Delvin heard the real name. He decided to tag the imprisoned Encyclopedia Brown with another label. "Yeah, SOB, what am I in for?"

Murphy twisted his body in an attempt to break loose of the grip. "I don't know," he said. "My sources can't be revealed, but they do come with the assurance of 100% reliability."

More guards were ordered to mess hall.

Delvin ripped Murphy's collar, but hung on. "Let me assure you of this. I don't want people knowing about me. See to it, or you're a dead man. You got it?"

Murphy nodded, failing to speak.

Loose tongues and investigations. That's what landed him in this hellhole, and he dared this man to intimidate him another minute.

Prison guards dashed from their posts as inmates scattered like children in a playground scuffle.

"Beat your feet!" one of the guards demanded.

The room was filled with the simultaneous sounds of batons drumming iron tables, lunch trays banging against walls, handcuffs clanging belt buckles and voices trimming open air.

A battery of guards took hold of Delvin and carried him off to confinement as they quelled the disturbance. As they rushed him through the block, a tall, African-American inmate with a Holy Qur'ân in hand said, "God must clear our hearts and minds of evil."

If the guard had given Delvin opportunity, he would have told the book-carrying inmate that there was no God in there.

A week had gone by. The smell of the prison library was unique: the pungency of masculine sweat, the dankness of grimy books, and the vacuity of cold steel amid sticky concrete.

In that 20 x 25 room, makeshift inmate attorneys hammered out cases for their paroles and appeals. Many spent all of their free time submerging their craniums into one hardback, then another.

Delvin weaved in and out of the rows of books eyeing the titles and holding some in his mind for later checkout. He had a strong notion that this was the very place he could enjoy a respite from inmates seeking out the fine details of his résumé. Or so he thought.

"So . . . you made it out of Siberia, huh, newbie?"

Stinson was like a stink that he couldn't be rid of. He had come from around a corner, slightly startling Delvin, but not enough to break his silence.

Stinson grunted. "You're too ornery for the hole to break

you. I don't see how you made it through that seven-day blickum looking halfway fit, considering all they give you is one square a day."

Delvin thought about the ease of choking that mess down once a day rather than three times a day. As far as he was concerned, Siberia had been a vacation.

"What made you crazy in the mess hall, man? We thought you were gonna kill Murphy. He couldn't do certain things on the toilet for about four days after that."

Delvin had hoped his stunt scared Murphy. He wasn't going to kill him, just make him think twice before spreading information.

Stinson pulled a toothpick out of his breast pocket, scraped it between his teeth, and nestled it back into the pocket. "He ain't said nothing else about you to anybody. And to shut him up that's a lot. You need to chill, though. You're gonna need a friend in this place." He snickered. " 'Cause the only time you'll want to be alone is when you masturbate."

Delvin glared up at Stinson. His prison mate didn't know that he adored opportunities to be alone.

Annoyed with his unwelcome shadow, Delvin walked over to the newspaper rack, a wooden contraption with half-moon slots holding reed dowel sticks. Each of the twenty-some dowels held an edition of *Washington Post*, *Atlanta Journal-Constitution*, *New York Times*, and other state, regional, and local papers. He picked up a copy of the *Courier-Journal*, hoping that Stinson would be able to decode his *buddy talk is over* signal. It didn't work.

"You probably get better stock market info from the *Wall Street Journal*, big shot," Stinson said.

Delvin heard him, but offered no response. His eyes did a quick read of the articles on the upcoming Juneteenth observances and the Louisville arrest statistics per capita, but halted on a small notice in the Real Estate Transfers:

Joseph B. & Monica Wright to Nathan & Edwina
Robinson, 4213 N. Lakespur Dr., June 2, $565,950.

He reread that section of the paper like the Cliff notes for an SAT exam question. His muscles contracted. Internal eruptions threw all his body functions off-base. Job Wright had sold his home for a fresh start; there Delvin was, standing still and going nowhere fast. His conscience wanted Job Wright dead. Delvin slowly and methodically ripped the newspaper to pieces, until they were smaller than if they'd been run through an electric shredder. He swept them off the table onto the floor.

"Storm," a guard said, pounding his baton into his massive fists, "you better have that cleaned up before you leave. Do it!"

"What's wrong with you, Storm? Are you trying to go back in the hole? You'll be in solitude for a month next time. These guards are crazy, man. Calm down," Stinson said.

Delvin looked around and saw that a few more guards and some nosy inmates had congregated in the library. He began placing the scraps in the garbage.

Stinson bent down beside Delvin and helped to gather up the scraps. He whispered, "Don't let the Ashland fool you. Minimum security doesn't mean they've got their backs turned. They'd find your silver-haired butt in these Kentucky hills blindfolded."

"Nobody's thinking about escape."

Stinson brushed his fingertips on his forehead. "I

know what your problem is. It's coming to me," he said, as if he was clairvoyant.

Delvin rose out of his seat, determined not to be disturbed any further. What he imagined was far from anything they could speculate.

Delvin sat in his cell, realizing that he had spent more time in solitary than in his personal space. For his library exploit a few hours ago, he was ordered to the 30-day task of dishwashing duty in hopes that he would, according to the warden, "Learn to do positive things with those bones and muscles."

He sat on his bunk, an iron object welded to the wall with a generic mattress less than three inches thick, with his head buried in his hands. Delvin screened out the random hollering that rung out into the dead space of the three-story cell block. He garnered more hostility toward Job and the past events that had landed him in his present situation.

He stood, kicked the bowl of his stainless steel toilet-paper holder-sink combo, and walked over to the metallic square on the wall that posed as a mirror. Delvin peered into it. Maybe he would see that he was dreaming or that his release had been sped up by several days or years.

His tan was gone and his chiseled facial features had withered. He needed an exfoliating treatment. His Clark Gable mustache was in need of a clipping, and his salt-and pepper hair warranted a trim. All forms of enjoyment were gone. No Porsche, Victorian home, designer clothes, or blushing women begging his bidding.

Reality was taking its hold, as though the mirror became an analyst, telling Delvin that his own actions had reduced him to this dilemma. But he refused to be swayed. As he looked back on particular incidents, all of the blame couldn't be placed on him . . .

He couldn't help but ask himself how Job was making out.

"Maybe next time you should read something that won't make you want to rip it up. Try this," said the voice at the doorway of his cell.

Delvin looked away from the mirror and stared the talking head down.

The man couldn't have been any more than five feet five, about one hundred forty pounds, with a hairline that had withdrawn from the crest of his dome. Wax was where hair had been. His face was ranch-dressing white, his expression was calm and his demeanor somewhat inviting.

"Here, take this," the man said, tossing Delvin a Gideon New Testament that was palm-sized with a Hunter green pleather cover. It flew between the bars, landing on the bunk. "My name's Shiloh Kimmons, the prison chaplain."

"You mean—"

"Yeah, something like that."

Delvin was going to call him the prison's God lunatic. "Who asked you to come see me?"

"No one has to ask—the first time. Most people here don't know to ask because they don't believe they need someone greater than themselves. So, I'll come the first time. After that, it's up to you." Shiloh pointed to the Bible. "Read it and let the words stir your mind. And if you want, we'll talk later . . . if you want."

Delvin sighed in bitterness.

"Mr. Storm, you'll never find in the Bible where Jesus ever ran after a person, forcing them to accept what He had to say. His words are a light. And what better place to come to the light than in prison?"

"The warden said the same thing."

"The warden's talking about his authority. What I'm talking about isn't in the same league, and you know it."

Shiloh's words brewed inside Delvin. He was convinced that the chaplain was at least worthy enough to break his silence. "I'll get back to ya."

"Remember that the Word doesn't need you, Mr. Storm. You need it."

Delvin watched Shiloh walked off in a slow, almost inaudible pace until he was out of sight. Inside his cell, midway between the mirror and the Bible, the atmosphere engulfed his flesh. He felt as though a decision was being squeezed out of him.

All consciousness moved to Delvin's legs; they no longer belonged to him. In the prison's darkness, he moved toward the Bible.

Chapter 3

Man goeth forth unto his work and to his labor until the evening. Psalms 104:23

On the following Friday, Job sat in the Paradise Valley School District's office, awaiting his opportunity for a final interview and decision from the Human Resources department.

Monica announced, during dinner the evening before, that Nine Iron Golf and Resorts had hired her as reservations manager.

After twenty minutes, he found himself across the desk from Assistant Superintendent Buddy McManus, as he thumbed through the employment file.

Buddy was medium height with a stocky physique and a jovial disposition that eased Job from feeling like he was trapped in a vacuum.

Buddy had taken advantage of every modern vanity technique with his mousse, slick, black hair coloring, and manicured nails with an onyx ring on his pinky. "I've got a few minutes. Let me show you around, Mr. Wright."

He began to tell Job about the family pictures on his desk. Then there was a brief tour of the massive suite with offices, a library, conference room, and file room with electronic and hard copies. Buddy's office had a wall-length aquarium filled with Characins, African butterfly fish and other exotic water life. One wall was lined with a contemporary collection of Southwestern art by Ballentine, Applegate, and others.

Job pointed to *Dancers Thinking*. "Wonderful piece."

"It's my favorite."

Job thought about the times when he not only appreciated finer acquisitions, but could also afford them. "I would have to put out my entire salary to deck a house out like this."

"C'mon, Mr. Wright, you . . . umm," he paused, flipping through Job's file, "were a real estate agent. Didn't you make pretty good money?"

"I've been down that money road, and it's overrated. What I'm getting ready to do now is for children and their needs." Job thought that was a decent comment, since he was trying to secure a job.

"You know, I am curious." Buddy rubbed the dimple on his pudgy face. "What made you decide to apply all the way out here, in Phoenix?"

Job hoped the silence wasn't too obvious as he searched for an answer. "You know, I have several reasons for our move, but the main one is that my wife is from Nevada. We really wanted to come out West to be near her relatives." He hoped that answer would keep Buddy at bay. It wasn't exactly a lie; not exactly the truth, either.

Buddy studied Job's answer with little concern. "I tell you what. I don't want to keep you in suspense any longer." He closed Job's employment file. "Congrats, Mr. Wright. Your application's complete, and the school board has approved you to be hired. Welcome aboard."

"I appreciate this, Mr. McManus. You won't be disappointed."

"Mr. Wright?" Buddy's timbre changed from a nasal twang to a low resonance, as if every word counted. "I would be remiss if I didn't tell you that Paradise School District prides itself in having a caring administration, honest and dedicated teaching professionals, and a cutting edge curriculum. We have a low tolerance for news that scar our profession. Do your best, and make us proud."

"I will," Job said, refusing to read anything into Buddy's statements other than for general information. He glanced at his watch. "I've got to run. Me and my wife have an appointment with a realtor this afternoon. I'd better find us somewhere to live or my wife'll kill me."

Buddy leaned back in his chair and smiled. "You better do your best to keep her happy."

Job sighed. "I know this search will be harder than finding a job."

It wasn't the fault of Hickell & Vonson's Realty that Job and Monica couldn't decide on a home to purchase. And Job didn't put any blame on himself, because his list of must-haves could fit in a single hand. The summer heat that day confirmed his desire for two items, and he made it plain to the broker. "Donnell, I need a garage and an excellent HVAC unit. If those things aren't in the house, we walk."

It was Monica who was vacillating from one decision to another. She wasn't in Kentucky anymore; brick, wood shakes, and vinyl siding had been replaced by stucco and adobe. The house hunting excursion had taken them from South Mountain to Pinnacle Peak, from Deer Valley to Scottsdale. There was no hope in sight of snatching a property off the market. Donnell Hickell had demonstrated a wealth of patience, but Job wasn't as accommodating.

"Honey, can you tell us what it is you're not seeing?" Job asked Monica.

"I'll know the home for us when I see it. I'm not trying to be difficult, but this money we're spending is ours," she said.

That point was well taken.

"There's a relatively new subdivision near Fifty-first Avenue and Bell. It's near a golf course, if you like that sort of thing," Donnell said.

Job wasn't keen on the idea. He thought that it would be another vain ride with no results.

"A golf course?" Monica asked. "If it's got real grass, let's go."

Job began to feel like they were mice lost in a grid. There was no getting away from the cacti, but the ground cover from street to street had evolved into a palette of desert colors.

"What's the name of the subdivision we're going to?" Job asked.

"Resi'Stanz." Over the dashboard, Donnell pointed out a small radius of open sky. He told them that they were in north-central Phoenix and Fifty-first was a main thoroughfare to downtown. "Here we are." Donnell grabbed his mobile phone and dialed a number. "I'm calling the listing service to get the gate code."

It was as though God had told Monica He had found her name in the Lamb's Book of Life. With the guide provided by the brokerage firm, she spotted one listing then another, until they pulled into a particular cul-de-sac. "If this home looks as good on the inside as it does out here, this is the one," she said.

Only five houses made up that circular pocket of asphalt, and the house she had her eye on was the deepest within 2333 Rong Street—

They spent more than three hours walking the grounds, testing the systems, prodding the adobe, and feeling the interior walls.

"By the way you're examining things, you seem to know a little about real estate," Donnell said.

"He ought to, that's—"

"What happens when you read a lot of books," Job interrupted Monica. "It's always been a fascinating subject to me. I might even go into investing one day." He tried to shoot Monica a "between-you-and-me" grin, but she didn't seem to go along with it.

Donnell explained to Job and Monica that real estate investing was a hot venture in the southwest. He proclaimed that turning properties and buying rentals was more popular than stocks and bonds, thanks to infomercial folks with promises of no down payment. "Good luck on investing, if you ever try it," he told Job.

Job thought back on him and Delvin, and his stomach churned. He didn't want to be involved in money schemes, legal or not. He peered over and saw Monica's stern, "we-can't-afford-investing" look; Donnell's comments raced right out of his mind.

Too much was going on for Job to make a decision right then. He felt the pressure of a salesman's pitch from Donnell. He wasn't fooled by the realtor's laid back performance. But the greater pressure came from Monica. She was silent. She appeared weary from viewing houses, but gripped in concrete and refusing to break away until she heard the words she wanted to hear.

Job caught himself picking at the buttons on his shirt. "I tell you what, Donnell, you've done a superior job of searching out a home for us," he said. He began knotting up in apprehension when he eyed Monica, but he drew in a breath and said, "We may need to wait. My wife and I will let you know."

Chapter 4

And they departed from the mount of the Lord in three days' journey. Numbers 10:33a

J ob didn't heed the warning from Phoenix natives about moving on peculiar days. A peculiar day was any day over ninety degrees and he defied good sense by choosing to move on the scorching Independence Day weekend.

On June 30, the Mayflower movers had packed every box and piece of furniture in Louisville and had gone on ahead, taking I-40 out west. But the Wrights' three-day journey took six because Monica wanted to veer off and take the scenic route, historic 66, from Oklahoma City to Phoenix.

After reaching the Arizona border, they called the movers, and gave them an approximate arrival time. They had already taken a two-day vacation. They drove up to the Resi'Stanz subdivision on July 6 to a torrid ninety-seven degrees. The movers were waiting for instructions to unload. The Wrights were drained from the trip, and were sure that their 2000 GMC Denali had been stretched to its mechanical limit.

"Okay, guys. Most everything is labeled, but if you have questions, just ask me or my wife," Job told them.

Between munching on burritos and tacos, the three men had the eighteen-wheeler unloaded before nightfall.

Job, Monica, and the movers were on the front porch taking turns tossing pebbles at the "Sold" sign in the yard and finishing the last few tacos. To everyone's amusement, one of the movers made a comment about wanting some dessert and Sangria.

Someone must've rubbed a genie's bottle, because it wasn't long before that part of the meal was taken care of by a couple of neighbors.

"Hey. We brought some cakes and a warm welcome. We hope you like lemon—baked fresh this afternoon. After all, we didn't know what day you were moving in, so we had to keep a watch out until you pulled up."

The lady making the grand presentation was about five-foot-four, chubby, with a pageboy hairstyle and China-doll skin accented by round, apple cheeks. She had an Edith Bunker nasal voice—minus the sincerity. Job gave a wave that was more of a brush off than a return of cordiality.

Monica slapped Job on the shoulder.

"Pardon my husband's rudeness. I'm Monica Wright. This is my husband, Job," she said, taking the cake. "Thank you so much."

"Why, you're welcome." The petite Caucasian lady introduced herself as Isabel Marriday. She pointed to the lady who accompanied her. "And this is Fontella Logan."

Fontella chimed in, "Praise the Lord. Welcome to the neighborhood." She was a statuesque African-American with the same mid-thirties look and caramel complexion as Monica. She had a short Afro enveloping her face.

"So we do have a neighborhood-watch committee," Job joked.

"Don't pay my husband any attention. He's having a comic moment that isn't funny," Monica said. "The cake looks delicious. I'm going inside to see if I can find a knife."

"Don't you worry about that," Isabel interjected. She had another Saran-wrapped package in her arms and presented it to Monica. "I made some cupcakes too. Eat these and enjoy that big cake later."

Monica took the cupcakes in her left arm, her right already holding the layer cake. "Oh my word. They look delicious."

Job said, "Here, honey. Let me help you." He took the cupcakes and removed the cellophane from over them. "Here, guys," he said to the moving men.

Monica went inside of the house with the cake. Fontella walked in behind her.

One of the movers told Job that they would get a night's rest before going back to Louisville. "Here's a copy of the manifest and bill." The gentleman tore away a canary copy from his clipboard. "Tell the lady over there, thanks for the dessert."

The movers got into the cab of the truck, and with a little maneuvering, pulled the huge green and gold rig out of the cul-de-sac and subdivision.

Monica and Fontella returned from inside the house.

"You two must've had a lot of furniture to secure a company that big," Isabel said.

Job refused to honor her overbearing curiosity with an answer. He made up his mind right then that he couldn't stand her. "So, which house do you live in, Miss Marriday?" he asked in a pretense of politeness.

"Please, call me Isabel. I live in 2300, at the entrance of the cul-de-sac."

"Me and my husband live next door," Fontella said.

Good, Job thought. At least the I-have-nose-trouble, busy-body, nothing-else-productive-to-do, call-me-Isabel, wasn't right next door. He pictured her getting late night glimpses of Monica sitting in his lap, or peeping in his bathroom, trying to figure out the brand of cologne he used. "What about this heat?" he asked.

Isabel instinctively took out a cloth napkin and patted her cheeks. "It's rather hot, but you'll get used to it."

"Sure we will," Monica said.

"Fontella and I were wondering what brings you to Phoenix."

"Don't put me into your wondering, Isabel," Fontella said.

Monica laughed out loud. "We don't mind you asking."

Oh yes, we do mind, Job thought.

"We moved here from Louisville. My husband is going to start teaching this coming school year in the Paradise Valley School District, and I'll be working for the Nine Iron Golf and Resort Club," Monica offered as an explanation.

"My husband's a member of that club. The one on Seventh Avenue?" Fontella asked.

"I start in August. What do you think of it?"

"Honey, let me tell you, I can't stand golf. But I go with Larry to an occasional get-together. It seems to be a nice place. You'll probably like working there. "

"We have wonderful schools here. The governor has come up with novel ways to finance each district. Did you teach in Louisville, Mr. Wright?" Isabel asked.

"Oh no," Job said. *You ladies are asking too much about our business.*

About the time Job completed his thought, Monica

suggested that they all go inside out of the heat. "I don't guess we have to tell you ladies to excuse the mess."

Isabel batted her eyes and said, "Of course not. We can help you with any unpacking, if you'd like.

Job did not want that to happen. Monica cleared her throat while Fontella turned her face in Isabel's direction. Nobody seemed to agree with that suggestion.

Job had pulled up four of the dining room chairs near the kitchen, and they all sat. Monica offered some water, which was the only available beverage, but everyone refused.

"God has apparently led the two of you to this area. You have to listen to the Lord," Fontella said.

I'm on another path, whether it's God's doing or not. Job looked at Monica. She gazed back at him, a curl in her lip. "I guess that's a good way of putting it," he said.

Monica nodded her head, a sickly smile on her face. "Speaking of the Lord, can anyone tell us about any good churches in the area?"

"There are several good churches in Paradise, South Mountain, Surprise; just all over Maricopa County. What denomination do you prefer?" Fontella asked.

Isabel cut in, "Now if you're Catholic, you can go with me to Mass at St. Augustine's."

"Thanks for the invitation, but we prefer a more charismatic service. We're black folks; we like to shout ev'ry now and then," Job said, amusingly.

Isabel's face turned flush. "We have African-Americans at our church. We even hear an occasional *Amen*."

Job shook his head and an index finger, *no*.

"I understand," Isabel said. "Shout on."

"You have any problems with a non-denominational church?" Fontella asked.

Job started to voice his opinion about what he had seen in, "New Age" churches. He went into an abridged filibuster on pastors that called their buildings "Worship Centers" and congregations that refused to take a denominational stand, but claimed to be steadfast on the Word of God.

Job paused a moment to contemplate his next phrase.

Monica shot him a disturbed look and beamed in on his tirade. "We're not bothered at all by non-denominational churches." She smiled at Fontella. "We'd love to visit."

Fontella grinned. "Great. Then let me invite you to mine. Our pastor is Roland Harris, the founder of Chapel in the Desert."

"How many members?" Job asked.

After a brief pause, Fontella said, "I think we have about fifteen-hundred members."

It wasn't the first time Job had heard churchgoers comment on the size of their congregations, and Fontella seemed to have that same arrogance, like she was comparing family size or something. Job asked her, "How can you be personable and be so large?"

Monica glared. Her face was beyond "please be quiet." It was a definite "shut up."

Fontella said, "We started four years ago with two-hundred, forty people joining on the first official Sunday."

"You all have grown fast," Monica said.

"The Lord's blessed us."

"Even I've attended a few times. It was different from what I'm used to, but I enjoyed service," Isabel said, apparently not wanting to be left out of the conversation.

"I'd like to invite you for this Sunday if you're up to it," Fontella said.

"Sure, we'd love to go." Monica cut her eyes at Job. "Wouldn't we, honey?"

Job rubbed the back of his neck, wondering what her hurry was. They had just moved into the area. Their feet hadn't settled on the ground good before her wanting to go cavorting with strangers. He believed that the Lord would understand their absence from church that particular week. Although he hadn't told her, he wanted them to take their time over the next couple days and do some unpacking, and on Sunday, watch an Arizona Diamondbacks game. The strangling look in Monica's eyes told him he'd better reconsider. "Oh, yeah. We'd love to attend."

"You all can follow me and Larry this Sunday. We start at 10:00 A.M."

"Unusual time for a Sunday service, isn't it?" Job asked.

Fontella grinned. "I don't really know why Pastor Harris chose that hour as a starting time; I'd be interested in knowing. Anyway, we leave around 9:25 every Sunday, because it's a little ways of a drive. And to get a parking space that's not in the next county, we need to get there kinda early."

"We'll be ready," Monica said.

"So, Mr. Wright, what are your thoughts on religion and different denominations?" Isabel asked.

Job's heart skipped a beat. He felt like asking her if her husband—although she hadn't said that she was married—knew that she asked so many probing questions of people. *Not your business*, he said to himself. He looked over at Monica, hoping she would chime in with a witty response—come to his aid. All she had was a void, unreadable look.

"You don't have to know everything in one sitting, do you?" Fontella asked. "C'mon, let the Wrights have a chance to finish getting settled before it gets dark." She rose out of her seat, grabbing Isabel by the arm.

Job's heart pumped with an appreciation for Fontella's good manners. At the same time, Monica's crossed, pulsating arms seemed to drain the blood from his body as Isabel and Fontella shuffled off to their houses.

Monica turned in Job's direction, tapping her shoe on the sidewalk. "We need to talk, Joseph Bertram Wright, but I can't find the words just this minute."

After the neighbors left them standing in their front yard, Job suggested to Monica that they spend the night in a hotel and awake fresh the next morning to begin the overwhelming task of unpacking.

She wasn't hearing him.

When they were inside the house, she dead-bolted the door with a sound that was no ordinary metallic click. She flipped her wrist with a malicious bend, as though it was his neck she was trying to snap. The next thirty minutes, she trounced between the great room and the kitchen, carrying boxes and exhibiting a variety of head motions, arm waves, and vocal inflections, but no understandable language on why she couldn't find words.

Job had no clue. He decided it was best to wait out the monsoon called Monica. He took a few boxes that had been labeled for the master bath and began emptying them, placing the toiletries, towels, and other items on shelves.

He had started arranging some of his personal grooming items—shaver, mortar and pestle, spare blades—in the cabinet under the vanity, his head buried deep in the opening. A few moments passed. He heard the soft steps of her shoes against the carpet and then onto the ceramic tile in the bath.

"Joseph Bertram Wright, we need to talk," Monica said.

He came out of the bathroom, through the master and down the hallway. On both sides of him were stacks of boxes arranged in a way that would make the claustrophobic ill, having no apparent end in sight. For him, a corridor of death under her control. "Where are you, honey?" he asked.

No sound.

When he reached the only vacant area on the first floor, he found her seated in the breakfast room, another chair facing her. The '99 Sedona Jazz Festival T-shirt and cotton shorts she wore had a grimy, sensual mystique that stirred him despite his weariness, but her facial expression was unsentimental, almost comatose. His mind and libido retreated into neutral.

She motioned.

He sat, still in search for the reason behind her anger and wishing for release from the oncoming detonation.

"This is our first night here in Phoenix," she said, keeping that same blank look while she voiced her words in staunch succession. "I want to get a good understanding before this night is up."

He licked his lips, striving to come up with a response, but nothing came to mind.

"You haven't breathed a good twenty-four hours in Phoenix, and you've started living a lie here. Might as well have stayed in Louisville. You can't make our future safe if you dance around your past like you did today with those neighbors. You did the same thing the day we were house-searching with the realtor."

Job wasn't prepared for questions from unfamiliar people and was unaware that Monica had paid such close attention. "Look, honey, we're going to be all right."

"I talked to our attorney about the possibility of making things right with the school district. She told me that I should keep the matter to myself. It's as if everyone has problems telling the truth."

"You asked Wendy for advice?" He sighed and looked away. "Man, I can't believe you did that."

"She's our attorney, Job. I couldn't ask just anyone for the kind of advice I needed to help you fix this. You've put me in a position to have to hold your lie, and that's not fair or good."

He tried to explain that his action was for the best, that she was making a big deal out of it. "I got the job. That's what matters."

"With me, it's not about the end result, it's about the process. *How* did you get the job? And if you'll lie, you'll be prone to steal. Just like Delvin."

At this juncture, he couldn't admit to her that he really knew about Delvin's business propositions, or that the thought of making additional money was intriguing at the time. "I wish you wouldn't say that. You're really intent on cutting me up."

Monica crossed her arms. "You haven't heard the half. What you didn't concentrate on when you had the partnership was seeing to it that the business stayed clean and that crooks like Delvin didn't foul up what you had worked so hard to create."

"Exactly, Monica." He pinched his lips. "Remember that it was Delvin who did this to us. We wouldn't be in this predicament if it wasn't for him," he said.

"What's so funny is that in the midst of it all, I still don't call moving here a predicament. It's got to be God's design. It has to be, because only He would have us land halfway on our feet despite the fool thing you did."

"I trust God, Monica." He said it more to be self-convincing.

Monica's gaze turned icy. She sighed and then told him, "You only trust yourself. And you should see that didn't work."

Job cleared his throat, and then raised his voice. "Jesus ain't down here having to deal with school superintendents, Isabels, and Fontellas." He relaxed and then apologized for shouting. "God has no idea what I'm going through." He started pulling at the edges of some wrapping tape holding a box together. "But what's been done is done. Move on."

Monica rolled her eyes. "God has no idea . . . you think God's dumb?" She went over to the stove and opened it, checking to make sure nothing was already inside. She then shut it, cut the oven on, and returned to her chair.

"We have a new life, Monica. A new life."

"I don't want a new life. I want a *better* one. When we lived on Lakespur down south, we had a good life. But we don't live there anymore. Now that you've got me in Phoenix, I want a blessed life."

Job looked around. He saw blank walls, and even they seemed to be telling him that a turnaround was needed. They were a bunch of blank canvases waiting to see how he would paint the portrait. Monica's words were on his brain. "I hear you, honey."

"I really hope you mean it."

On the following day, Job awakened to piled furniture, unpacked boxes, and a knowledge that he and Monica would be in close quarters as they worked to gain some order at 2333 Rong Street.

He had always contended that their home, no matter where, was his castle, but the layout was Monica's domain. That Friday was devoted to her telling him where to set a box, hammer a nail, blasé, blasé.

With few exceptions, that was the sum of their conversation that morning.

He tried breaking the monotony with light discussion that required her to respond with more than short answers. By lunchtime, he had run out of fresh topics. Disgusted with the silence, he decided to try a fresh approach to kicking off a chat.

"Look honey." Job snatched a Bible from the bed stand and began shuffling through the pages for any scripture that may force her out of silence, but impatience made him give up on finding one. Content in relying on his memory, he said, "The Bible talks about going to bed angry. This place is the wrong place to let the sun be against you."

Monica twisted her mouth, put her hands on her hips, and gave him a discomforting look. "And you're the last person to quote a book you barely believe in."

Her words pierced his thoughts and soul. All Job could say was, "It was a joke. Lighten up."

Monica let out a snappy, fake grin. She turned and went back to work.

That evening, she was courteous enough to let him know that dinner was ready, but the meal was silent except for an occasional slurp or chew.

Before they went to sleep for the night, she turned over and said, "I was unpacking some files in the office when I ran across something that I bet you've forgotten."

Job was turned away from her, staring at a dark, blank wall, hoping that it could give him some relief. "What?"

"The '99 taxes you haven't filed."

"I'm gonna get to it."

"Um hm. That's what I'm talking about. You don't pay attention to what's going on around you. Frankly, it makes me sick."

Job didn't respond.

With that, she rolled in the opposite direction, and they said their good nights.

Saturday was the day silence was broken. Job was resolute not to let the first waking hour go by without having an entertaining conversation or some interaction without the tension.

At Monica's every turn he was there, cracking a joke, asking a question, or making faces to make her laugh. Job struggled until one of his performances worked.

"Okay, okay! You're getting on my nerves. I'll talk; just give me some space," she said.

Job granted her wish.

Around ten, he suggested they cruise Phoenix, take time away from unpacking and check out the city. No planned agenda, just run headlong into a suburb, see a few interesting attractions, and act on impulse.

To his surprise, she took him up on the idea. They ran up under a shower, donned color-matched linen outfits, jumped in the SUV, and took off.

It was a thirty minute drive down Bell Avenue to Scottsdale, where Job picked up a few items at a local drug store. For the most part, they window shopped.

They doubled back a ways, heading south down Seventh Street to Bank One Ballpark, home of the Diamondbacks. They picked up a schedule of the remaining home games. They stopped in the BluesLight Jazz Grill on Fifty-first and Indian School for a late lunch, and then spent a short time at the flea market on the Arizona State Fairgrounds.

Job glanced over at Monica, who had her feet propped up on the dash, flipping a city map from back to front. She eyed him without a blink, but she extended her hand. He touched her for a moment and then returned his attention to driving.

Job dug his heels into the floorboard of the vehicle. "Hey baby?"

"Um hm." Her response sounded soothing, almost benevolent.

"We're going to pass right by Coral Gables Boulevard. Mountain River High is on that street. Let's drive by there on the way home. I'm trying to get used to going there from any direction."

"Why not?"

Job considered Mountain River, in comparison to other public schools, as an ingenious piece of architecture. The exterior was made of material native to the Southwest—a mustard colored adobe hewn out of a set of hills. It faced away from the daytime heat and was covered by metal roofing.

He thought it peculiar that the gate was open with a few cars in the parking lot. Curious to see why the school seemed accessible on the weekend, he pulled in.

Monica frowned at him and popped her lips. "I thought we were only driving by. I should've known better."

"We might get to see my classroom."

Job parked the car and asked if she was getting out.

Monica adjusted her seat into a more relaxed position. "You're on your own. Leave the car running." She leaned back, unbuckled her seatbelt, and turned on the radio.

Job went to the front entrance, knocked, and then realized the door was already unlocked. He heard a chirp as he started down the main hallway, guessing that it was an alert that someone had entered the building. He had passed a few classrooms that appeared to be used for science: Bunsen burners, rows of test tubes, the formaldehyde smell.

He was met by a gentleman who was about 5'10" with sledge hammer hands, sunburned skin, satin black, shoulder length hair, and a thick Spanish accent. He had a tape measurer on his belt and a broom in his hand.

Job's Spanish skills, one thing he'd have to work on if he were to survive in Phoenix, were limited at best. Somehow he and the custodian were able to come to a verbal understanding. His name was Enrique. He was using the remaining Saturdays as extra time to make last minute preparations before school began in August.

Enrique said, "Principal," pointed down the hall and then said, "*Izquierda.*"

Job wrenched his brain for a Spanish-to-English interpretation. He figured that the principal's office was nearby and she must be in.

Enrique gave him an, "Adios," and went on his way.

The administrative offices were in a remote corner at the end of the central hallway. Job entered through the door, which was accented with a frosted glass. Inside the offices was a massive counter that measured about four feet high. There was a partition for three large desks, columns of file cabinets, and a monstrous safe.

Job smelled coffee. It must've been instant, with a hint of mint. There were faint sounds of someone on a phone. He followed his ears.

He was led to a woman who was shuffling a set of multi-colored papers and talking on the phone.

She halted her conversation when she noticed Job standing in the doorway, and hung up. "Mr. Wright," she said.

Job's mouth hung open. How did this woman know his name? And who is she; a teacher?

"Oh, I'm sorry. I don't mean to startle you." The woman placed the paperwork on the desk in front of her, saying, "When you applied to Paradise School District, you sent in a picture. The principal where you're assigned, always receives a photo of the potential employee. I'm Bianca Rizzo."

This couldn't possibly be the principal. He shook her extended hand and looked at her without appearing to gawk. He could see the Italian in her; the light cream skin yoked by burnt almond hair, the retroussé nose, thin lips, and honey colored eyes that were accented by a pair of red Art Nouveau spectacles. Her wide smile gave him the impression that she was personable, yet with an authoritative intellect. He couldn't get over her youthful look. She seemed only one year the other side of her high school diploma.

"I didn't expect you until Monday. Superintendent McManus called and told me that you would be moving in and getting settled this weekend. Dedication. I'm impressed," Bianca said.

"Don't be so impressed, Mrs. Rizzo. You're the one here on Saturday actually working. I'm just looking around."

"Ms., please," she corrected.

"Oh, I'm sorry."

"Don't be. I'll get married when I find the right man. Meanwhile, I'm concentrating on my career."

For a fleeting moment, Job felt a slight awkwardness when she voiced her current marital status. "Good thing. Concentrating on your career, I mean."

"Humph. The district expects me to be here any day of the week, so it doesn't count. I'm a twelve-month employee. And the principal."

Bianca thumbed through a stack of student attendance records from which she pulled one. "So, what brings you by here?"

He checked his watch and began to get uneasy, remembering that Monica was out in the car. "We took a half day's break from unpacking to drive around and see what we could see."

"We?"

"My wife and I."

Silence.

Job took the initiative to clear up Bianca's perplexed

look. "Monica—my wife—is outside. And I better be getting back to her before she kills me."

"Well, Mr. Wright. I hope you were able to see some interesting sights, although there's nothing much around here to see." Her dark eyes were shieded under the part in her hair.

He shifted his eyes to a different direction. "I really must go."

"I won't be here much longer myself. I need to begin a weekend. What's left of it. Umm, Mr. Wright?"

Job, who had begun heading toward the door, spun around. "Yes?"

"Have a great day." The inflection in Bianca's voice sounded more like she had just asked a question than given a suggestion. Job thought it was a slick reprimand for walking away without speaking. "You, too," he said with a hint of nervousness.

When Job returned to the car, he found Monica asleep, curled up in the seat with the street map unfolded over her.

When he awakened her, she reeled right into him with a few loud, unrepeatable comments. After a moment or so, she calmed down and asked, "What were you thinking, leaving me like that? You're standing on thin ground with me anyway, and then you have me out here on a practically deserted parking lot." She rolled her eyes away from him.

"I met the principal and a custodian," Job said, trying to sound matter-of-factly.

"How was he?"

Job was reminded of Bianca Rizzo. The youthful look, the resonant voice. In the same exact moment, he felt both guilty and fortunate. He did his best to respond with as little excitement as possible. "Oh, the principal? She—"

"She?"

"Yeah." Job breathed in a portion of nonchalance. "She was okay."

Chapter 5

The wicked plotteth against the just, and gnasheth upon him with his teeth. Psalms 37:12

Delvin pulled his hands out of the water, thankful that they were protected by industrial gauge rubber gloves. Kentucky Corrections required chlorine bleach in the dishwater, but he was pale enough without sticking his bare hands into the chemical of the servant class. He had heard of bleach being used before. He knew that outside of prison, it was how the Chinese laundered his shirts and the way his stylist lightened hair.

He was astounded at the perspective he could gain just by peering into and pounding through dishwater. It was the last day to bust suds on his thirty-day, ninety-meal punishment. He made a mental note not to wish for the assignment again.

Inmate after inmate filed past his area, depositing their plastic trays into what they called the Bean Chute, a 12" x 12" square that had been cut into the wall and trimmed out in welded metal. He took a rubber spatula and cleared each tray before plunging it into the hot, murky water. There was a nauseating odor of human skin and leftover scraps from that evening's meal: Salisbury steak, green beans, corn on the cob, and fruit cocktail.

Standing still, watching soap bubbles take shape then burst, gave him time to plot, plan, and analyze. He hadn't forgotten where he was and that Job Wright wasn't there with him.

Delvin wanted redemption and soon. He knew that, although he was incarcerated, he could make arrangements to put a free man in uncomfortable positions. What better way to feel better than to pawn his former partner off, have *him* to think he had been placed in a little prison?

All it took was a little ingenuity, cold hard cash, and a relentless person to damage their target. Delvin possessed all three. All he lacked was a contact on the inside. He had plucked out a name from among the ranks. But Stinson had not come through the line just yet.

Tall, dumpy, slim, and overweight—a barnyard of roosters clucking after a late feeding came through that little hole for a brief visit. He refused to look up and make any one face recognizable. For him, each man that evening was just a shadow, a talking head with legs. With one exception.

"Aw man, don't do that. Didn't anybody tell you?" Stinson asked as he scratched the chest hair sticking out from his shirt. "You're throwing away the goods."

Delvin's heart pounded. "What goods?" He took quick glances at several trays. Nothing looked salvageable on any of them.

"I still gotta lot to teach you." Stinson took his bare hands, reached into a few trays and yanked up the corn cobs, each devoid of a single kernel. He tossed them into a nearby plastic lined 50- gallon container. He brushed his forehead and a few corn silks stuck above his eyebrow. "You're trying to keep us from making this week's hooch, huh?"

Delvin was silent, yet confident that Stinson could see confusion written on his face.

"Never mind, Storm. I'll give you the low-down later. Just don't get rid of these." He held up another cob.

Stinson continued to chatter on about one topic then another; he was either unaware or unconcerned that he was holding up the line. It occurred to Delvin that this man might be the very one he needed to befriend. Or better yet, use.

Delvin cleaned the last tray while the container of cobs was whisked away to an undisclosed destination. He peeled off the gloves and hung them on a nearby high pressure sprayer. He tipped his head to the guard then exited out of the galley area. He walked into the cafeteria and over where Stinson, Saks, and Murphy were standing around one of the tables, engaging in what seemed to be a lie-telling contest.

Delvin directed an intentional gaze at Stinson. "You have a minute?"

"Who? Me?" Stinson asked. His biceps popped repeatedly.

Saks and Murphy took the hint and gathered themselves into a remote area of the room, about thirty feet away.

Stinson hoisted himself onto a table and planted his feet on the bench. "What's on your mind?" he asked.

Delvin looked around, assured that no additional ears were joining the conversation. "Need something."

He grunted. "Oh, this is grand. You come to me—for something. Must be a cold day in hell." He turned his left hand until the palm was up and then scratched it with his right.

"You have a way in this place," Delvin said.

"You're telling me stuff I already know."

Delvin seethed underneath, but appeared composed. His daily discourse with the inmates had been far from cordial. The majority of his interactions had barely been above a hello. He was being tested by the very one who had attempted to befriend him in the past. It was a sickening feeling, having to depend on another for anything. "I want something. That's all."

Delvin was growing impatient, a minute regret that he had even approached the man he believed was the most conceited inmate in Ashland. "So, are you the man or should I look for another?"

"Let me ask you something, Storm." He shook his head. "Are you blazed? Something wrong with you . . . like . . . crazy?"

"No. Why?"

"You must be, because you don't get the picture. What's in it for me?" Stinson was loud enough to cause Murphy and Saks to look in their direction for a brief moment.

Delvin backed away, squeezing his fists so tight the blood left his hands, leaving the knuckles eggshell white. "See, I knew you were homosexual. Trying to pretend like you have my well-being at heart. Back off."

Stinson's eyes opened up. He began a hard laugh, continuing until he began to choke. He straightened up, pounded his chest, and regained his composure. "Man, I told you I ain't into that. I meant it. You ain't seen nothing outta me that told you I'm a siss—get real."

Delvin was confident that Stinson was resourceful. Above all, he knew the network inside the hole had laws that ascended above the warden, with a hierarchy of its own. "I'm going to put together a list. Things I want while I'm here."

"Contraband?"

"No. Some papers, books, and stuff."

"That shouldn't be hard."

"But it won't be things you can find inside, necessarily."

Stinson cocked his head. "I figured that."

"Might take me a few days to compile the list. I'll let you know when it's completed."

"The person who actually secures the goods won't be me."

Delvin leaned in, wondering if his time had just been wasted on the wrong person. "Why am I talking to you, then?"

"You have a thing against patience, don't you? Be cool."

Stinson was in control and Delvin hated it. Having to wait for someone else to put a plan into motion was not his forté, but he had no choice. "You haven't told me what you wanted out of this."

Stinson rubbed his face, twisting his cheeks as if in a whirlwind of thought. Moments passed. He sighed. "A toy."

Delvin, had expected something more profound. Then he asked, "What? A set of Chinese tension balls? A stainless steel abacus? What?"

Stinson belted out a laugh to confirm Delvin's ignorance. "Naw, man. A regular toy. Hoola hoop, Slinky. In this place, a toy makes problems light; gives a ray of hope. It brings out the child inside no matter how old you are. Murphy taught us that."

Delvin looked beyond their immediate conversation and thought back on that day he wanted to give Murphy a lesson in keeping his trap shut. He remembered, too, how it had backfired on him. "It's not something I need."

"It will be. Good piece of advice. Go ahead, get one for yourself. It'll do you a world of good."

"What do you want, specifically?"

"Think about it. Surprise me."

With the round-about explanation he'd been given, Delvin thought about putting on his list the first junk toy that came to mind. Then he took a second for more intelligent thought. That thought told him not to make Stinson an enemy. That man was his free-flowing water line, and he wanted to keep the bill paid.

Stinson barged in on his thoughts and said, "Got a bit of advice for you, Storm."

"What's that?"

"Bitterness clouds your thinking. All the more reason why you need to start paying attention to your surroundings. You don't need your thinking clouded."

Delvin felt him trying to dig below his surface; he wasn't having it, so he felt a change of subjects was in order. "Hey, what was with the corn scraps?"

Stinson rose up from the table, causing a screeching noise that echoed through the room. It startled both Murphy and Saks, who seemed impatient from the wait. As he walked away from the little huddle, he told Delvin to, "Keep your eyes open. You'll see."

Chapter 6

Remember the Sabbath day, to keep it holy. Exodus 20:8

Job stuck to the bed early Sunday morning, yearning to stay right there. He tried not to think about the day and what it represented.

"In all things, you gotta have faith," Monica told him the day that the Louisville Real Estate Commission put the proverbial chains on his company door. "This came out exactly like it's supposed to. It's the way God planned."

"Faith didn't help, Monica," he told her. His countenance fell under the soil when God didn't do His job. Then what was the purpose for attending church?

He wanted Monica to understand that he believed there was a God, but that life's situations needed more than a prayer or a fasting. He wanted to hold fast to the belief that God helps those who help themselves.

Her words did little to convince Job that the Lord was always around, moving for the betterment of his life. Since college graduation, his credo had been one of self-reliance, but he would give anything to garner the faith that Monica spoke of. According to her, his lifelong existence could be one continuous, indefinable dilemma if he didn't go with her to church on that morning.

Monica had risen out of bed and taken over the master bath.

He grabbed his overnight toiletry bag and a towel and went to the full bath on the second floor.

Thirty minutes later, they retreated to the master closet, dressed, and convened in the foyer.

He studied her from the cobalt blue, wide-brimmed hat down to her stilettos. To Job, she made Macy's Couture look good.

He wasn't in the suit mood, but felt that he needed to make a positive impression since this was their first time going somewhere with a new neighbor to a new environment, a new church. He chose one of his favorites—a Jones New York, navy and white shirt, gold silk tie, black platypus Stacy Adam's.

Job heard a car horn.

Monica said, "It's Fontella and her husband in the drive." She grabbed her purse and headed out the door while taking a glance at her watch. "Wow, like clockwork. Nine twenty-five. We haven't had time to get to the truck."

"In this sun, who wants the time?" He locked the door, and they walked off the porch.

Fontella suggested that Job and Monica ride with them instead of following, especially on their first time attending the church. Her husband, Larry, welcomed the Wrights to Phoenix and the neighborhood. He apologized for not making their acquaintance earlier. "Pharmaceutical sales keep me busy, away from the house during the week. I'm glad my wife saw to it that you were welcomed properly."

Although Larry was at the driver's seat, Job estimated

him to be every bit of six-foot-seven. It was more than a coincidence that the Logan's family car was a Navigator. Larry appeared to be navigating from the back seat.

"Monica, Fontella tells me that you have a position at Nine Iron Golf," Larry said.

"I begin in about three weeks," Monica replied.

"I'm sure I'll see you there sometime. I have a membership."

Job resented the fact Larry felt comfortable enough to bring up topics revolving around luxuries his present salary couldn't afford. *Can we talk about something else?* His petition was answered.

Fontella asked Monica, "What does the Lord Jesus Christ mean in your life?"

Monica looked over at her with a whitewashed stare. "Huh?"

Fontella's eyes sparkled as she let out a small giggle. "It's the question that our pastor has made a part of the witnessing ministry. It's the question of our church culture."

"Oh. That's interesting and different," Monica responded.

"So? What does He mean in your life?" She focused in on Monica, seeming to wait for an answer.

"I think God has me and Job on a journey. It's not an easy one. I just pray and trust in Him. I guess that it's all we can do," Monica said.

Fontella shouted, "Aw girl, testify!" The women slapped a high five.

Fontella interrogated Job within moments of Monica's answer, and all eyes were on him. Larry's face filled the rear view with Fontella twisting in from the front passenger seat. Monica was at his side. There was nowhere to turn, run, walk, or drive away.

"W-well, you know. J-Jesus has showed me some

things. God's all right with me. I love Him," Job stammered out. He was thankful as the next ten minutes whisked away. That was the length of time he heard silence—before arriving at the church.

Chapel In The Desert emerged from a strip mall abandoned during a five-year urban renewal that took place in the mid '90s. The congregation was blessed to have expanded down three blocks on Sun Valley Parkway at Grand Avenue in a suburb of Phoenix called Surprise.

"I guess now you see why we have to be on time for service," Fontella said.

Parking was a phenomenal task as cars congregated like a swarm onto the parking lot. People rushed from their vehicles to the entrances labeled *Faith*, *Hope*, and *Charity*.

In the vestibule, columns of pink Italian marble shaped in Corinthian style lined the hall and towered well above fifty feet overhead. Human-size floral arrangements of Yucca, Matilija Poppy, and Beavertail Cacti were along the walls with Bird of Paradise trees in an intricate pattern on the floor. Glass encased posters offered picturesque details of the various church ministries. A scrolling message board announced activities and provided scriptures defining why people should worship. Men and women with brisk handshakes and broad smiles were greeting, making sincere attempts not to miss a single person.

Job looked around at the people and their manner of dress. The wardrobe styles—tees and jeans, pant suits and sandals, casual linen pastels—had him exchanging glances with Monica. He could feel her saying to him *You know? We could've worn what we had on yesterday and been more in keeping with the people here.*

Monica whispered to Fontella, "You should have told me that the attire is more casual."

Fontella responded, "Girl, we don't pay attention to what you have on." She patted Monica on the hand. "You're fine."

As they were ushered to seats, Job navigated his eyes forward to the pulpit. A small group of musicians had assembled themselves on an elevated part of the stage that held a physical set-up equaled to that of Frankie Beverly and Maze. They settled in and tuned and cranked up an assortment of songs as mega screens projected lyrics.

He heard shouting behind him and looked. Young people had filled the aisles waving banners and flags. The congregation joined in singing, "We have come into this house, gathered in His name to worship Him . . ."

"This is just too much to take in at one time," Job bellowed out in hopes that the Logans would believe he was well-versed in good-ole conservative Baptist tradition. He laughed to himself in embarrassment; back in Louisville, he rarely attended church, other than on Christmas, Easter, and Mother's Day. Any other Sunday while Monica was at church, he would be found at home, catching an old movie or a football game.

A quartet of singers, two men and two women, came to the stage in front of the pulpit. They each grabbed a mic and led the congregation in singing one tune after another. Job sang along as best he could, even though most of the songs were unfamiliar. He made out pretty well on one by Donnie McClurkin and another by Dallas Holm.

Forty minutes had gone by. Job leaned in and whispered to Larry, "When is the offering?" He figured that if the preacher called for the money, then the sermon and benediction would soon follow.

Larry told him tithes and offerings were place in wooden boxes stationed in the vestibule as they exited. "We don't take up offerings during worship service."

Job laughed, hoping not to draw attention. "You've got to be kidding," he said, putting emphasis on each word.

"No. That's really how we do it. Pastor Harris says that Christians need to embrace a level of trust. If someone robs a church offering basket, they rob God, and the wrath will be more than they can bear."

"Yeah, but you don't dangle the carrot. You're asking for trouble."

"This body of believers is blessed," Larry said. "We've never had a single incident of mishandling or theft."

Job shook his head in disbelief. He had been used to deacons taking up the offering, whisking it to the back office where one counted and another two or three watched. After church, under heavy guard, the money would be taken to the night depository. Monday morning, it was double-checked to see that it had been handled properly and received by a bank officer, who issued a stamped receipt. A set of watchdogs. A back-up to the back-up.

A middle-aged man, about five-foot-nine with graying hair, beard and mustache, came onto the stage. By Job's sight, either the man was void of a single blemish on his café noir skin, or the pixels on the mega screens perfected him into Ebony Fashion Fair status.

"Good morning, saints, worshippers, and friends," the man proclaimed.

Job and Monica exchanged glances. He reached over, clasped her hand and whispered, "This is a trip, ain't it honey? No reading of the scripture. No singing of "Amazing Grace" before the preacher gets up. Makes you wonder, huh?"

"What?" Monica asked with a hint of aggravation in her voice.

"If it's a cult the Logan's are trying to get us into."

Monica backed away from his lips, licked the poison

on hers, and stared him down as though she cared less if anyone heard what she was about to say. "I never thought Louisville had a monopoly on how church services were supposed to be carried out. Now be quiet."

He did just that.

Pastor Harris made a few announcements regarding ministries within the church that had gatherings scheduled for that week. He instructed those with birthdays and wedding anniversaries in the remainder of July to stand, and then had visitors to stand.

Job and Monica were of one mind at that moment. They refused to rise despite Fontella's coaxing. Job looked out over the part of the congregation he could see, amused that the church found praise in such simple gestures as welcoming what they labeled, "the potential membership."

Pastor Harris clapped his hands and the sound system helped him send a deafening reverberation through the sanctuary. "Now," he shouted, "let's get some Word into our systems."

Those words had not left his mouth good before the entire room went up into an unprecedented cry, unlike any Job had ever heard. Not at a concert. Not at a ballgame.

Pastor Harris cupped the thumbnail mic on his headset. "C'mon, saints. We can get excited over everything else." He began a strut that, in steady rhythm, evolved into a high-stepping march. "We go crazy over things that can't help us, things that don't matter. Then let's get excited about the Lord and what He's done. C'mon, c'mon!"

The congregation's response didn't seem to get louder, but thickened, broadened. The musicians added to the fury with chords and cymbal crashes.

"Be seated, if you can," Pastor Harris said.

The congregation began to mellow and a scriptural text was given.

"I want to speak to each of you today about breaking new ground. All of us live in what we call the desert, barren ground. Phoenix and Scottsdale are physical places where we reside, our domicile," he paused, ironing the side of his slacks, "but I'm now talking about where our spirits live."

The congregation was prompted to turn their Bibles to Ezekiel, thirty-sixth chapter. Pastor Harris began reading from the ninth verse. "'*For behold, I am for you, and I will turn unto you, and ye shall be tilled and sown.*' You see saints, the Lord used this prophet to talk directly to us. He's saying that God is with us. No matter what the trial. No matter the circumstance. He—I'm talking about the Lord," he paused for the sporadic *Amens* to wane, "is allowing us to be turned or plowed under and for new ground to show. Amen?"

Job heard shouts and affirmations from different directions.

"Then," he bobbed his hand up and down, "God wants us to know that He'll plant us. This means we have the Master placing us in good ground, with good seed. C'mon, somebody."

"Say it, Pastor," was one of many expressions from the congregation.

"Then . . . well, look at verse eleven near the last part of the verse," he commanded. "'*And I will settle you after your old estates, and will do better unto you than at your beginnings.*' Stop," he shouted.

The reading ceased for a moment, but the praise started all over again.

"Hey now, let me finish," he commanded. "This means that what you had in the beginning, is nothing compared to what God is about to bless you with now; heah!"

Job consumed himself in a thought. *If this man said "boo", would they shout off that?* He pitched his eyes toward Monica, believing he could get an are-you-thinking-what-I'm-thinking glance from her. Instead, she had her hands raised, eyes closed and her head bobbling like she was disjointed at the neck.

Pastor Harris bellowed, "God, thank you. Thank you for your provisions. Thank you for your caring. I know you will do better for me now than at my beginnings!" He whipped a finger out to the congregation. "That's the Word for today my people. Be blessed. 'Cause, when you've said all you know—"

"It's time to go!" the congregation chorused.

As if on cue, the musicians broke into a postlude while Pastor Harris exited.

The congregation praised and disbursed. Larry reached for an offering envelope as Fontella rose from her seat and moved to hug Monica.

Job sat in amazement. "It's over?"

Fontella stopped hugging, leaned against a seat in the row in front of them. "What were you expecting?"

Job creased his forehead. "Well, a longer sermon than that."

Fontella chuckled in a way that didn't make Job feel brainless, but embarrassed. "You heard songs of praise, testimonies, prayers, scripture text, a sermon. You need something more?"

"Well, I—"

"It doesn't take all day for the Holy Ghost to do His work," Fontella interjected with a smile.

Job looked at Monica, who had one eyebrow higher than the other. He was losing the battle in the Holy Ghost discussion, and she appeared to be waiting to see what came out of his mouth next. *She's no help at all.* "We should get something to eat," he said.

* * *

Larry insisted that he and Fontella take them out for Sunday brunch. He asked what they had a taste for. They had no preference.

He chose the Sheraton Crescent Hotel on W. Dunlap, telling the Wrights that they was known for their eggs Benedict, their Southwestern omelets, and the best Arnold Palmers in town. It was a twenty minute drive there from the church.

Their orders were taken and they were well into the meal when Fontella asked, between bites of a Belgian waffle, "Well? What do you think of Chapel in the Desert?"

Job, hoping that Monica would explain for both of them, glued his mouth shut with a forkful of Southwestern omelet.

"Oh my goodness. What can I say? The service was wonderful, and I'm glad you invited us," Monica said.

"Our worship experiences are always unique, always blessed. I hope that the approach of our church service doesn't hinder you from wanting to come back."

Job did an internal snicker, thinking back on how different the service was from what he had always known. *It was unique all right. To tell you the truth, it was strange.* "If the church service is always that short—"

"They are," Larry cut in.

Job sighed. "Then, we'll definitely be back." He could tolerate anything for that short amount of time. He would attend, for Monica's sake.

Fontella asked, "Did you get what you needed?"

Nosy. Job was beginning to believe that she was as fond of digging into people's business as that stubby little Isabel they met when unloading the moving van. He figured Fontella's curiosity must've been in remission that day. But now, it had come out of hibernation. "Get what I needed?"

"To me, church isn't about the shouting, although, I guess, some people need that release. Or that's just how they praise." Fontella took her fingertip and circled the top of her glass. "For me, church is where I come every week with a question. That question is an actual need."

"Every person should take that approach. I know I got what I needed. This move has been a little stressful, but today's worship service made this last week worth it," Monica said.

Larry's eyes had been ping-ponging from one person to another with an intent look. He said, "It is good to see another married couple in the neighborhood. And possibly, coming to our church."

Job feared the women had hooked Larry in. "Okay. I don't want to be the bad person in this subject. I did enjoy church. I just think you all are making religion out to be more than it really is."

Larry faced Job eye to eye. "So tell me something. What did you get out of Pastor Harris's sermon?"

What made him ask me that? He could tell Larry's question wasn't meant to be meddlesome. It carried a wind of sobriety, as if the answer would only provoke another question to chip a soul. Job's soul. But he didn't feel like class was in session. Not for him, anyway. "What did you get out of it, Larry?"

"Ezekiel. Thirty-sixth chapter. Ninth through the eleventh verse," Larry recalled.

Fontella and Monica were both wide-eyed, fixated on him.

Job was upset that he couldn't remember the scriptural text, let alone any meaning from the sermon. At that moment, he wished he had listened with a purpose.

"If you're going to live a life free of the past, fresh,"

Larry stated, "believe in the Lord God, and just start living."

Job became suspicious of Larry's comment, believing it was an underhanded effort to send him a message. To him, the validity of a belief system could be argued, and he had heard too much emphasis on God that day. And besides, *living* was what he thought he and Monica were doing.

Chapter 7

Whosoever therefore resisteth the power, resisteth the ordinance of God: and they that resist shall receive to themselves damnation. Romans 13:2

Delvin passed over breakfast. He wasn't up for ramming Egg Beaters down his throat, spending the remainder of the day on his personal throne. Instead, he decided to arm himself with a pencil and scratchpad and sit in his cell, letting his thoughts heat and his focus intensify.

He heard thunder, but there was no immediate rain. The earth's ovation was the only sound that accented his writing that Sunday morning.

After an hour of toiling, Saks came by and stood at his cell door. "You going to chapel service, man?"

Delvin's hands froze. He rolled his eyes up without moving his head. "Does it look like I'm about to shuffle my feet?" he asked with such an intended jaggedness that Saks caught the message and walked away as if treading on cotton.

He resumed his writing, hoping that another inmate wouldn't come by and spill out another foolish jawful of words.

Five items. He had devoted two disgusting hours to

his list and had come up with a quintet of measly things. His mind wandered back to his pre-prison times. Given two hours, he could've cranked out an entire business plan down to the micro-detail with projected costs and profits within a three-figure range of error. Now, he couldn't put together a mere grocery list of items that anyone with a cerebrum could salvage in a day's time. *This place is making me pitiful.*

That was his mind. Then, he began to dwell on his body.

He stood up from his bunk, stretched his torso and rolled his neck. Every bone and joint ached. He would have given anything for a Pilates workout about now. The high fructose injected juices the prison had in full supply was running through his kidneys, seeping through his skin in the form of adolescent-like pimples. He shook his head in hopes of rattling appalling thoughts and feelings right out of his presence.

The marching of feet outside his cell signaled to him that a transition from the Catholic mass to the Protestant service was taking place on the lower level, outside perimeter of C block. After that, he was able to regain some tranquility. He would have had total peace were it not for the water pounding against the asphalt pitched roof. What would have been a refreshing natural sound to most was an irritant to his psyche.

Delvin had exhausted any hope that he would finish his task at that time. He stuck his pad and pencil between pages of the Bible he had been given.

"Guard," he said.

It took a few moments for the cell block overseer to reach Delvin, swinging keys and leaning on the bars. "Whatcha need, Storm?"

"You can unlock my cell. I think I'm going for a walk."

"You'll be using your single privilege for the day. And

you have to remain either in the yard or the library after you take your little walk. You're out until 1:30. Understand?"

Delvin had been careful not to abuse his freedom. If he hadn't been planning some deviance at that time, solitary confinement wouldn't have been a terrible living arrangement. At least he would have undisturbed minutes, hours. But he needed the liberty for human contact, so he walked the chalk line.

"Back up, Storm." The guard pulled out an object the shape of a beeper and flashed it toward the door. The latch opened and the door swung toward the hall. "Let's go."

He moseyed out and down the hall. He peered into each cell as he walked, but did not allow his eyes to fixate on any inmate's personal space. He had a fear of retaliation.

About halfway down that floor, he met Stinson. Delvin wanted to know if progress had been made on his request from the day before, so he asked the question with his eyes.

Stinson responded with a look, no speech. *Give me time. The hook-up is on the way.*

Delvin bowed his head and walked by. They understood each other.

Another fifty feet or so, the stairs that led to lower levels within the cellblock somehow drew him. What he heard was more of a rhythmic undertone, or breaths echoing like ghosts leaving a small room to stretch out into open space.

The sound drugged him, led him on a virtual leash until his scales were removed and he found himself looking into the opening of the prison chapel. The leash had released its grip, but not before he had locked eyes with Shiloh Kimmons.

Delvin's internal heat blew up the Celsius scale. He had avoided that man since their first meeting, and cursed himself for not knowing where the chapel was located.

"God is a wondrous God." Shiloh raised a hand above his head and then lowered it toward a front row chair.

Delvin didn't want the good chaplain to consider him a coward, but he wasn't making the twenty foot stride down that aisle either. He finger-combed his hair, wiped any lingering surprise off his face, and chose a seat in the last row.

"The Lord is someone you have to want in your life. He doesn't come to you and take residence just because He wants to. Invite Him in," Shiloh declared.

"Umm," a couple of inmates mumbled.

Delvin heard their response and wondered about the meaning of it. "The preacher isn't saying anything worth anything. What do you idiots think you're listening to?" was what he wanted to say. He pondered why he even took a seat, filling his ears with this nonsense. He just knew that the chaplain's ranting wouldn't aid his present situation.

"Don't treat this time of worship as a fashionable thing to do," Shiloh said, as though he heard Delvin's thoughts and was extending a warning. "Don't play with what others depend on to live."

Delvin scanned the chapel and wondered if the chaplain proudly called his working environment a form of living. There were about ten hand-me-down chairs and a pulpit that had names carved in it, no scandalous sayings or street graffiti. Maybe they were the signatures of the builders, probably former inmates that bode their time by woodworking. On one wall was a faux stained-glass window, plastic. It hung like a picture frame by some tattered yarn. The whole room was lit by a single incandescent bulb with an illumination power of about forty watts. And the room smelled as though everything non-salvageable from the floors above had settled there.

Delvin chuckled to himself, knowing that in his neediest of days, he didn't live that frugle. Then he remembered that Shiloh Kimmons, prison chaplain, could come and go as he pleased.

Delvin Storm, the prisoner, couldn't.

"Jesus loves you, no matter how dark your sins, no matter what you've done," Shiloh proclaimed. He reached over to a small table and turned on a tape player. The music was scratchy and sounded like a band of toddlers. "Do it today," he continued with an emphasis that anyone within earshot of him should make a decision. "Come to Jesus, just now."

To tell the truth, he could've been an amputee, because not a soul budged.

Shiloh seemed undaunted by the lack of prisoner participation. He thanked everyone for attending the service, challenging each to return next Sunday, and he reminded those leaving to be respectful to those coming in, as a young man from the Nation of Islam would be preparing to conduct the next service for those of Muslim faith. He then stood around for a short while, committing himself to shaking each inmate's hand.

Delvin bowed his head and wedged between a couple of inmates who were headed out the door, but his hopes to escape the chaplain's grip were dashed.

"Have you been reading the Bible I gave you?" Shiloh asked.

Delvin felt a tinge of insult in that comment. "A little."

"Umm hmm," Shiloh mumbled. He had an analytical facial expression—something between a puckered, sour lemon look and a staunch jaw, clean slate face.

"Look, preacher, you're wasting your time. This religion stuff, I've never been into it."

"I'll come to see you later, Mr. Storm," Shiloh said, ignoring Delvin's remarks.

"You said you weren't pushy. I haven't invited you."

Delvin decided to work down some lunch and then return to his cell. The thunderstorm had formed a mud hole in the courtyard area, which meant the inmates would be inside for three, maybe four days. Most were napping out of plain boredom. He sat on his bed and picked up the Bible that Shiloh had given him. Fanning the pages, he stopped at Psalms 37:4, only catching the part that referenced him receiving his heart's desire. Those few words were the last ones he remembered before he dozed off.

He and some real estate colleagues were setting up the week's business meetings over brunch and Merlot at the Wet Kitty. He had inside information that Stonefield Trace had some wonderful lots at a half-mil and up. A lot of money to be made. He left the joint with the intent of getting Job in on the action, but the chump had too many fearful hairs on his chest . . .

"So, you've been reading." Shiloh stood in the opening of his cell, leaning on the bars. "And from the looks of things, you've been taking notes, too."

Delvin wiped the dream from his eyes, imagining he had taken a sleep aid so that, when the medicine wore off, he'd be sprawled on the couch of his posh downtown condo. Had to be the most potent drug he had ever taken, because it wasn't wearing off.

Delvin stretched in an attempt to gather together his body and mind. "Don't flatter yourself, Chaplain," he yawned. "This is hardly any notes from that trash you were feeding this morning. *Thus sayeth that; whither thou goest this.*" Delvin spanked the Bible shut.

"So that's what you thought of the sermon today, huh, Mr. Storm?"

He sneered, not believing the obviousness of the question. "I haven't seen one piece of evidence that a being—whom I cannot see—visits a prison to protect me and comfort me." Delvin tapped his chest. "For protection, give me a glock. For my comfort, give me a woman."

Shiloh's forehead creased.

"What good does it do?" Delvin paused to move closer to the bars. "Why believe in any god, unless it works on my behalf?"

"Jesus works for your behalf," Shiloh corrected, "but not in a fashion where you dictate to Him. He's not your prostitute. Far be it for Him to be your beckon call boy."

"Look, preacher, I can't tell you this any other way than straight out. You don't seem to understand that the only way you get ahead in this world is with money and power, and plenty of it. You don't have anything without them. You'll be nobody, and you'll get nowhere."

"So, you call this getting somewhere?" Shiloh's head did a quick turn down the cellblock, then back on Delvin. "It's true, Mr. Storm. We do have to live in this world. But the things you talk about, money and power; they're so temporary. So superficial."

"This world can eat you up. Money and power has the tendency to be a great equalizer when the other dung in life brings you down. But I understand, preacher. You don't look like the type that's ever tasted the corporate world. Where I come from, greed is a commendable thing. It's better to be a wolf than a lamb."

Shiloh's face was nonchalant. "Strange you would use that analogy, considering Jesus is often called the Lamb slain for our sins."

Delvin stuck a finger in Shiloh's face. "See? That right

there tells me this Jesus couldn't have been much of nothing."

Shiloh rubbed the top of his head, traced his hand down the side of his face and began squeezing his chin. "What's the cause of your rebellion? A friend? Brother?"

Joseph Bertram Wright. Delvin's former partner's name had settled down to his stomach, taken residence, agitated his inner being. Through all the physiological imbalances he was dealing with, he had to try and remain silent on that issue. But he didn't.

"The nigger's no brother. He sure isn't a friend. I haven't heard from him since I've been in here," he rattled off, realizing his mouth had skipped way ahead of his brain. "Look, preacher. I've had what I thought was a friend. He let me down, in more ways than one."

Shiloh kept his eyes down in puzzlement. "How so?"

Delvin boiled inside. It hadn't felt good, keeping his thoughts and feelings locked up. But Shiloh seemed to be an attentive listener and not a judge, so Delvin didn't mind letting the chaplain know a few things. "A friend will tell you when you're wrong, even when they may be afraid to say. And when a situation turns for the worst, a true friend, I think, will admit the part they played in a scheme, rather than keep their mouth shut to save themselves."

Shiloh caressed his forehead. "So . . . you've been hurt. It makes sense." The calm in his voice and demeanor kept Delvin off-guard, unnerved.

"I haven't been hurt. I don't let people do that to me," Delvin insisted. "I was disappointed. Nothing more." He sprung off his bunk, trounced over to the mirror and brushed the stray hair from his forehead.

He could feel Shiloh eyeing him, and he was doing it

without a blink. "Before you leave from here, your search for ultimate satisfaction will end on a positive note."

"Oh really?" Delvin did a split second survey. Nothing in present surroundings had smelled, tasted, or sounded right. In fact, nothing could've been more wrong. "There's no positive in this place." He then thought about Job and what he was planning. "Well, maybe *something* positive can come out of this."

In ignorance to Delvin's meaning, Shiloh said, "Oh, yeah. If you put your mind to it."

You don't know how much truth you just spoke, preacher. "If you think that Jesus-thing is your tool to convert me, then find yourself another tool. But I respect you sticking to your convictions. We need more men like you around here."

"I have time to see a major conversion in you. You'll be around here at least until your first parole board hearing."

That's three years from now. "Don't hold your breath, preacher. No far-fetched religion can change me."

Later that evening, Delvin could see that the library was unoccupied except for the librarian and what appeared to be a couple of spectacled, bucktoothed white males chatting among themselves in twentieth century pseudo-scientific jargon. Delvin figured them to be computer geek criminals trying to keep abreast of the latest technology. They appeared to be no threat by the way they scratched their greasy heads, painted fearful looks on their faces, and took off in an opposite direction.

He pulled up a chair, propped his feet up on a table, and began scanning the most recent copy of *Business Week*. He had become engrossed in reading when a thin hand emerged over the page he was on, almost to the point of touching his face.

The man's voice flowed like a heart that never skipped a beat. A Spock-like smoothness. "I understand that you have begun a sequence of data collection and tactics necessitating my expertise."

Delvin was startled because of the suddenness and angered by the intrusion, but overjoyed at the revelation. *Man. It took long enough.* He realized that he was staring into the eyes of the hook-up. It was the prison's resident encyclopedia. Murphy.

To think that this man could even gather the nerve to approach him. Surely he remembered that their initial meeting was far less than cordial.

"Why do you talk like somebody's English professor or something? Come off it." Delvin had to ask.

Murphy pulled up a seat. "Storm. What good did it do for Webster to have created a dictionary and thesaurus if he didn't expect the American people to take advantage of the English vernacular?"

Take a breath. Delvin felt his brain begging for an aspirin. The five-dollar words were being spouted off faster than he could decipher them. "I guess you've made your point." He reached beneath his undershirt and pulled out a folded, tattered sheet of paper. "I need these things. ASAP."

"You do realize, Storm, that our present state of affairs somewhat hinders the definition of ASAP to be effectual, do you not?"

"ASAP means as soon as possible—but we're in jail—don't expect miracles. I got it," Delvin said in frustration.

Murphy unfolded the paper, smoothing each fold as he progressed along. His eyes dotted the page from top to bottom as if he were studying a fine piece of poetry or prose. "A couple of the guys told me that you were present, accounted for at chapel. I did not perceive you as the religious type," he whispered.

Delvin curled his fist in clear view and twisted his face. "I'm not."

Murphy's eyes widened. "Don't misunderstand me, Storm. I have no animosity toward those who recognize omnipotent powers; gods and the like."

"I've just told you where I stand on that subject."

"I understand." He returned the paper to its folded state. "What do you want with these items?"

Delvin gripped the outer edge of the table. "I didn't realize that for you to secure these items, you had to know what I want them for."

"I only need the reassurance that your undertakings are upright; that they won't afford me additional incarceration time."

"You needn't worry."

"Storm, I want you to know that—as I've heard some inmate say in a broken slang—*the buck will end with you.* This is, of course, with the assumption that there's any trouble."

Delvin took a few seconds to let Murphy's words sink in. He knew that the list of items in and of itself wouldn't yield him any trouble. It would take someone who had known him on a past, personal level to put all the sections of his enigma together. Nobody fit that bill at Ashland FCE. "You're in no danger."

"Excellent."

Delvin snapped his fingers. "Let me see that list again right quick."

Murphy pinched the paper between the fore and middle fingers of his left hand and reached over.

Delvin grabbed it, whipped out a pen, wrote down a few words and handed it back to Murphy. "I added a toy for you. Stinson told me to."

"He made that proposition, did he?"

"Yeah. Some malarkey about every man needing a toy.

Boy, I tell ya. You guys have the weirdest thought patterns—"

Murphy interrupted. "Piaget. You should do more reading. That is, on a more philosophical level. Piaget, the French educational theorist, resolves that you can learn tremendous things from an individual when you observe them at play."

"Funny. Stinson said the same thing. Well, sort of."

"Hmm."

"Thus, we have toys. It's very simple."

Delvin listened to Murphy's intellectual dissertation, wondering how such a diverse thinker could land himself in prison. He was beginning to believe that great thinkers could have a criminal side, too. "I didn't think you would be the contact, but I shouldn't be surprised. You were the one mouthing off about having information." He then thought about the day he was elbow-deep in suds and the inmates' dishes. "Speaking of information; you know anything about some corn cobs Stinson told me not to throw away?"

Murphy sat back in the chair, patted the paper in his pocket as if he was giving Delvin some sign of assurance, and then he sneered. "Ahh. The remnants of our maize." He laughed. "You'll see."

Chapter 8

Give her of the fruit of her hands; and let her own works praise her in the gates. Proverbs 31:31

Morning traffic didn't bother Monica as she drove through Maricopa County's traffic grid, taking the time to make Pastor Harris's sermon personal. "And I will do better in the present than at my beginning." *God, I hope so.*

Monica surfed radio channels, settling on KPXQ, 1360 AM, and programmed it on her Camry. Chuck Swindoll was giving an inspiring message on his *Insights for Living* broadcast. It was her sequel to yesterday's religious experience. She pulled into Nine Iron Golf Resorts, certain that she would have a great day.

At nine o'clock, she walked in through the clubhouse entrance where she stopped at the rotunda and admired her surroundings.

In the center of the rotunda was a desk where a receptionist greeted her.

"Ms. Wright, the CEO would like to meet with you before you see your office suite. Please, have a seat," the lady said.

Monica had never seen so many tanned, taut bodies in

one place in all her life; not in person anyway. Men and women were arriving at every moment. Some dressed in dull but pricey business attire and many in designer sportswear prepared to go onto the golf course, the pool and spa, or the exercise suites. These same individuals would be making reservations for friends and associates through her office, she figured.

Minutes that seemed like eternity passed. She took a glance at her watch. Nine-fifteen. She snapped open her briefcase, a stainless steel piece given to her by fellow employees from her former job. She decided to spend the next few moments perusing the Nine Iron Golf and Resorts full-scale brochure and handbook, but the endless chatter and laughter hindered her concentration.

"Mrs. Wright?"

She looked up after getting over her slight shock. Cory Drummond, the CEO, had sprung in from nowhere it seemed, which couldn't have been difficult given the veil of hall noise that covered him.

"I'm sorry to have you waiting so long, which is the reason I came out to greet you myself instead of having my admin to show you in." He sounded sincere.

Cory wasn't a complete stranger to Monica. She had interviewed with him in late May, a process that lasted four hours and was spread over two days. During that time she looked for, but didn't detect, arrogance, self-pity, alcoholism, or any other sociological offenses in him. He appeared to be charming, professional, and committed to Christian beliefs. He was careful to point out that he took hold of his position in the company despite the reservations of other prominent and respected shareholders who wanted a chief officer with more experience.

"On my first day," Cory told Monica during her interview, "I had five voicemail messages from elite club

members saying they would be watching me and report-
ing back to the board of directors on how I was doing.
That was seven years ago." He told her that since those
first days, he has earned the establishment's respect. He
ended the conversation by telling her that was his expec-
tation of her.

During those next few moments, Monica had to pinch
herself because Cory Drummond was leading her to an
office inside of the building.

They terminated their walk at the very end of the hall,
in a conference room where six men were seated. There
were three Caucasians, two of Asian descent by appearance, and one African-American. All of them were dressed
in Brooks Brothers-style suits with drab ties and glowing
white shirts. Before them were thin black portfolios with
Monica Wright plastered on them in dead center with no
other writing.

"Please, Ms. Wright, have a seat," Cory said, keeping a
tedious facial expression and tone.

There were two seats available, one at the end of the
table with a clear view of the others. She decided not to
take that one.

She sat, positioning her briefcase at her feet and looked
around. There was silence.

Cory slid an envelope near her. It was sealed with no
writing on the outside. "We've run into a serious problem, Ms. Wright. I had to assemble as many directors as I
could for this person-to-person meeting, with the others
consenting to give me their thoughts, et cetera, by
proxy."

They're terminating me already.

Cory continued. "Our management situation has
shifted, causing a tremendous gap in our company that
has to be resolved. I've looked the situation over care-

fully, taking into consideration all of the angles and repercussions that could come up."

Monica uncrossed her legs, sighed and crossed them again.

"We have made a difficult, but needy decision." Cory broke out with a wide grin. "We can't offer you the reservations manager's position. Given your obvious qualifications, talent, skill, and strong willingness to learn, the board has consented to accept my recommendation of making you the new Vice President of Operations. Congratulations!" The entire room, minus Monica, chorused in laughter.

Her body had tensed like a wire, but loosened with her gasp of breath. "Why did you do that to me?" she asked in a shout. "I wondered why the plate on the office door had a different title than what I'd interviewed for. I was too scared to ask you why, Mr. Drummond."

"Mr. Drummond is my dad. Call me Cory," he demanded playfully.

The board members dispersed in sporadic fashion, still falling into fits of laughter when they exchanged glances with Monica. With her new position revealed and her tension eased, she could return the humor.

Cory sat on the edge of the conference table, flipping through a set of memos that his administrative assistant handed him. He smiled at some of the messages, frowned over some and then tossed them all at an empty ashtray. "Monica," he said, "don't leave just yet."

Her mind was on getting to her office and settling in. Maybe grab a relaxation snack. Instead, she opted to smile and sit.

"Open the envelope I gave you."

She had forgotten about it. "Should I be afraid?" she asked.

Cory pulled out a Mont Blanc from an interior coat pocket and began twirling it through his fingertips as he molded a sly look on his face. "Depends."

She broke the seal of the envelope and pulled out the folded sheet. It had her name on it, and a salary figure that made her feel like holy-dancing and praise-shouting. She swallowed to assemble her nerves, and asked, "Is this for real?"

"Think you can be happy with that? Hubby should feel all right too," he said.

She peered at the paper again, folded it and returned it to the envelope. She calculated the salary to be thirty-five thousand more than for the previous position she'd been offered. "This has been confirmed?"

"With health, life, and 401K. Of course, complimentary membership. Welcome to the life. Work. Enjoy."

"Thanks, Cory, for your confidence." *Thank you, Lord.*

When Monica arrived home and saw Job with his feet propped up and his behind resting in a recliner, she wanted to strangle him. Four disassembled boxes appeared to be the only work he had done all day while she slaved at the corporate plantation. She brushed by him and looked into the kitchen, where she smelled food cooking and saw pots on the stove. She turned and looked at Job, whose grin disarmed her anger.

"Mmm. You cooked, so you're forgiven," she conceded.

She unfolded the details of her first day, which included her express ride up a rung on the management ladder. "Eighty-thousand dollars," she exclaimed with emphasis on every syllable, and then she repeated the amount with less bravado.

Job's eyes glinted, then immediately did an opposing expression that Monica couldn't read with any certainty.

It was a facial snapshot she'd never seen from him before. A portrait she hoped never to see again.

"How are the people?" he asked.

Her mind reversed to that morning assembly with the CEO and board members. "They seem to be pretty easy to work with, but they can be jokesters at times. They love to laugh, so I guess it's a good thing." She went on explaining that she had to hire her own assistant. "I'm treating everybody with kid gloves right now."

"Which is the very reason I don't give out my past to folks who pry."

"I know I'm on a honeymoon with my job right now. The real in people will eventually come out. That's why I'll go slowly, choose my friends carefully, and make sure I'm always truthful."

Monica was not as concerned about the behavior or responses of friends or co-workers as she was about Job's truthfulness, and whether any of his truths or lies would ever resurface.

Chapter 9

. . . Therefore suffered I thee not to touch her. Genesis 20:6b

School had been in session for several weeks and Job's teaching space, he thought, was shaping up. His computers, internet, intranet and all, were up and running. Brand new text and workbooks were on the shelves. Posters with vocational messages and class rules had been strategically placed around the room. He even had a peace lily and an aquarium to liven up the place.

"I have a proposition for you," Bianca said as she walked into Job's classroom.

The door wasn't open. Can you knock? Okay. You are the principal.

He stopped jotting the next day's lesson on the dry erase board and swallowed the shock of her presence. He wanted some clarification out of her quickly, before he got the wrong impression.

"Wow." She strolled along the walls of his classroom, turning on occasion, giving an approving look.

Job didn't want to be overconfident of his teaching at that point. Compared to the rest of Mountain River's Business Ed faculty, he was a veteran in the corporate community, but an apprentice in the classroom. A critique of his instruction techniques had to be around the corner. Even more, he wanted to know, with some reservation, the basis to her proposition.

Bianca concluded her parade around the classroom. She stopped and leaned against a corner of his desk with her arms folded and her legs crossed at the ankles. "How're you adjusting here? Is everything all right?"

He walked over to the opposite corner of the desk and put his pen and lesson book down. "Truthfully, I'm making out pretty good. No real problems to speak of."

"Making out pretty good," she repeated.

Job wasn't sure whether the soft, pampered look she gave him was real or a daydream. "Yeah."

Bianca eyes seemed fixated on him. "I'm glad. I don't want you to ever think that we don't care about our employees. We want you comfortable. To feel like you can talk to us when you have a problem. Work-related or otherwise."

Job could do nothing but drift. Bianca's body movements and words seemed premeditated. Not a syllable wasted. She took charge in a corporate, but boudoir sort of way.

"I know you're in your first year teaching here, Mr. Wright. But I've been watching you."

"Thanks."

"As is normal procedure, and for your protection, your duties have to be limited in your beginning years. It gives you time to hone your skills as a teacher. So, I've decided to give you only one assignment that pays one-fifth above your regular salary."

"I appreciate it, Ms. Rizzo."

"It's just us talking right now. You can call me Bianca," she declared. Her face showed that she meant just that. "Anyway. I've decided to assign you to the VOES pro-

gram." She unfolded her arms, revealing a large envelope that strained at the folds. She placed it on the desk
in front of him.

Job opened the package and pulled out the contents to
a point where he could glimpse, but not take the materials
out of order. Student application forms, parental consent,
course descriptions—much too much for a five-second
look. Each sheet or pamphlet had the initials VOES at the
top. "What in the world is that?" he asked about the program name.

"It's the Vocational Occupational Educational Series.
Our students receive opportunities to get hands-on training and compete in contests from the regional to national
scale."

"Why me?"

"Because your résumé includes years of practical business experience. You were the obvious choice."

Job's heart rate leaped. His hands began clamming up,
fingertips dropped in temperature. "Résumé?"

"Why, yes. Your workforce experience can be a testi-
mony to the students who will participate in the group."

I can't seem to get away from my real estate mess.

"Not every student is college material. But every student needs practical preparation, which is the whole purpose of the VOES program."

Job mentally let off some tension. "Oh. I see."

"Superintendent McManus and I have discussed this
extensively. You're the man for the job. Being the freshman Business Ed teacher is irrelevant to us, so come see
me tomorrow during your planning period. There are
regs in this program that have to be followed. We'll discuss them." Bianca pulled at the top of her two-piece suit
and then reached out her hand. "Congratulations."

Job shook her hand, meeting her eye for mysterious

eye. At the same time, his body heat raised to levels he didn't want to go. He would have to wrap a belt of discipline around himself when it came to his boss. She was sending confusing signals. Was she business, pleasure, or a mixture of both? He had had enough trouble to overcome without creating something new.

Job had to give her a firm grip then let her go.

"Remember," she cooed, "My door's always open."

Oh Lord, Job thought after Bianca left. The way she moved and talked struck him in a manner that sent his gears moving in ways he hadn't felt since the beginning of his marriage. *I can't refuse to be in her presence. She is fine, but she's my boss.* He slumped in his desk chair, relieved that particular sensations were fleeing.

He only wished Monica had the capability of tingeing him like a desert wildfire, but she was always fussing and focusing on his shortcomings.

Ms. Rizzo's—Bianca's—words don't hold criticisms. "Gotta stop thinking like this," he said out loud. Only the classroom's echo answered back. He sprung up from the chair and left the room, slamming the door behind him. The safest place for him right then would be 2333 Rong.

Job spent every second of the twenty-minute drive home trying to clear his head. *Help me shake this.* He had little faith that his sound bite prayer would give relief because little, if any, ever came his way.

He walked through the door that afternoon to the sounds and smells of stir fry, thinking Monica had stopped by the Golden Buddha on Forty-fourth Street, a high-end bistro that Larry and Fontella had introduced them to. That would have been good. No. Monica was busy doing her slave-over-the-stove Chinese food thing. That was better.

"You know we're supposed to begin attending couple's class this evening." Monica rolled her eyes and smacked her lips. "And don't tell me you forgot."

Job gritted his teeth. He wouldn't have to make up stories to get out of all the churchgoing, if it wasn't for Fontella's sales pitch on how wonderful the church's ministries are, and for Monica's desire to be involved in some religious activity.

Above all, when it came down it, he had forgotten about the couple's class for that evening. His mind was busy creating a game of its own. *Should I? Shouldn't I? Tell. Don't tell. Is there something to tell? Is there not?* "I've really got a lot of work honey. Can we skip tonight?"

Degrees of Disgust was the portrait on her face. "You start missin' one thing and then you'll want to miss another. Before you know it, you're not going to church altogether."

"You've done read too much into missing *one* couple's session. It ain't all that. Just this once, c'mon."

She picked up the Kikkoman's bottle and sprinkled a little soy sauce into the pan. The outline of her jaws showed that she was gritting her teeth. She said in a malicious tone, "Joseph Bertram Wright, let's be committed to at least one thing without a ton of excuses."

Job felt like he had swallowed rocks and a boulder had landed in his pit, commanded to stay there for sheer punishment. Her words solidified his thought; anyone else's speech right then would be a balm, a respite from the usual verbal tensions.

She grated about a teaspoon of ginger, added it to the wok, now sizzling. "We're not missing anymore unless it's a good excuse."

Before he could consciously put a halt on his response, he shouted, "Get off my dern back, Monica. Ain't you ever got anything good to say?"

There was silence with the exception of the food, which seemed to have a conversation with itself.

Job's body tightened and cool tracks of sweat rolled down his back. "It's just been a day, Monica. I'm sorry. Really."

She cut the stove eye off. The wounding look she gave made him believe eating was impossible anyway.

"You brought me out here. We're working toward what you might call *doin' fine*," she said. "I want to keep doin' fine."

"Yeah, but—"

"Don't interrupt me, man. And for God's sake, don't cut off our blessings. It's one thing for God to allow us to be tested on our faith. It's another for us to do things that cause problems. Things we can avoid."

"You're making this out to be more of a deal than it is."

Monica's face had flushed, and tears started to form. "Take care of me, Job. I'm begging. Take care of me."

Chapter 10

But Sarai was barren; she had no child. Genesis 11:30

The corporate culture of Nine Iron had given Monica a baptism during her first thirty days on the job. Being a vice prez gave her Carte Blanche to all the amenities it offered, and she did take advantage of an occasional spa treatment or the tennis courts. Not to the extent, though, that she would drown in the culture.

But what she viewed others doing was, in her eyes at the least, sinful and damaging to the human body and soul. Far be it for her to be a part of that social wave. She would let others flaunt that life.

Some paid for the privilege. Others were employed into it. Corporate slugs and socialite honeys sipping on Courvoisier. Dick and Jane puffing Cuban cigars after hours and at power lunches. Scheduling the wife or husband in for a break at noon. Brokering a deal at five. Working those same and similar indulgences out of their systems before heading to their respective personal addresses.

Golfing, Nautilus machines, concierge service and the other amenities were a religion to many, but far from a spiritual one. *But, hey. Not my problem.* Her daily prayer was that she didn't get lassoed into the ambience of it all.

On the previous day, Monica had listened to Pastor Harris as he concluded a three-part sermon on Expecting Blessings. She likened his comments to the blessings she and Job had received since moving to Phoenix. The job, despite its pitfalls, was a key blessing for which she was indebted to the Lord.

She pressed the pager function on her phone. "Nami, can you come in here for a moment?"

Monica signed off on a couple purchase requests, tossed them into her OUT box, and checked the reminder on her palm pilot when the administrative assistant came into the door.

"Yes, ma'am."

Nami Delacroix. Fontella recommended the assistant job for the twenty-three-year-old single mom who had been a member of Chapel in the Desert for the last several years.

Nami was a native of the French Quarter, but had no accent, probably because she moved away at three. It could be debated as to where she got her eyes because their color spoke Grand Canyon brown or Mardi Gras gold, depending on a person's preference. A Creole and black full-figured woman who walked with such feline grace that the well-heeled power brokers frequenting Nine Iron forgot all about the Barbie dolls when they eyed her.

Monica was proud of herself. She had taken the opportunity to give another sister a chance at corporate America. And Nami had been anything but a disappointment. Her wit and effervescence made her an asset to the company.

"I'm out of bottled water. I checked my fridge," Monica said, somewhat apologetically. She reached for her pocketbook and pulled out a few dollars. "Here. Buy me a couple bottles at the NIC [Nine Iron Commissary] until we can order a couple cases."

"Okay, but I have several bottles chilling in my office fridge. Save your dollars." Nami handed the money back.

Monica reared back into her chair, rubbing her belly. "You don't mind?"

"No. I'll bring you a couple bottles."

"Thanks."

"You all right?"

Monica tried not to show any grimacing looks, but Nami was observant, a trait she valued. "I'm fine . . . I think. Just some queasiness."

"If you have some salty crackers, that may settle your stomach," Nami suggested. "Works for me."

"I'll try that. And when you come back with the water, bring me the fiscals for August, last year. I want to do some comparisons."

"Sure will."

"And umm, when you leave, would you close the door behind you? I need a few seconds of quiet time."

"Yes, ma'am." She left.

Monica waited a moment before thumbing through her Rolodex, pulling up the Logans' home phone number. Fontella told her yesterday at church that she would be home all day Monday. So she dialed their residence.

"I'm not calling just to be social," Monica declared after the hellos. "I need to know the name and number of that OB-GYN of yours."

After much pleading and a last minute cancellation, Dr. Jason Jones was able to fit Monica in that day during a two hour lunch break.

"You show signs of pregnancy. Surprisingly, even

physiologically," he said. "I can see why you were convinced it had happened." He wrapped his stethoscope around his neck.

She began pulling the clinical top over her body. "You see something unusual?"

"Well," he said, with a puzzled inflection in his voice, "the tardiness of your cycle, the lightheadedness, and other indicators would make you think that you've conceived. But you're not pregnant, I assure you." He picked up her chart, thumbing the pages while he pursed his lips.

She was certain Dr. Jones's real interest wasn't in the chart. "Doctor?" She wanted Dr. Jones to wipe the asinine look off his face. Unbeknownst to him, his look became her instrument of pain.

"Sometimes, a woman can have such a strong desire to be pregnant, that she will exhibit the symptoms of pregnancy without it really being so. This is your case."

"No, please," she pleaded, "don't tell me that."

"Do you all want to have a child?"

She paused for a brief moment. "More than anything," she admitted. She was clear about her desire for a child, but she was foggy about how Job felt on the same subject. She was, however, certain that if she and Job were together in that desire, well and good. If they were not, then she would use him as a sperm bank, and pray that God would take care of her and her baby. Without Job.

Dr. Jones perched on a stool and then rolled himself over to a small desk inside the room. "I'll be able to get your med records from Louisville with the release you signed. In the meantime . . . do you know of anything physical that prevents you from conceiving?"

"No." Nothing that she could recall.

"Pray, concentrate on you and your husband's act of love. You'll get results in due time. Meanwhile, I'm prescribing some pre-natal vitamins. Sometimes they aid in triggering a woman's body into conception."

"So I don't need to run to the pharmacist and get a Clear Blue Easy to double-check you?" she kidded.

"Naw."

Monica returned to the office and began to wade through a stack of memos arranged by importance. She had told Nami that she preferred not to be disturbed unless it was vital, but Job paid her a visit that afternoon.

"I've known all-weekend long that I was going to surprise you. Today was a half-day for students and an option for certified staff," he said, "so I left a little after the last bus rolled off.

"You really got me, boy." She did her best to be jubilant, despite the day's events. She refused to give him details until that evening.

"Well look, girl. Let's press. Your work will be here tomorrow."

"It wouldn't look good for me, taking off on the same day I get my first check."

Job was silent with a fevered, corrupted look.

Monica wasn't sure whether it was from her refusal to go along with his plan, or that her salary outweighed his. "We'll go out on the town tomorrow evening. I promise. Do a jazz club or something," she insisted.

His lips pursed. "Sure. Sure. Okay."

"You might as well cheer up; you have something else you need to do. Something much more important than frolicking with me."

"That's not how I'm seeing it."

"That's not how I'm seeing it," she repeated with sarcasm. She whirled around, snatched up her palm pilot and began tapping the stylus on the screen. "You're forgetting today's date?"

"August 14. What's the big deal?"

"You should be at home. It's the deadline for you to have our taxes filed. The extension?" Monica put a Cheshire cat grin on her face.

"Aw, man."

After work, Monica and Fontella met at a local sub shop where she unloaded the news of her doctor's visit. They touched, prayed and agreed for the Lord to bless her and for His will to be done.

When Monica arrived home, Job looked like the day had piled up on him. He was in the yet-to-be-set dining room, among a slew of boxes with stacks of receipts and government tax forms on top, squeezing his forehead. He crumpled up some scrap paper and tossed it, under-handedly, at her, then laughed.

"How're you coming?" she asked. In a way, she felt sorry for him. "You created this predicament. Deal with it."

He breathed. "Don't remind me."

Monica sat on a sturdy box. *Well. No time like the present. Here it goes.* A can of Arizona tea and a safe deposit box full of nerve was what she used to furnish the hour by hour details of her day.

Job swallowed, easing his look. "Umm. I don't know what to say."

"Say what you feel."

"You're forcing me to do too much thinking right now."

"I want us to work together as one loving couple. I'm having a hard time believing you'd be happy if I became pregnant."

"It's difficult for me to know where we are in our marriage, or what I want. You spend too much time pointing out my short comings. Every time I turn around, you're always onto me about one thing or another. "Maybe not every time, but a lot."

"Where's all this coming from, Job?" She shook her head and smacked her lips to conjure up more to say, but could only come up with, "Give me just one example."

"This." Job held up a stack of tax filings.

"That's not me pointing out where you're lacking. That's just diligence." She realized that Job still had an abundance of work before him and that her day had been anything but smooth. She felt her eyelids sagging. "This discussion is longer than the next five minutes."

"I know. We won't resolve it tonight. But we do have to talk—"

"We can't just talk about it, we've got to do something about it," she said.

Chapter 11

For the Lord knoweth the way of the righteous, but the way of the ungodly shall perish. Psalms 1:6

Delvin's face wasn't buried as deep into his breakfast plate as the other inmates'. He picked up a cup of coffee. And there it was.

YOUR PLACE @ AFTERNOON MAIL CALL was the note in its entirety. He looked around, seeing if anyone looked out of the ordinary. Maybe he could zero in on the messenger. He wondered how. In a prison, activities seemed to take place so covertly, with such ease. *What took so long for my request to be fulfilled?* It didn't matter. It was a sign that his day had come.

Two-thirty P.M. It was easy to hear, or not hear, the myriad of he-motions and responses from individual cells when packages were received. He thought their overuse of passion was silly.

Then, Delvin's turn came.

He was caught off guard by the person who was standing at his cell door. The man was beyond what he would describe as "robbed of good looks." His right cheek showed evidence of a third-rate skin graft job. He didn't smile. He didn't talk or even grunt. His appearance could've landed him a starring role in MJ's "Thriller" video. The man pushed a plastic cart with an upper and lower bin, which only added to his hideous visage.

"You got something for me?" Delvin asked, praying that the man didn't sense his bona fide fear.

The man bent down, pulled out a 12x12x18 box from the bottom bin, handed it to Delvin and walked away.

Delvin asked, "You have a na—"

"His name is Pilchoevsky," interrupted Murphy, who had done his usual slithering onto the scene. "But you should refer to him by the same sobriquet as the rest of the residents here in Ashland. We call him Deliverer. And believe me, he always does."

Delvin asked, "Why Deliverer?"

Murphy confirmed. "Because in this crack of inhumanity, he's the supreme entity behind inmates getting anything accomplished that's worth meaning in their decrepit lives. Deliverer doesn't talk because he doesn't have to. Or maybe, he can't. Nobody really knows."

Deliverer took hold of the cart, bowed his body and walked away.

Murphy whispered, "Deliverer doesn't choose to involve himself with others' affairs. Unless, of course, you pay him to."

"What happened to him?"

"He used to set up off-shore accounts for high-dollar crimes. Computer fraud and the like. On the day the establishment moved in for the sting, Deliverer hopped in his Jag, trying to outrun them so he could get to his awaiting Cessna for a flight out of the country."

Delvin found the deformed mail clerk's story fascinating.

Murphy leaned on the crossbars and continued. "The establishment attempted, to no avail, to convince the guy to give up, surrender to the authorities. He ran his precious automobile into a parking meter and sat while the cops surrounded him. Poor guy. He tried to swift-kick his door open, but it wouldn't budge. Stupid. An overexcited cop and stupidity."

"I can imagine."

"He climbed over into the backseat, I guess to get out of the car. Anyway, he failed at his chance. That officer shot; hit that gas tank." Murphy looked off into the cell block's open space. "Jaguar's just weren't meant for that."

"What?"

"A bullet. It caused the fuel reservoir to burst, catch fire, splattering flaming fluid on his face."

Delvin began tearing away the layers of sealing tape that held the box together. "Better him than me."

Murphy flared his nose. "I can see that story reached into your inner being." The twists and turns in his voice made the sarcasm evident.

"Yeah. Well." He lifted the flaps, moving the Styrofoam peanuts aside. He looked at Murphy from the corner of his eye. "Everything seems to be in order."

"Let me give you fair warning, Mr. Storm. Never, ever try to bypass me to go to Deliverer. The information and distribution network doesn't operate in any manner other than the one established."

"You have no argument out of me."

"Also, remember this, when Deliverer sets wheels into motion, there's no spiraling in the opposite direction." His eyes sharpened, the brows pointed to each other. "So be positive of any requests you make."

"I consider myself warned." Delvin reached into the box, pulled out a box labeled *Trivial Pursuit Genius III*. "For you."

Murphy stared and then smiled. "Ah. Excellent selection. A game that will stimulate my eclectic knowledge. I thank you."

"If you see Stinson, tell him I have something for him too."

He wanted time alone and got it. *Did Deliverer secure everything?*

Delvin considered the contents of the box as individual treasures, a collective bounty. His skin increased with sensitivity as he looked at each item:

Ream of white paper.

Stamps, envelopes, clear tape dispenser.

Plastic three-ring binder.

Latest issue of the *Robb Report*. He would be able to at least pretend his exquisite tastes were being catered to.

A copy of Sun Tzu's *Art of War*. His plans would take strategy. Just the read to get him in the mood.

Back copies of Louisville's *Courier Journal*.

A 1992–93 Syracuse University yearbook.

Rubik's cube, the toy he would give to Stinson when he came around before lock-up that evening.

A 1988 copy of Nashville's Hume Fogg yearbook. Job's old high school in the year he graduated.

Later that same evening, Delvin heard an unfamiliar sound in the hall, a two-step dance of human feet followed by a clanging and light crunching of items bouncing against each other. He couldn't make it out, so he waited as the sound came his way.

Stinson showed up at his cell door with about six liquid-filled containers in a bag.

Delvin picked up the Rubik's cube and started to make a comment, but Stinson held up a finger to his lips. Silence, which was a first for him. He took the toy and exchanged it with one of the bottles.

Delvin accepted the plastic container, which was shaped like milk man delivery bottles of the '60s. He whiffed. It was grain alcohol with a mysterious animal-decay aroma. He took a sip. The answer to those corn scraps became clear. That night, his bunk, that bottle and the knowledge of his request fulfilled became his relief. His senses numbed, his worries fogged. His ills, just for a moment, were forgotten.

On the following day just before noon, the cell doors had opened and the majority of the inmates had gone down to the cafeteria. Delvin decided to forgo lunch, recognizing he had more important matters, and he could satisfy his hunger with snacks from the canteen should he so desire.

He looked toward his cell door where Murphy had made his usual reptilian entrance. "You're compiling quite a collection there. A hobby?" He referred to the conglomeration of news clippings, scribbling on notebook paper, and other diverse material covering the bunk.

Delvin had worked through the night to plaster an eclectic selection of articles, pictures and correspondence. Any person with a reasonable amount of intelligence could've walk into his cell, glanced at the mural, and made accurate determinations about his schooling, vices, and dislikes. "This occupies my time."

Murphy informed Delvin that Shiloh had inquired about his whereabouts. "He hadn't seen you since the first time you went to chapel. He wants to know if it was something he said?"

"The whole religion thing isn't for me. I thought I

made it clear to him." Delvin ripped an article from the *Courier Chronicle* that read:

WRIGHT AND STORM
REAL ESTATE TWENTIETH CENTURY STYLE

It went into his spiral notebook after a nauseating thought of his past partnership fluttered through his mind.

"This place is sneaking up on you," Murphy said. "It's an aggression you haven't worked out as of yet. And you've been here, some—"

"Never mind that. I need you to do something for me."

"Alright. I am here to be your conciliator. What's your desire?"

If you must know, destroy Joseph Wright. Equal partners in business should feel equal pain when put out of business. Well, it couldn't be totally equal. There was no way of seeing Job in prison. What he did want, and felt he could do, was to put his former partner, classmate, and friend in a dungeon-like position. And to do it, there was a fundamental piece of info that he needed to know. That's where Murphy, Deliverer, and anyone else connected to the prison's vita-link came into play. "I need someone found."

"Blunt and to the point, eh?" Murphy asked. "You'd like to initiate an endeavor. An extant human being or someone assigned into the most recently departed?"

"They're alive and doing too darn well. At least, I think they are."

"More than one person."

"Just one. Well, truthfully, he's married, so I guess his wife can be buried with him. Wherever he is."

"That's the gist of it. You aspire to have someone located."

"Yeah." *That'll do for now, anyway.*

"So. What will you pay to have Joseph Bertram Wright located?"

How did Murphy know that? Job's full name was given with such an assured tone, as if he was a soothsayer reading Delvin's palm. And the revelation was real, no hoax.

"You have a peculiar way with things."

Murphy told him, "Like the R&B tune, 'it's written all over your face,' and I rarely use euphemisms. I don't regard them as academia. Pictures of the two of you together. A copy of that man's high school annual in your possession. Other paraphernalia obtained at your request and at your disposal. How could I not have deduced? But, for the life of me, I can't determine how you ended up with him on the cover of *Black Enterprise* magazine. You are, by no means, black."

Delvin explained to Murphy that his lineage was Israeli on his mother's side and a mixed-bag on his father's, his paternal grandfather being part black, Italian and Creole.

"A percentage of what you described is of African descent," Murphy concurred.

"But the fact is I'm *non-White*. And *BE* wanted to recognize us as partners, together in the realty firm." Delvin felt a peculiarity settle in his gut. "And besides, Joseph Wright was recognized as the actual founder of the company. And there's no doubt that he's black."

Murphy widened and then narrowed his eyes. "Oh. I see."

Delvin knew that Murphy was trying to sum up exactly how a major African-American magazine saw fit to include him as a major feature. But what was the point in trying to figure it out? What had been done had been done. And it was because of that thought, that Delvin's response to Murphy was, "I'll bet you see."

"None of us have purity running through our veins." Murphy laughed, which sounded more like a hiss. "Get past your apprehensions and misgivings, Mr. Storm. Information—I told you—is my specialty. It would stand to reason that I'd figure out who it is in whom you have such deep-seated interest."

"Having to work through a third party gives me cause for suspicion. Anyway. I'll admit it. You're right. It's Job Wright who I want found. And don't take long. I want this to happen while I still can breathe under my own will," Delvin declared.

"Oh, the enigma that the lack of concrete knowledge creates. Don't let me unnerve you. Guys like you couldn't get your needs fulfilled without gentlemen like me."

"And capital. This is far from an ordinary request."

Delvin knew that on his end it would take a few days, a letter and some phone calls to his attorney, who had taken power over his financial accounts, to pull cash aside for his bidding at the moment. He had developed some confidence in Murphy's abilities, and handing out cash as the incentive would be worth the reward. "How much are we talking?"

Murphy took a brief scan of their surroundings for unruly ears that might be clinging against the cell bars. He turned back, his eyes widening. "I'll have to check with Deliverer on the financial measures. Then, he'll come through with positive results."

An evening shift guard came marching through the cell block, rapping his baton on the bars. "Start heading to your rooms, gentlemen," he hollered.

Delvin nodded to the guard when he looked in, and walked on down the line toward the end of the block. Confident that the guard was out of sight, he handed

Murphy a small piece of ruled paper where he had written bits of Job's personal information. "This should aid you in finding him."

Murphy took the paper, stuffed it in his right shoe under the sock. "May I ask why you want this man's whereabouts, Mr. Storm?"

Silence.

Murphy must've seen the scowl on Delvin's face. He returned a fearful look of his own. "You know what," he said, "forget I asked. It really does not matter. I'll pass your request on to Deliverer."

"Good." The fact that Delvin had just commissioned an APB on his former partner from a private cell inside Ashland Prison didn't mean that it carried no relevance, or that it was an impossible feat. He was confident. Alive or dead, Job Wright would be found.

Chapter 12

. . . Whosoever looketh on a woman to lust after her hath committed adultery with her already in his heart. Matthew 5:28

Amazing.

A little more than a year seemed to have gone by as fast as Job could flip thirteen calendar pages. He was grateful that a considerable amount of time and distance had come between his past and present life.

In fact, until that morning, there had been no mention of it. Monica, who seemed to have become adept at raising difficult conversations, tried her hand at a verbal combat while she fixed breakfast. But Job wasn't having it, and she backed down.

He had surged right into his second year at Mountain River after radiant evaluations of his first year performance. The students' response to his teaching style and classroom decorum had been positive; his students helped him shape his classroom mannerisms. The faculty and staff had shown their respect when it came to his opinions and input on matters of curriculum and school improvement.

His end-of-year observations and evaluations came from Bianca Rizzo, who insisted on doing them, which was a responsibility ordinarily reserved to one of her assistant principals. According to Frances, her administrative assistant, Bianca claimed Job as her "personal project."

After Job's second period class that morning, he reported to Bianca's office to turn in his progress report for the school's VOES program.

Frances didn't bother to escort Job to the principal's office or look up from her work. She angled her head in the direction of the principal's office.

Job hadn't achieved a decent level of comfort when he was alone with Bianca, even after working with her for over a year. He couldn't help but to be attracted to her grace and sensuality—qualities that seemed to be ingrained into her DNA. Nothing would've pleasured him more than to raise the topic of their interactions and hear his own words, "Bianca, I feel the magnetism between us, but nothing's going to happen," without sounding ignorant or hostile. And he didn't want her response to be misunderstood, unreceptive, or aggressive. He had tried to convince himself that in time, the sparks would go away, but the longer his tenure with her, the brighter his flame. Thankfully, he'd managed to only visualize a transgression and not turn it into action.

"Aw c'mon," he said to Frances, hoping she would take time and be his segue to meeting the boss. "Ms. Rizzo may be doing something we're unaware of. You might want to look in and announce me."

Frances took the pencil in her hand and waved it in the direction of the principal's office. Despite his anxiety, he had to go it alone.

Job walked up to the door, and stood face to face with a poster that read, "MY FACULTY IS MY WELCOMED DIVERSION." Although the door was cracked, he knocked. "Ms. Rizzo?"

Bianca's eyes were glued to the television mounted from the ceiling in a corner of the office. Its volume was startling. She nodded indefinably, and without comment, gestured for him to enter.

Job closed the door behind him. "You think you've got it loud enough?" He took a seat in one of the twin burgundy leather chairs, taking a moment to eye her office, a dimly lit space decorated with furniture and other pieces of understated elegance.

It was the first time Job could recall Bianca acting like he wasn't there, her fixation on what sounded like a news commentator's account.

"Oh, my God!" she shrieked. Her skin, usually a deep olive color, was a pale, morbid hue. Her hands had cupped around her mouth.

He could tell that she wasn't ready to hear about his group's progress, regardless of how positive it was. He placed the written report on her desk, and then moved around to see what she was viewing that apparently had her stunned.

"I thought I was watching a movie, a joke. It's real . . ." Her lips trembled and her voice drifted off as her eyes reddened, lifting up a well of tears.

He stood, reeling in confusion and wondering what kind of predicament he had walked into. "Tell me what you're watching," he demanded.

She gazed at him, eyes so white and wide, as though she had no pupils or irises. "You don't know?" she screamed. She wrapped her arms around herself. Her skin returned, in that moment, to its normal tint. "I'm sorry, you wouldn't know."

Just then, the CNN broadcaster interrupted:

**. . . AND THEN A SECOND PLANE CRASHED
INTO THE SOUTH TOWER OF THE WORLD**

TRADE CENTER AT 9:03 AM EASTERN TIME. THE CRASH LEVELED THIS TOWER UPON IMPACT . . .

"New York. Towers. Early this morning," she said.

Job listened to the broadcast, this time more closely, trying to pick up a few definitive details to place between Bianca's speckled explanation.

"That was over three hours ago," he said under his breath.

The news commentator repeated the time of the event. Job fought to think of something he could say or do to lighten the moment. He seized a couple Kleenex and handed them to her. "Maybe you should go home. Or I can get Frances."

"There's no way I can leave school right now. Everyone will be torn up over the news. I've got to help keep things going, keep it together." Bianca turned around to him, burying herself into his arms, molding into his body. "Hmm."

She moved against him with such quickness that he was prohibited from making a sensible thought or physically resisting. Her eau de toilette (he was confident that it was Chloe) wafting up his nostrils didn't help the situation.

He felt a rush of the forbidden, an alluring embodiment of wholesomeness. He was thankful her office door was closed with no window, just a solid piece of wallboard. He curled his arms around her, winding his fingertips into the small of her back. He tried to think of himself only as a comfort to her. He limited his thoughts to that.

She purred in response to the closeness.

He managed to wrestle one arm away, lock his hand around the TV remote and turn the volume down. He took her shoulders with a gentle grip and nudged her to an arm's distance, giving her a concerned look. "You gonna be all right?"

Her cream colored blouse was tearstained. She pulled strands of her hair behind her ears, but her panting caused them to fall back out of place. "Yes. I'm fine." She wiped her face. "I can't believe people could be so mean." She pulled in closer, nestling her face on Job's chest.

His psyche kicked in. Skin itching, muscles contracting and expanding. *Please* was all the prayer he could think of.

He had a feeling that she knew the embrace was out of place—using heartrending reactions to the 9/11 attacks as a catalyst to make her advances.

Tempted? He couldn't deny.

Over the past months, Monica had managed to fill him with a paranoia and bitterness from her constant complaints and her undying desire to start a family. She blamed him for it all.

Bianca could be the ideal escape from his tribulations. Her responses at that moment proved to him she'd be a willing candidate.

There was a flip side to his thoughts, which said, "*no.*" Bianca wouldn't be trouble-free. His boss and lover? Disturbing his marriage wasn't worth all that.

Then the unmentionable happened.

Bianca yanked at the cinch in his belt, drawing them waist to waist. She worked her delicate mouth onto his, locking him into a passionate kiss.

The combination of sudden movements threw Job off-balance. Bianca's desk was the only support that kept them from falling, intertwined, on the floor.

Job felt the wetness of her lips as she drained the last liter of innocence and sensuality from his body, a smooth transference of stored-up urgency.

As Bianca backed away, she sighed, slowly opening her eyes. "Oh, God, I've wanted to do that for the longest," she said, not allowing Job time enough to think coherently. She swayed over to the back of her desk, the small slit on the back of her skirt widened, revealing her thighs. She sat. "See how easy that was? Proof that we can be intimate and professional if we allow, no matter what we do or the circumstance. Don't you agree?"

Shock was the only way to describe how Job felt as he tried to steady himself. "You're my boss." He shoved his wedding band in her face.

Bianca's forehead creased into confusion. "I am your boss." Her response was flat, mimicked. "You're merely consoling me in the time of need. I do have feelings that require consolation, sometimes."

Job listened to her explanation and lost all poise and grace. "I just can't do this." *I feel like I want to.* "I just can't."

"I know you think you're going to stick to that position. But time will tell." She batted her eyelids.

Job knew that was for sensual effect and, in a sense, it was working. "How'll we work together now?" he asked. "What about my job?"

Bianca's visage changed to a blank slate. "Why would I consider firing you? You're doing your job in a professional manner. People like and respect you."

"I know, but—"

"Oh no, I've got plans for you," she said in a mysterious tone of voice. "And if, on a given day, you say your final word is that nothing can happen between us, then, your job will remain intact."

Thank you, Jesus. He sighed, more for the salvation of his job than anything else.

It was plain to Job that she was a vixen behind wraps, able to do her thing like a hydrant; smooth, able to cease and resume on a whim. If he yielded to her, deciding to make a connection, fine. If not, things would still appear copasetic.

Bianca relaxed into her chair. "I see that I've overwhelmed you. Go to class, Mr. Wright. We'll talk later, for sure, because I have some news that dwarfs your report on the VOES program. But I can tell that you wouldn't be able to handle my news right now."

Job wanted to ask what she meant by that statement, but he walked out of her office with unanswered questions. For a moment, his vanity did an uprising, believing that with his looks and intelligence, why wouldn't she try and make a play for him? Then he took another look at himself, knowing he didn't want or need the drama. He did realize, however, that his love for Monica was shakier than he thought. He was in a power struggle of the human, magnetic kind.

During lunchtime, Job sat in the faculty lounge wishing the last bell would ring. He remembered opening his mouth to chat with his colleagues, but he couldn't recall, with any amount of certainty, the topics raised or his responses.

He decided to try feeding his nervousness away by bingeing on lemon-filled doughnuts, hoping the sugar rush could help him decide whether to tell Monica what had happened earlier, and if he did, how to explain it. No matter how he tried to spin the story, it didn't come out digestible. In the middle of his indecisiveness, Bianca came through the lounge door with two reams of copy paper in hand.

"Mr. Wright, I'd like to see you for a moment, please. It's nothing earth shattering," she said, beckoning outside toward the hall.

"Just a minute." He shoved the last bit of doughnut in his mouth, wiping his lips with his fingertips.

Bianca was in the hall, bobbing her head up and down. Job couldn't help but notice her UltraBrite smile. "Congratulations, Mr. Wright. You've accomplished what many have tried."

"Help me out, because I have no idea what you're talking about."

She let out a breath. "Each year, our school district selects a school to submit a name and application to Disney for a program that honors educators in various disciplines. Teacher of the Year awards. It's a big deal where teachers get a trip to Disneyland, the award itself, money—the works—but you have to be nominated. And the opportunity to choose came around to our school this year."

It's got to be a catch. "Umm hmm."

Bianca looked around. The hallway was clear. "The requirements are that you've got to be nominated by your admin, and there's an extensive form to complete, showing your work, personal accomplishments, et cetera."

"Oh," Job said, hoping she didn't catch the foolishness of his thoughts because that wasn't quite the stumbling block he expected to hear. "What do you need me to do?"

"I'll bring the written form around to your classroom in a little bit. You also have an essay to complete, and I've heard the Disney folk are finicky about the appearance of each submission." Bianca turned. "See you later. This stack of papers is beginning to feel like lead."

"Okay, but I doubt that I'll be around here too long after school dismisses. I've got to check up on things at home."

Bianca turned around. "By the way . . . how is Monica?" Job was caught off-guard. Again.

"Don't answer that, I don't mean to pry," she said. "I'll meet you before the last bell rings."

He spent the rest of the school day going through the motions of teaching, while his mind wandered in and out of the events that had taken place. *I've been nominated as Teacher of the Year.* Should he drown in excitement? How did Bianca pull that off? More than once, he had to draw himself back into the reality of the moment.

When Bianca mentioned Job's award nomination during the school's afternoon announcements, she ended her comments with a tag on how proud she was that one of her faculty members was going to receive such a prestigious election. The last bell could hardly be heard above the students' shouting out his name.

"Get outta here, folks!" Job swung his classroom door open and stepped aside as the young scholars cleared the room like they'd had no home training whatsoever. Once he could hear students' voices echoing outdoors, he felt safe enough to collapse in his chair and sigh in relief.

That day was almost at an end.

Bianca appeared at his classroom fifteen minutes later, looking from head to toe an icon of classic Italian beauty. She strolled across the room with her copperhead snakeskin briefcase in hand and a matching purse over her shoulder.

"Sorry I'm late," she said. "I meant to see you before the last bell, but you know how it is."

"Yeah." Job took a stubby pencil and began digging at the edges of his wooden desk. "Now help me understand. How is it that I am receiving this award? Aren't there other teachers in this school more deserving?"

"You don't beat around the bush, do you?"

"I've had an exhausting day. I'm ready to go home."

"I know . . . to Monica." Bianca placed her briefcase on his desk. "Let me assure you, Mr. Wright. What happened this morning in my office has nothing to do with your being selected for this award."

He heard sarcasm through her dramatic sincerity, especially when she made a reference to Monica. *My loving, faithful wife.*

"Now, concerning the autobiographical essay you have to compose for Disney. If you don't mind, I'd like to read it for editing before you submit it. It's your work, and I'm not trying to tell you what to do. I just want to make sure you put your best foot forward on this. You're representing our school as well as yourself."

"You kinda jumped subjects on me."

"Really? How's that?"

Job put the pencil down. "Well, for one thing, how do we proceed after what took place this morning in your office?"

Bianca stood in place at the edge of his desk for a moment, surveying his question. She moved within arm's distance of Job, narrowing her eyes. "You have to ask? I mean, really. What exactly do you see in front of you?" She pouted.

Strange feelings and sinful thoughts began to creep into Job's conscience. He began focusing on his desk, thinking an inanimate object would be a safe haven for his eyes, but Bianca was using it to her advantage, making circular strokes on it with her index finger.

"What I'm trying to say is that—"

"Let me help you out, Mr. Wright, 'cause it's evident you have problems expressing what you want or telling me what you feel." She moved in closer, causing Job to spring out of his chair. They were face to face. "We fit, you cannot deny it. And you wanna take it, you want me. You're just not sure how to go about it."

Job couldn't speak, no matter how hard he tried.

"This is the Hoopla Capital of the Northern Hemisphere, so what you do here while you're married, single, gay, straight, nobody cares. Make your decision." She backed away from him a short distance, and Job couldn't smell her mint fresh breath any more. Then Bianca said, "I've put it out on the table. You have to let me know when, where, or not at all." She picked up her briefcase and headed to the classroom door. "And whichever way you decide, it'll be no hard feelings, trust me."

Job had no misunderstanding after that. All he gave was a one-word acknowledgement that he couldn't recall. Life would have been easier if she'd just left him alone to teach and only teach. Bianca's passionate approach wasn't something he'd ever had to deal with before, and what she had done that day made him prey for a kill.

She had added another dilemma to his already confusing mental mix, and he couldn't make a rational thought. And he still had to put on a good face for Monica that evening.

Chapter 13

And the keeper of the prison told this saying . . . now therefore depart, and go in peace. Acts 16:36

That same morning of September 11, Delvin was eating breakfast in the cafeteria. Grace seemed to have been extended as a leftover from Labor Day. That day, the usual compost prison administration called food had been raised one quality point above garbage. The eggs were still of the bulbous, liquid variety, but the bacon had been replaced with ham, pork chops, and loin.

He had just about completed his meal when four strategically placed televisions came on.

The news of apparent terrorists' attacks and subsequent grounding of commercial air flights scrolled at the bottom of the monitors.

Thank goodness for protective screens. Some of the inmates began tossing food and trays at the TVs, but without harm to their function. Delvin could only figure their response was to the news or plain foolishness.

"Hey, Storm," Stinson yelled from the adjoining row of benches, "aren't you from New York?"

I'm from upstate New York, crazy idiot. There's a big difference. "Syracuse," he eventually answered.

Stinson boomed out, "Still New York."

Delvin could feel a snarl engulfing him, a tightening of his face and neck. He had to twist his upper body for comfort. "Right now the nation's issues aren't my problem. Terrorists? That's not my problem. In fact, they probably did me a favor. Some of my worst enemies worked in those buildings. So what, somebody died. If *I* could murder the world, I would."

"Let me leave you alone." Stinson stood, brushed off his pants. "You're getting into one of your funks and I don't want to be around for the aftershock."

After order was restored, the warden dealt out reprimands to the culprits of the breakfast melee. Liberties were given to the rest of the inmates by noon.

At 1:00 P.M., Delvin relieved his tension during a conjugal visit inside a normally vacant 75x30 room detestably called The Reformatory. Here, inmates with visitors could have sexual relations under armed watch. Prisoners sought relief and guards sought a thrill under the guise of voyeurism, but it was better than nothing.

To Delvin, Nadia Van Houten-Storm was far from some flighty, jet-setting twenty-six-year-old man-pleaser. The Dutch femme fatale worked to attain her U.S. citizenship and had become an accomplished sculptor and art restorer. She had diplomatic wit and keen intellect. And she was the epitome of sexy.

Delvin's wife had, according to the prison's grapevine, "moved on to a liberated man," by dating some international playboy named Meritorious, whose money was fresh and legal. It was apparent that after Delvin's imprisonment, she wanted a man that didn't spend his nights in a cell for an apartment. Meritorious was a lucky man—if Delvin had his freedom, Mister Fresh and Legal Money would be dead. Then, he would consider whether Nadia was worth keeping.

Delvin didn't have proof positive, but he was convinced that at some time past, Nadia had done some felonious dirt without getting caught. Regardless, he had a complex trust in her, limited to certain of his financial affairs while he was stashed away in prison.

He rubbed his hair back, flicking away the droplets that had formed on the ends of each strand. He tasted the water that remained on the ends of his fingertips.

Nadia palmed his rib cage, her narrow, puckered lips parted—the look of a gratified vixen.

He meant to make that conjugal visit memorable. He had a mission for her, knowing that if she was going to cater his bidding, he needed to tattoo his motion on her body.

"Oooh, Del. What was going on in that mind of yours?" Nadia asked in an accent fired with a molten lava edge. She shook her shoulder length tresses, darkened from humidity and magnificence in the moment, and rose off the blanket ridden table they had improvised as a bed. "You bare your soul. I feel."

I'm sure you did. "I was ready for it," he said. He yanked up his pants and zipped them. "Weren't you?"

Her tongue peeked from her mouth and then charmed its way back in. "Yah. It was the way you hung to me." She batted her sapphire blues. *"Dank je."*

"You're welcome. Anytime." He didn't want to hear anymore of Nadia's meowing over their lovemaking. He knew that he'd added an unfamiliar aggression to his erotic responses, taking them to a summit that left them both exhausted and her in wonderment. But the hourglass was running in their time together, and there was unfinished business to be handled before she departed.

"Nadia, I have a package for you to deliver to my attorney tomorrow morning." Delvin's lawyer was Edward Kirkpatrick, a tight-fisted, no nonsense Southern gentleman brat who had limited power of attorney over an off-shore account made clean by device. Nadia would deliver a package and give Edward instructions to disperse funds once given the directive.

"I do it. For you," she cooed.

"It's very important. Now you don't have to fret over the prison inspector at the gate."

"He won't take?"

"No. I fixed it so that it appears to be legal stuff. Sure, he'll look through it, but it's nothing threatening. It'll pass."

"Okay."

He gave Nadia the manila envelope. "Don't forget to take care of that for me, Nadia. Tomorrow."

"I'll do."

Delvin put on his shirt remembering that she had Mr. Worldwide Lover at her disposal. Meritorious could take up where he left off. Nadia didn't know it, but Delvin felt he had been given more than a quarterly sexual release. He had given her a role in the overthrow of Job's happiness and success.

After Nadia left, he waited a nervous sixty minutes for a word from prison officials on whether she had made it to the outside with the package in tow. If she had been detained and the package confiscated, he would soon be in Siberia or given some god-awful duty. After that hour went by without incident, he relaxed, convincing himself that he must be one of the fortunate; believing his Machiavellian pursuits were heightened because the stars aligned in his favor.

Delvin was spent and ready for a catnap, but he dared not admit that to Nadia, who seemed to have energy for days. But he couldn't rest just yet.

"Warden wants to see you," the cell block supervisor

growled without speaking the last name of any inmate in particular.

Delvin heard the stocky, oil-slick-haired supervisor, but was too engrossed in his fantasy ride to Shangri-La to believe he was the one being summoned. That was, until the supervisor raked his baton across the cell bars. "Move now!"

Delvin left his daydream long enough to start getting a proper shirt on and let the supervisor know, "I heard you. I'll be ready in a minute!" Then he went back to his flight of imagination.

It was about 3:00 P.M. Dinner's aroma was already ghosting its way throughout the cell block and smelling quite tasty. It was a shame that it took a national tragedy to give Ashland civility.

But civility—and Delvin's personal Shangri-La—had been interrupted.

"What does Warden want?" he asked.

"You'll never know 'less you move a lot quicker."

The only perk for any warden's job had to be to lord over resentful subjects, because Delvin didn't see why or how Grambling Cox spent his waking hours in that trap called an office suite. It was more like office soot. Warden's work place appeared to be in the early stages of diamond formation; coal. Everything was black or variations thereof. Tables, chairs, desk. Black.

Delvin guessed the State Dept of Corrections did their best to requisition dollars for furnishings in the only part of the prison with no vertical iron linings. But their best wasn't best enough.

Warden's head offered the only distinct color contrast in the entire office. His hair was a natural copper hue. Ditto on the mustache and goatee. And he had light freckles on his face.

Above all, Delvin knew that everyone had a side of them that others would regard as distinct and bizarre. Warden's—Delvin thought—idiosyncrasy was his affinity for the occult and science fiction. Volumes upon volumes on shelves, at the feet of the man's desk, others against the walls. Thick, dusty reads on the subjects of warlocks, futurist theory, satanic worship, and other topics, all bound in Olde World leather—black.

Christmas couldn't even have brightened those surroundings. It was questionable as to whether the warden celebrated any holiday in a religious or a secular fashion.

The supervisor said to Delvin, "I'm gonna put some jewelry on you, Storm. No offense. For Warden's protection in case you disagree with what he's got to say."

He remained silent while the handcuffs were snapped in place. He was seated in a simple, splinter-laden chair facing Warden's desk. Delvin asked, "Can I keep them?" holding his hands high, the metal flashing off the light.

"What for?" the supervisor asked.

"For my next conjugal visit," Delvin replied. His mind had just enveloped Nadia's bare body.

"Sickening." He shook his head, then spat on the floor. "Wait for Warden."

Only minutes went by before Warden Cox came into the office with a wet dog appearance. His head was a vat of melted pennies as his fingers raked the dome. "Mr. Storm," he announced with a suspicious pleasantry, "guess you're wondering to yourself: self, why am I in the principal's office, huh?"

If that was meant to be comedic, it didn't work. Delvin was perturbed because his daydream had been interrupted. To answer Warden's question, no. The handcuffs kept him from feeling jovial or making guesses on his fate. "Suppose you tell me."

Warden took in a belly of wind and laughed it out.

"You got a sense of humor. I like that, if it's held in proper perspective." He sat behind his desk, pulling out a cigar of the discount convenience store variety. "Well, I'll tell you."

Delvin eased his body. "Listening."

"Mr. Storm, rumor has it that you have settled into this facility with a few bumps along the road, but they've been smoothed out. If you can call it this, you've become a model prisoner, for lack of a better term.

Now who put the blinders on him? "Okay."

"Well," he paused to light his cigar, "I can pick any inmate I want, Mr. Storm, to become one of the individuals at the top of the pyramid. Yes sir. I want you to become a trustee."

"Trustee?"

"Lemme tell ya what it involves. Quite simple. It starts out—until I see you can be trusted with the freedom you'll enjoy—with you listening and doin' what I tell ya. How 'bout them apples?"

Delvin wanted to grab and choke him. He rethought the urge. Warden Cox was a human testament on how to reside at the bottom rung of a ladder while feigning to be at the top. "I don't guess I'd mind being a trustee, Warden."

"And you'll enjoy, eventually, free access in my little kingdom. Under the constant watch of an armed guard, of course. Think you'll like that?"

Free access? When Delvin looked around and spotted the Dell Inspiron sitting on Warden's desk, his mind started tossing. Electronic entry to the world. "I think I can handle that, sir." *I'm a rascal.*

Delvin blocked out the majority of the cell block's noise on the remainder of that Tuesday. There were three exceptions.

The wind danced its way around between razor wire and the sharp-shooter's tower, composing countless avant-garde tunes making the beams and joists of Ashland quake, disturbing the countenance of the inmates. A higher power sending what was thought to be an otherwise undeliverable message.

Then there was the journalism commentary shipped in by public address from the prison's central electronic ignorant box. CNN, MSNBC, or some other cable news channel with minute-by-minute updates of the 9/11 cleanup and search efforts. Listening to that was enough to make him lose his sanity.

Above all, there was Murphy, standing at his cell opening, leaning. All he needed was a cigarette and fedora to have the appearance of a g-man from a black and white flick.

"Took long enough," Delvin said. "Whatcha got?"

Murphy rubbed his fingers against each other, causing a sandpaper-to-raw-wood sound. He seemed unstirred by his barking, given the way he invited himself into the cell, sat on the bunk, and responded in an unvarying, conventional hum. "Have you secured the financing?"

"I've got the goods in place." Delvin explained that his lawyer would receive instructions from Nadia to make funds available once Delvin knew the amount to fork over.

He didn't make Murphy privy to the fact that he had a back-up to the back-up if Kirkpatrick fell through. He'd learned a valuable lesson when he was on the outside. The thing about eggs and baskets was cliché but true. Therefore, he had placed another account, capital that had been established by legitimate means, with a different individual. "How much is this venture going to set me back?"

"I'm pleased that you engaged yourself and followed through." Murphy placed a slip of paper between his thumb and palm, concealing the note with the other four fingers. He handed it to Delvin palm-side down as if he was passing the killer spade in a high-stakes card game. He held to silence during the entire ceremony.

Delvin read the note. *Thirty thousand? Huh. I thought they'd want some real money.* "How do you want to get it?"

As if the question had been anticipated, Murphy handed over a second note with the same bravado. A moment went by before he asked, "Is it clear to you?"

Delvin unfolded the note. It was a series of letters, numerals, and the odd name *Garrison Tenpenny*, meant nothing to him, but he figured it was meaningful to Murphy. "Yeah. It's crystal."

"Memorized?"

Delvin glanced at the note again with an alert effort. "Why?"

Murphy whisked the note out of his hand, tossed it in the toilet and flushed. "Write it in unwritten places, Mr. Storm."

"Why you—"

"No evidence. Not a shred. You want a nickel added to your chronological passage through this institution?"

"I'm doing the time I've got and gettin' outta here."

"Then, no evidence."

Delvin began burning the information in his memory. *Garrison Tenpenny.* "We'll play it your way. How long will it be before I see any results?"

Murphy stepped outside of the cell opening. "If you blink, you'll miss the first phase. As plebeians say, the wheels are set in motion. Have a superb sundown, Mr. Storm."

The day was made perfect when the dawdling, sole-scrubbing footsteps of Deliverer could be heard on the floor of the cell block late that evening. He paused in front of Delvin's cell, rested a *Reader's Digest Condensed Volume* on the bars, and went on his way.

When Delvin pulled the book through the cell bars and opened it, he found a note, which because of the dim light and someone's vain attempt at encryption, took quite an effort to read:

JOSEPH WRIGHT. NotinLouisville.Notin Kentucky.Believedtobeinpartswest.StayTuned.

Chapter 14

Can two walk together, except they agree? Amos 3:3

Monica left the paperwork from her job in the car seat. It was intentional; she needed a few moments to relax and reflect while she waited in the office of Dr. Karen Najib, a specialist in obstetrics and gynecology. At any moment she would be called to the back, but the soft music had lulled her into thought.

It was in those idle moments that a suppressed anger over what had transpired between her and Job during breakfast earlier that day resurfaced. She just wanted to talk, that was all. As usual, Job wanted to skate over the facts.

She had witnessed, over the last few days, that whenever she and Job were invited to a restaurant, church or some social event, he would find an excuse to pass it up. She thought his excuses were lame; so lame, in fact, that she couldn't remember any excuse he invented.

She declared that he was acting like some fugitive from the law. "Louisville is over, Job," she told him, referring to his refusal to endear past experiences—even the trying ones—and learn the lessons from them.

He wasn't hearing it. "I don't even want my dreams to remind me," he told her.

"So I can safely assume you haven't been in contact with any of our friends back that way?"

"Like you do," he retorted.

"I do," she told him, "I call and I write."

"That's you." Job's eerie look and the contempt in his voice gave away his embarrassment.

"One thing I've learned in my few years on this planet," she told Job, "is that a woman can't change the mind of a hard-head man. Only God can soften him, call him to his senses."

He is doing better in some things she told herself. She was elated when Job filed last year's taxes before the April 15 deadline. *And without one word from me, too.* But still, she wasn't going to let a charred history close her out of a future packed with friends and acquaintances.

Monica snapped out of her daydream and picked up an issue of *Women's World* off the table. She flipped through the pages, pausing at the article *What Celebs Depend On To Get Through.* She thought about her strength and who she relied on to get through troublesome periods.

Chapel in the Desert had been her spiritual filling station since arriving in Phoenix; so much so that she looked forward to becoming a member and forced Job into the same, and together they rarely attended another church. She could count the number of times that she came away from the Sunday service without a VHS of Pastor Harris's sermon. Monica regarded her pastor as an upright and prophetic messenger, possessing the gift to relate the Bible as the supreme guide for people in contemporary times. Her time.

"Dr. Najib is ready for you now," the receptionist announced.

Monica snapped back into her present surroundings, her level of anxiety rising to an unforeseen height. Her annual physical was an event she didn't wish on her worst enemy. She had told Job in past conversations that, "You men couldn't handle what we have to go through to stay healthy. God knew what He was doing. He gave this burden to the right gender." But it wasn't the routine of the physical that had her concerned. If she could hear a positive opinion from Dr. Najib on her ability to conceive, her anxiety would go away.

The RN took her blood pressure and heart rate and performed a couple other organ checks, writing the results in a newly created file. Monica peered at the stack of papers and asked her why her patient file looked so full, as though she had been a long-standing patient. The RN told her that the file was filled with records the clinic requested from Louisville and from Dr. Jones, the physician who examined her when she first arrived in Phoenix.

Dr. Najib entered the room with a life-sized, full color chart. The lighting from the room bounced off her waist-length, blue-black locks that were pulled back into a ponytail. "We're going to have physiology lesson today," she said with the flair of a comedienne, her voice revealing the fact that she had not lost her mid-Eastern accent.

Monica chuckled to herself, glad that she was seated on the exam table and realizing that she would have towered over the petite Dr. Najib had she been standing. She squelched her amusement, knowing that the doctor would soon have the upper hand once her feet were in the stirrups. "I must be okay. You're coming in here with jokes."

"Let's just say the tests I ordered gave me information I need," Dr. Najib responded, still smiling. She carried on some small talk, asking about the Wrights' move and if they were settling in all right. The conversation switched to Monica's job, which went on for several minutes. "I'm a member of Nine Iron Club, though I seldom get to visit," she said.

The three women shared another laugh or two when the RN, recognizing a signal from the doctor, rolled a tray of medical instruments closer to the exam table.

Dr. Najib reached into a box of latex gloves and put on a pair. "All right, Monica. You've been a woman long enough to know." She leaned over, helping Monica to lie back on the table. "We're ready for the part you hate."

Monica would have agreed with Dr. Najib given any other year during any other annual exam. It wasn't thrilling being prodded every which way, and then left in wonder over answers to questions unique to the female anatomy: Cervical, breast or colon cancer? Urinary tract infections? Some other unknown, untreatable ailment? On this day, however, she felt an assurance that the news her doctor was about to give would be optimistic; conception was possible.

Dr. Najib and her RN had left Monica in the exam room alone while she dressed. She had had enough time to dress, search through a couple issues of *Fit Pregnancy*, and peruse the medical posters on the walls before the doctor returned.

"I'm sure you're ready to be out of here, considering today's excitement, aren't you?" Dr. Najib asked.

"What excitement?"

"New York plane crashes. You heard?"

Monica expressed her surprise, so Dr. Najib brought her up to date. Her mind then became divided. Half of her brain tried to digest the news while the other half wondered whether Job was aware of the national dilemma.

"Let's not dwell on it. Too much depression for the world. I guess this will even make me a suspect," Dr. Najib said, pointing to herself.

Monica figured that although her OB-GYN didn't appear to be a bomber or terrorist, she would be dumped into an accusatory pile just like others with a similar appearance. It was nothing new. Being part Native and part African-American herself, Monica had been a victim to that type of profiling all her life. "Nobody would suspect you to have anything to do with that," she tried to offer consolation.

"Hope you're right. Let's get on to you." Dr. Najib walked over to the life-sized chart. "I guess you say this is about to be bad news, good news. Better than none at all, eh?"

Monica called herself holding a breath. "Let me have it, doctor."

"Alright. Bad news." She pointed to the chart. "You have fibroid tumors. Looks like three. And I believe this is the main reason you're not getting pregnant."

"Tumors?"

"Yes."

Monica clamped her eyes shut, trying to kill her faint feeling. "C-c-cancer?"

"Oh no, dear," Dr. Najib said with a sound of confidence. "Benign. And a very common problem in women of African descent."

"Surgery. And no children."

"Wrong on both counts." Dr. Najib used the chart to further explain how Monica's blockage was occurring and that surgery would not be necessary, according to her test results. "You will have a non-surgical procedure called Uterine Artery Embolization."

Monica sighed, opening her eyes in surprise. "What . . . outpatient?"

"Yes and very little recovery time."

Monica swallowed, gathering the energy to ask, "Will . . . everything . . . still be in place?"

Dr. Najib giggled. "Mrs. Wright, get ready. Your insides will be, how you say, wide open. For some reason, it goes along with this procedure. Like opening flood gates."

"And this has been done before? This procedure, I mean."

"Hundreds of thousands of times."

"That's comforting, considering."

"There doesn't seem to be any other medical reasons why you should not have children. Has your husband had a check-up? Sperm count, et cetera?"

"Oh, yes." Monica's knowledge about Job's health was based on what he had told her. She sighed and thought for a moment that she may need to alter her answer. In other words, she didn't rely on his information with absolute certainty.

"Oh." Dr. Najib leaned against the edge of the exam table. "Then the two of you have been taking the appropriate steps. Eliminating the negatives. Fantastic."

What Monica didn't tell her was that it had been her express desire to have children. She realized that, while Job never spoke against starting a family, he'd never let out a cheer in favor of it.

"Now if you like, you can get a second opinion about my diagnosis. Feel free, if you question my findings."

Early that morning, Monica had come to a decision that whatever the diagnosis, she was going to seek advice from another physician, but Dr. Najib's calm demeanor and frankness convinced her that it wasn't necessary. "I want what's best for my health regardless of whether I have a baby or not."

"Well, let's schedule the procedure, umm, when?"

"ASAP." *Got to tell Job the news.*

"Wonderful. I will have to check my calendar and tentatively put you on the hospital schedule. Is Phoenix Baptist okay?"

Am I ready for this? And my job? A baby? "I'm sorry, doctor. Did you say—what did you say?"

Dr. Najib smiled a comforting smile. "I asked about Phoenix Baptist for the procedure."

"Fine," Monica said. "I drifted. Sorry."

Dr. Najib jotted more notes onto Monica's file. "Understand. This is a big step. But the sooner you do it, the better you will be. Then we can begin the steps to get your body ready for pregnancy."

"Yes." Getting her body ready to accept pregnancy was the easy part. Job? In that name, lay the difficulty. "I'll do whatever you need me to Doctor."

"I'm sure you will. And please, give my regards to your husband." Dr. Najib wrapped her stethoscope around her neck. "You should be elated, Mrs. Wright. Your future is brightening."

"You're right, doctor." Monica shouldered her purse and rose to leave. *Yeah. Our future. God help. I've got a lot to tell my husband.*

After she left the doctor's office, Monica attempted to reach Fontella at home and on her cell, but ended up leaving messages. She was able to reach Job, who was busy in the school's faculty workroom copying assignments. She asked if he had heard the news about the plane crashes and he acted as though she hadn't asked a question, giving her a jumbled explanation about some award nomination. When he got around to asking how her physical exam came out, her lone response was, "We definitely need to talk this evening when we get together. Don't try to get it out of me now. It's too much to tell."

*   *   *

Job hoped the homemade tamales and the strolling mariachi band of Aunt Chiladas restaurant just off of Seventeenth Avenue would curve his nerves when he met Monica that evening. Too much had happened that day to suit him. He felt free enough only to tell some of that day's event. Then there were parts he decided to keep to himself.

He wasn't revealing his encounter with Bianca from earlier that day. No spin in the world could fall between Monica's ears, to make her understand that his actions were only consolation in a time of emotional distress. Fortunately, he had been in enough fresh air to get Bianca's perfume out of his clothes. He was positive that Bianca's advances were one thing Monica didn't need to know.

"I'll have an Arnold Palmer. She'll have a Coke," Job told the waiter, who was pulling a miniature cart filled with chili sauces and other condiments closer for their inspection.

"If you have any questions about the menu, I'll be glad to answer them," the waiter stated. He turned to a young lady dressed in a Latin-American costume and spoke a few phrases in Spanish. "The cocktail waitress will be back with your drinks."

"Gracias." Job looked around the dimly lit room, allowing his eyes to consume the walls that were decorated in Southwestern colors, the elaborate water fountain and masonry fireplace. The applause from the surrounding tables died down as the mariachi ended their rendition of *La Cucaracha*. "It's good to know that what happened up in New York hasn't really dampened spirits here," he said, trying to sound cheerful.

Monica's smile appeared to be more fabricated than authentic. "It's nice, real nice." She dipped a chip into the restaurant's signature salsa and took a bite. "Sorry. Just got a lot on my mind, that's all."

"I understand." *I've got a lot on my mind, too.*

"No, you really don't understand. But you will—after I've told you everything." She explained the details of her doctor's diagnosis for ten minutes, interrupted only by the waitress asking for their menu selections. After they had each ordered an appetizer of cold Gazpacho, Job asked not to be disturbed for about fifteen more minutes. Then they would order entrees.

Monica's inner thoughts must've run deep, because tears formed and ran down her face.

Job reached for her hand, interlocking his fingers with hers. "You'll be fine." He sipped his drink. "I gotta ask . . . will you be all there? I mean—"

"My uterus will still be in place, if that's what you're working up the nerve to ask." She wiped a tear with her free hand. "It's not like a real surgery where they put you under a general anesthesia, but this procedure is supposed to correct my problem. According to Dr. Najib, pregnancy becomes a distinct possibility. She said get ready. Those were the doctor's actual words."

Job's thoughts made him wander off into an unknown zone. He looked down at their table and spotted the soup before him, and he realized he'd lost some time in semi-consciousness. *Pregnancy.* He responded, "Oh."

"What's wrong with you, Joseph Bertram Wright?"

He swallowed a spoonful of soup, wishing that his dish was *muy caliente,* deadening his tongue and sending his brain into euphoria. "What?"

"You look peculiar. Your forehead is beading up, and it's cold in here. It's like you're either in shock or something, or you have a problem with what I've told you."

Job tried to moisten away the twitching in his lips. "I

don't know what you see, but I don't mean anything by it."

"Yes, you do." Monica drew in a breath and did a rigid exhale. "Come on out and say exactly how you feel."

The problem was that he wasn't sure how he felt. "It's going to change our lives. Are you ready for what the changes could be?" he asked in an attempt to delay a response to a topic he hadn't given any real consideration to.

"It's not hard for me to say, Job. I'm ready for a baby, babies, if God allows it to happen. It's the one thing that always surfaces on my mind and has for the longest now. But you know what? I refuse to go down this road by myself." She pulled her hand free from his, as if in defiance. "Job," she said in a blunt tone, "are you trying to tell me you don't want a baby?"

Ping-ponging his questions and explanations was over. Her taut expression meant that his next words needed to be austere and to the point. He twisted his neck to relieve the building tension. "I wonder if the timing's right. Children—it's just new to me."

"We've had some ups and definitely have had downs, but we've gotten through them all. It seems pretty clear to me; there couldn't possibly be a problem we can't get through."

"Okay," flowed out of Job's mouth.

"Okay, so the timing's right. Our child wouldn't have to witness the stuff we've already seen, all of the situations that we've endured. It can only be good times ahead."

"You've made your point, Monica." He scraped the bottom of his bowl. "For some reason, I believe we have better times ahead of us. But we don't need to rush into a new avenue. Children? Jesus."

"*And*. A child is God's way of blessing a marriage. Our

child will be a testament of our union, not one that's the result of a crime or infidelity."

Infidelity? Why in the world did you say that? He thumped his water glass, remembering that she didn't have a clue about his most recent intimate secret.

Monica rambled under her breath about how her job status may be affected, how she might have to convert to an at-home wife and mother. She followed that statement with more unrecognizable monologue. "We've got some planning to do," she said.

Oh, Lord. The day wasn't drifting away fast enough for Job.

The waitress returned to see if they were ready to order entrees. Job used the opportunity to catch a breather and to initiate a more pleasant train of conversation. "Let me tell you about today," he said after the waitress excused herself.

Monica took a sip of Coke and then looked at Job with what seemed to be anticipation. "You were trying to tell me about an award?"

Job went on to explain about how Bianca was pleased with his work, so much so that he was nominated for the Disney award. When he finished his narrative, he sat back and smiled.

The glare that Monica fashioned collapsed the room around Job. He thought he had spieled out good news, and he couldn't imagine the meaning behind the furrows in her face.

"So," she said as she dug her elbows in the table, "I guess I'm supposed to be elated at that, huh?"

"Well . . . yeah."

"Why would I be happy for you? All I'm hearing is that you're trying another meteoric rise to fame." She took her hand back, slapping over a small bottle of margarita salt. "All that, and you couldn't be happy when I

told you a doctor is resolving a health problem that puts
us on the road to beginning a family."

Job's body tensed like a tightrope. "What? Is that what
you think I'm doing? This award wasn't something I was
trying to pursue. They came after me!" He lowered his
voice, apologizing. "Sometimes in life, people really do
show their appreciation without having to be coerced
into doing it. This just happens to be one of those times,
so you need to come off it, girl."

"You aren't fooling me. I know you all too well. You
love attention."

"I'd be crazy to turn down thanks simply for doing a
good job. As far as I'm concerned, you can take it anyway
you want, 'cause I can't stop you from thinking like
you're going to think."

Monica grunted. "You're right. You can't."

Job decided he should agree to disagree. The ambience
of the restaurant was festive, but the remainder of their
dinner was consumed in silence, which was all the better
for him. That way, he had no more explaining to do.

They arrived home, splitting toward neutral corners.
Monica got the television remote in the family room,
claiming to catch up on the latest 9/11 news accounts.
Job retreated into the upstairs office. In between answering the individual questions on the Disney application
that was due, he made time to have a lengthy phone conversation with Larry Logan.

"Man, I can't begin to tell you how much trouble it is
just to have a calm, decent conversation," he told Larry
over the phone. Although Job was aloof when it came to
seeking advice on his personal life, he felt at ease with his
neighbor, but not enough to let him know about Bianca.
He slumped into the desk chair, propping the cordless

phone against his head. "Every single incident with that woman turns into an argument."

"Have you told her that?" Larry asked. "I mean, if Fontella starts getting on my nerves, I sit her down and show her the reasons why we can't come to agreement. I tell her nicely, but when I'm done having my say, she doesn't walk away guessing how I feel."

Job was multi-tasking pretty well. He answered a couple more application questions while telling Larry, "I don't know what I'm doing wrong with Monica. Lately, I can't seem to find the right approach for her. Whenever we talk, it's always loud and erratic. We never get anywhere." Job remained vague in the explanation of his and Monica's dinner conversation. At the same time, he wanted Larry to side with how he thought Monica was being unreasonable. "Is there something wrong with accepting an award from your colleagues?"

Larry didn't immediately answer. "Sounds like the two of you aren't listening to each other, or attending to one another's desires. You need to seek the Lord on that. Let Him give you some answers. I can't help you."

"I'm in a marriage-go-round, and that's the best advice you can give me?"

"Pretty much. It's what works for me after I've tried everything else."

Job hated what he was thinking. Comfort was all he wanted, and Bianca's charming sensuality was beginning to look like an option that couldn't go wrong. Seeking the Lord, as Larry advised, wasn't something he had tried. Venturing after the company of another woman was also unexplored territory, but it appeared to be easier to translate the operator's manual once he broke the seal. It was just a question of should he? Shouldn't he?

Chapter 15

. . . Let not the sun go down upon your wrath. Ephesians 4:26b

Job awakened that night; jumpy, wide-eyed, and covered in damp sheets. The Bacardi Silver he gulped down as his reward for finishing the Disney paperwork, had resulted into a headache instead of the sleep aide he had hoped it would be. The amber LED on the clock read 2:30 A.M. His body had had two hours of restlessness. Three hours remained before it would be time to prepare for a new workday. He reached around for Monica, although he wasn't positive she had come to bed. He didn't remember getting a kiss. No rub on his head. No brush along his back. A "go to Hades" would've sufficed.

He managed to grab a handful of camisole. Sometime during that evening, she'd found the bedroom and slept through his stirring.

Bianca was the reason he couldn't relax. She had negotiated her way beyond his conscience and tunneled into his subconscience. It wasn't right for her to violate his sleep, to be in his presence during a time beyond his control. She had been in his dreams. Now, even his imagination was guilty.

He left the house and Monica at 6:30 A.M. with unspoken good-byes and an unrepentant countenance. He wanted to say something apologetic or witty, something that would draw a from-the-heart response, but time and pride overtook him. He settled for letting their communication remain unfixed.

His driving time was reflective, and he opted to keep the radio muted. On his way to school, a brief detour to the corner drug store on Thunderbird and Fifty-fifth Avenue for Visine cured his insomniac red eye before the first period keyboarding class.

The hallway was filled with chatting students who seemed to be indecisive about whether to do the right thing and attend class, or give in to truancy. That morning, it wasn't just the students acting that way, it was everyone. Given the previous day's events, Job understood the unsettling atmosphere.

It was between his first and second periods that all his fear, confusion, and desire ran together. Administration was approaching from the far end of the hall.

Scottsdale's Max Mara must've outfitted Bianca because she was doing justice to designer black that morning. Her contours were a vision on canvas, stretching the seams of her dress to their material limit. Her hair, that same color and glistening against the fluorescent lights, fell into equal motion with the rest of her body.

Bianca twisted her shoulder to dodge a rushing student, and then paused beside a series of lockers. "Mr. Wright, I hope today is better than yesterday, don't you?"

Job wasn't into discussing the weather or the national dilemma at that moment. He was fearful that sensible talk would get casual, leading down paths he wished to avoid. "I finished the application and essay for the award. I'll bring them to your office later on."

"Fine." She looked around to see who might be listening. Job did the same for his own assurance. The hallway was clear except for a few lingering students about to face a late bell and a pink slip.

"The invitation stands, you know," she said.

No explanation necessary. Job knew what Bianca meant. Yesterday's kiss and invitation had done enough to wound him and make an indelible impression on his mind. She wasn't taking her pursuit any further. It would be up to him to make the move. That was just her way of reminding him that she didn't mind being the prey.

"I'm married," he whispered. He knew it sounded transparent, but marital status was his best defense and the most convincing statement he could come up with.

She pursed her lips. "Umm hmm." One of her manicured fingers traced the spine of a ledger she was carrying. "I'm in the book. You make the call."

Bianca's slam-dunk statement gave Job a cold, suffering feeling. Monica preferred to argue with him. Larry offered spiritual advice. Bianca proposed an alternative. What to do? God help him for what he was contemplating.

Job avoided Bianca the rest of the day. He even delivered his Disney award application and essay via one of his A-plus students.

Job took a scenic route home in order to rehearse his reconciliation with Monica. Maybe he would do or say something to put them back on the path to marital bliss. He stopped at Nell's Flower Box for a dozen roses and an *I Apologize* card; his way of knocking the wind out of her at first sight. There wasn't enough time to find the Anita Baker album with the song of the same title.

Once through the door, he quickly realized eighty dollars had been wasted.

Monica greeted him with a curious look, and accepted

the flowers without a verbal acknowledgement. She found a leaded glass vase, a wedding gift with years of dust, and the Mikasa label stuck to it. She filled the vase with water, sediment and all, and plunged the roses into it.

Job sat at the counter facing her. He tried not to allow her drama to upset him. "I'm tired of us moving from room to room and not speaking." He would *make* her talk if necessary. He came home in the evenings to a fine but annoyed spouse. At work, a voluptuous, starry-eyed woman hung onto his every sentence. It was getting to be a temptation unequaled by any other. So, if the love of his life wanted to wait until dinner was prepared before he lunged into conversation, well, oh, well, she would just have to multitask.

Monica was busy doing that classic clang-bang of dishes, pots, and pans, her means of showing displeasure without saying so. "What do you mean? I am speaking to you."

"This ain't speaking to each other, and you know it." Job swallowed his embarrassment. He realized the nonsense of her drawing him into a quarrel, and he didn't want that. "You know what? Let's slow down, take this a step at a time."

She said, "Okay," with a trace of frost in her response.

He rubbed his jaw, taking a second for the air to clear. "Honey, I love you," he said with as much sincerity as his heart and voice could put into words.

"I know that. But I'm getting to the point that love isn't enough. I don't ask for much, just that you'd consider the fact you don't live by yourself. You have a wife."

"Which is the reason I'm making every effort for a calm, loving evening. No fighting. No arguing or accusations. Me and you working through issues needing to be in the open."

Monica told him that sounded decent, but a little fore-thought—calling her at work to let her know his plans—would've helped. "I have a previous engagement."

"What? I didn't know about it."

"Of course. You wouldn't. We weren't talking, remember?" By all indications, she didn't want him to answer. "Pastor Harris is having a special night of prayer—the nation and the victims in New York and what have you. A lot of my clientele have missing business associates who worked in the World Trade Center. Some of the blue-collar employees had relatives working for the Port Authority. Even Cory mentioned a couple of friends that worked for Euro Brokers. Nine Iron was a graveyard today. Playing golf and tennis wasn't their priority."

"What does that mean?" he asked.

"It means I feel a connection to their pain. Besides that, praying for someone else may help me feel better."

"Prayer. Whatever. You feel that strongly? Going to church and leave us hanging in the balance? I don't believe this."

"Say all you want to try to make me feel bad, but I'm going."

It had been too long since Job experienced her honey-comb taste, supple touch, and her opulent smell. Getting reacquainted with her senses was at least another day away. Monica seemed to be forcing him to choose door number two. Why couldn't she be like . . . ? Nothing. He lacked the power to resist thinking about it. But he wouldn't resist forever.

Chapter 16

. . . and behold, it was burned with fire; and their wives . . . were taken captive. I Samuel 30:3

Six days later, the Wright's were still at odds. No conversation. They didn't have strength to argue or the desire to come to the table for the sake of the marriage. They didn't admit it, but the bonding cords were breaking strand by strand. They made a pact to set aside their differences and present a united front on the morning of Monica's embolization procedure.

Dr. Najib had advised her not to eat for twelve hours as part of her preparation. When Job told her that he wouldn't eat as well, she asked, "You're fasting with me? Praise the Lord." She viewed his willingness to participate in her medical prep as a genuine show of strength and concern, something she hadn't seen in a while.

Then he responded, killing her spirit.

"I wouldn't call it fasting," he said, "let's not take it down that faith road. I'm just not eating."

Prior to the procedure, she did her best to remain unruffled and witty, although on the previous evening she had had bouts of anxiety. Under a local anesthesia, her anxiety became a distant memory.

* * *

"The embolization didn't take long, everything's fine. How you feel?" Dr. Najib asked Monica.

Monica placed her hand down the center of her body and along her legs. All her body parts seemed to be in place. She felt fine.

Job looked like he needed nausea meds. He explained that his nose was playing mind games, making him believe he was in a sewage cavern with no means of oxygen. The facility had a medicated, pristine aroma. When Dr. Najib gave details on the side-effects of the procedure, he appeared faint.

"You okay?" Monica asked Job.

Dr. Najib also had a look of concern. "I say something not proper?"

Monica chuckled and then flinched, possibly from the slight pain the physician told her she may sense. "No, Doctor. Men can't stand a thing, which is precisely why God gave us the baby-producing job."

Job's appearance seemed to worsen.

Dr. Najib grinned. "We're done." She handed Monica a prescription for pain, if necessary, and then told her that she could return to work in a couple of days. "Resume as usual."

Monica needed to ask a few more questions, but Job's cell phone beeped. She gave him a stare as he excused himself and went into the hall.

Dr. Najib was in the middle of answering questions when he returned.

"Ms. Rizzo called," Job announced to Monica. "She wanted to know how you're feeling, and to let you that she's thinking of you."

"That was considerate. Tell her thanks when you get back to school."

Job placed his cell onto his belt. "She also let me know

that the contest officials at Disney called. A package is forthcoming which details the award package, travel arrangements, and prize money. Ten thousand dollars." He opened into a wide grin.

"Congratulations Mr. Wright," Dr. Najib said.

"And five grand will go to Mountain River; that's the school where I teach," Job said, directing that statement toward Dr. Najib. "And . . . it will be in newspapers all around the country. Hey, honey, isn't that great?"

Monica asked him, "Now, you haven't actually won yet, have you?

Job's eyes cut toward Monica. "No." His answer sounded defiant.

"Then, why are they sending a package?" she asked.

"I guess so each applicant has one in case they win. I imagine that's the reason."

Monica's pain overrode her expression at that point. Above that, she marveled at his ability to put on such a show, knowing they were at odds with each other. The only person who could be impressed was Dr. Najib.

"The news is wonderful," Monica said under her breath. She said it so that Dr. Najib wouldn't pick up on the fact that she wasn't moved by his announcement.

When they returned home from the clinic, Job began annoying Monica with his constant, "You need anything?" or, "You all right, honey?" Well, Honey was just fine and only wanted him to leave the house and get out of her hair.

She told him to drop the pseudo-thespian antics, and that there wasn't an audience observing him.

"How long is this going to go on?" he asked.

"Until you're sincere." Monica sat back in the recliner and waved him away, not wanting to hear another word.

He responded to her message with a slap of his side. He faded away to the home office.

She went to bed that night, but couldn't rest for Job's periodic trips to the bathroom, splashing water or fumbling around in the dark. Monica smothered her face a couple times to keep from laughing so loud.

The next day, she awakened to find Job sprawled across the bed and out cold. She was aware that he fell into a deep rested state after having a glass of Chardonnay to, "Calm my nerves," he had told her.

She had risen and showered. She moisturized herself while still half-wet. After a few moments of pacing around the room, she made a decision to be a socialite instead of a couch potato. She dressed for success in a navy two-piece. By the time she retreated out of the bath, Job was awake, still on the bed, but with a flushed, groggy appearance. He still had a few minutes before he would be pressed to get to school in time.

"What're you doing?" Job asked.

"Going to work, what else?"

"Aren't you supposed to take a day or so off from work? That's what the doc said."

"Don't dictate to me, Job. I feel fine." She reached over the top of the dresser and picked up her prescription bottle. "I can always take these if the pain gets unbearable. Got to get out of this house, especially if you're going to be here." She sprayed Chanel behind her ears, which perked her senses.

Job sprung into an upright position. "That's just plain stupid. You ever heard of a setback?"

Monica adjusted a bracelet on her wrist. "Umm hmm, and I'm still not hearing you." She hurried through the bedroom door before he could say anything else. "Have a great day."

She had been at work two hours when Job called, telling her that he decided to go on to school before he died from boredom at home.

"I'm dealing with a major issue here," she told him. Monica didn't feel the need to ho-hum him with any details, but she was in the middle of settling a servicing dispute with an organic fertilizer contractor who was named, ironically, Pete Moss. Above all that, she was feeling a little pain and didn't want to give him the satisfaction of knowing he was right about the possibility of a setback.

"I don't have a lot of time anyway. I'll let you go," Job said.

Monica hung up, peered at her watch, and huffed. It was 11:00 A.M., very early in the day. She yearned to leave work as the seconds rolled by. Job was right. She should've stayed home.

Her meeting with Pete was coming to an abrupt halt as she allowed him to brew and stew over her counter-offer. He shuffled his sod-laden feet, probably coming to the realization that he needed her more than she needed him. When he conceded, she pressed the intercom call button on her desk phone, asking Nami to prepare some contractual documents while she offered Pete a conciliatory Coca-Cola. She decided it would ease his bruised ego.

With the essential meeting of the day completed, she thought it best to return home to recuperate. She phoned Cory to inform him she was leaving early, and he told her not to worry. "Your work is in Nami's capable hands. She's a pro." What he said about her administrative assistant was nothing but true. And she wasn't worried; she was in pain.

A couple of hours later, Monica found herself dragging into the kitchen to fix a turkey bacon, egg, and cheese sandwich, and get some apple juice to wash it down. With a TV table in front of her and the remote at her side, she planned to become one, in harmony, with her couch. It would be all good.

After the usual barrage of soaps, detective shows, and *Lifetime* movies, she lost all track of time and fell asleep.

She awakened, with the urge to rub her stinging eyes and nose. Above her head was a series of crackling sounds which were soon overrun by a peculiar metallic hum and then the blast of a horn. The noise pinched her nerves.

Her wind seemed constricted, and she picked up on a pungent odor and what appeared to be massive clouds of dust throughout the family room. She sniffed again. When she realized what it was, her body heightened into panic. The more she gasped for air, the less she received. *Fire!*

The smoke had already lowered itself to the top of the couch, within inches of her nostrils, just enough space to catch a glimpse and breathe without catching an eyeful of fumes and a chest full of carbon monoxide.

She rolled off the couch and to the ground, crawling her way to the French doors by the kitchen. The doors were blocked with flames coming from the outside.

She didn't know the direction of the fire so, she bumped into the half wall of the kitchen counter and kicked over some bar stools. *Gotta find the outside.* She prayed that the front door, if she made it, wouldn't be obstructed by anything, especially flames.

Choking even more, she crawled along the foyer wall, getting caught in the telephone cord. *Telephone.* She pulled the phone down from the bar ledge, and the cordless receiver fell on the floor. She stuffed it into her robe pocket and continued to grope the floor and crawl. She managed to make it to the front entrance and tapped the doorknob. It was cold.

She squinted, hoping to wash away the grainy sting

paining her vision. She peered just above her head where the smoke seemed to do a limbo. She took in as much wind as her jaws could hold, stood up and bolted out the door. When she was out on the porch, her knees began buckling. She'd made it as far as her strength could carry her.

"Mrs. Wright, Mrs. Wright?" Isabel Marriday stood over Monica with a befuddled look in her eyes. She was rubbing her shoulder. "You alright?"

"What happened?" Monica asked. Her voice felt scratchy and sounded guttural. Her eyesight was constricted by the oxygen mask over her nose and mouth. She was lying on a stretcher in the back of an emergency rescue vehicle.

"I think you passed out, dear. You were holding onto your home phone," Isabel said. She had a wide-eyed gaze, and her shrill voice sounded like a distorted amplifier. "I hate to tell you this . . . the back half of your house is gone."

Gone? Monica's heart felt like it was about to throw her off the stretcher. She swallowed and then asked, "Where's my husband?"

Chapter 17

Thou hast set our iniquities before thee, our secret sins in the light of thy countenance. Psalms 90:8

After rushing off the phone with Monica, Job went to the faculty lounge during his planning period. He was certain to find a Maricopa County phone book, a simple commodity that was often seized for personal use and never returned, or damaged beyond recognition.

He blamed Monica for his decision to accept Bianca's invitation and get her home address. If any circumstance prevented him from getting there today, he was convinced the deal wasn't meant to be closed. His plan was fast-paced. Less apprehensive that way.

He opened the door to the lounge and found Frances directing the other administrative assistants on how to set up light refreshments for the faculty. Petit fours, vegetable and fruit trays, and punch were available for the staff to come, sample and go as they please. Too many nosy people in that room to suit him. But without the address, he wouldn't know where Bianca lived.

His hands got clammy as he thumbed the pages in the white section. The RIL to RIZ page was extensive, but Job found that there were only four Rizzo's. It was just as

Bianca said. She was in the book. He held it in his lap, peering around for any onlookers.

It seemed like everyone was occupied with their own business. He wiped his forehead and reached into his pocket for paper and pen. He scribbled her address on the paper, crumpling it in his hand. Before anyone asked questions, he stumbled out of the lounge without sampling the repast.

He went straight to Bianca's office, sidestepping France's empty desk. He knocked and refused to acknowledge his brain waves. *Make that about-face. Go to your classroom.*

Bianca was at the door, standing in the opening. "Well. You're not avoiding me today?" she asked.

"No reason to."

She moved aside, allowing him to enter. "Is your wife recuperating?"

"No. She thinks she's superwoman. She played hardhead and went to work."

"Oh."

"You know how you women are. Can't tell you anything."

"Please don't try lecturing on our gender. We could go all day telling men about themselves," she said jokingly. Bianca gestured for him to have a seat, but Job refused.

"I'm not staying long. Just came by . . ." He folded his lips inward and moistened them. "Does your offer still stand?"

Every item in the room, every molecule in the office, stood still as Bianca's eyes narrowed. Under any other circumstance, she would have responded quicker with a witty answer, but that moment was different. She needed contemplation time.

"When do you want to see m—"

"Today," Job interrupted. "I wanna see you after we leave work. You okay with that?"

She moved a strand of hair away from her face. "Sure. Yeah. Umm, today's all right."

"Fine. I'll see you then. What? Three? Three-thirty?"

"Three-thirty. I don't know what to—how did you— what made you decide . . . ?

Job had a fleeting regret for what he had done. It passed as fast as it came. He sighed. "We'll talk it over this afternoon. I have the address."

"Okay," she said. There was a question in her reply.

Job stood and left her office, surprised and satisfied that they'd just danced, and she allowed him to lead.

The drive from the school to Bianca's was a considerable distance, which Job appreciated. The time was useful as he gathered his thoughts and strength. *I want to talk to her. I only want to talk.*

Bianca's subdivision in Deer Valley looked similar to Resi'Stanz. There were few streets, few houses, and each path ended in a cul-de-sac.

"Well, hello." Her words dropped from her lips as tiny crystals in a path. Her boss-to-employee demeanor had taken a back seat. She widened the massive, ornate door for Job to enter. "What route did you take to get here?"

"West on Bell. Up Tatum."

"Good choice. You avoided the heavy evening traffic that way." She closed the door, walking him into the living room.

Job couldn't help but watch her. She couldn't help but be seen. Her business attire had been shed for some washed-and-worn crop lounge pants that left the midriff for the imagination. She didn't fill out the backside as well as Monica would have, though.

There was an aroma creeping in from the kitchen, intense with garlic and tomato. She wanted to return there and check on things. "You know, there's a bottle of Chianti on the buffet. Why don't you open it? Let it breathe."

Job uncorked the bottle and placed it in a copper-laced bucket swimming with ice and water. While sniffing the cork, he took inventory of his surroundings. From its exterior, Bianca's home was any ordinary Southwestern residence composed of adobe and enclosed by a cactus yard. The inside, however, was a Tuscan cornucopia of brilliance with terracotta tiling in the foyer. Drapes and seating were burnished orange. Oak pieces accented the soapstone fireplace. A billiard room with a life-sized picture of Al Pacino on the wall. The only thing missing was someone to hum the *Godfather* theme, and then the Corleone would've been proud.

I only want to talk. Right? I only want to talk. Job changed his cell phone to SILENT mode while he waited for Bianca to return from the kitchen. He sat on the sectional, face to face with the entertainment system. The various equalizers, players, and amplifiers seemed to take life, telling him to power up. He obliged, found Boney James's *Ride* album, and popped it in.

As the tenor sax filled the cool air with syncopation, Bianca returned with a tray of various cheeses, pickles, and olives.

A mood was being set, he couldn't deny. The food, the music—well, he chose the music—everything he heard, smelled, and watched was sucking him in. Right then, just about any woman could've wooed him since it had been weeks since he and Monica had attempted to enjoy each other. But Bianca had the look, intelligence, and vitality that fared above just any woman. If Job wanted to call a halt to the proceedings, it would have been difficult.

She sat next to him. There wasn't enough room between them to place a Coke or a smile. He clamped his eyes tight enough to see a kaleidoscope and sighed.

"Are we off the clock?" Job asked her. "I mean, right now, are we Mr. Wright and Ms. Rizzo, or are we Job and Bianca?" He shifted positions. "I want some clarity, 'cause I don't want to have to face any kind of retribution later."

"Hope you like pasta." Bianca edged closer. "Manicotti," she purred.

Job took in the mint from Bianca's breath, and then he shook off its effect. "Did you hear what I said?"

Her gaze traveled up the length of him. "Honestly, you think this is about trying to test the limits of my power?" She plucked a huge olive from the tray. "At this very moment, we are Job and Bianca, stripped of our titles. Now, here . . ." She squeezed the appetizer between his teeth. "Chew."

He did as she requested. He crunched the oil from the olive while considering where he was and what he was doing. He swallowed.

She tried to feed him another, but he caught her hand. "Why were you approaching me in the first place? We've got to be way beyond anybody's professional code of conduct."

"It makes it so intriguing, doesn't it?"

"What's behind this . . . this . . . whole seduction?"

She reached over to the far end of the table, taking a magazine with a black glossy covering, and flung it by the spine onto the table. When it stopped swirling and Job read the cover, he knew she'd done her research.

Bianca stabbed the magazine with her finger. *Black Enterprise.* August. 1999. Cover story read, *"Louisville's Power-Brokerage Duo."* She started rambling out loud. "Isn't this something? You. On the cover?" The sneer on her face spoke volumes.

Wow. Such an in-the-face reminder of the recent past. He used to make the high dollar in the family. He used to rule a piece of Louisville's financial pie. Now, the only pie he saw was the kind donated to the faculty lounge.

Bianca moved back into his personal zone. "I can see ambition isn't a new thing to you. Neither is success. That's evident. A man as fine, intelligent, and ambitious as you deserves unbridled attention. Stop trying to tell me that you don't like the interest I show you."

"Hmm." He needed to tiptoe around that admission. She was well-versed in what to say and do. Her seduction was melodious—a song not being played on Rong Street.

"So," Bianca raised her eyes to meet his, "why have you given in to my pursuit? Actually, you know, you were pursuing just as strong. Explain that to me."

Stick to what you rehearsed. "I came over to talk. That's all."

Bianca chuckled.

Job tried to ignore her. He looked away and then turned back to her. "I go home. Nothing happens. We eat in silence. We spend the majority of our evenings in opposite ends of the house. She wants things. I want things. What we want out of life seems totally different." He cringed when he realized he'd just itemized his problems to someone who probably cared less.

"And lovemaking?"

He paused. "Forget that. Nonexistent. No . . . I can't lie. It hasn't been great. You know, when you can't have a decent conversation about the simplest of things, making love doesn't cross your mind." He wondered how she dared bring up the sex subject. But it was he who wanted to talk. Any topic was fair.

Bianca threw him a quick glimpse. He shot one back.

She said, "I don't see how anyone could get by without sex. Good sex, I mean." She stood up. "Want a glass of wine?"

He nodded. He wanted to see her stroll toward the ice bucket. It gave him an opportunity for his mind to ricochet about the way she had said *good sex*.

She returned with the wine saying, "Successful black men are a rare find here in Phoenix. I've never been with one, so I'm ready to take my chance."

"But I'm married."

"Is this the only explanation you can come up with? It's a poor one when you look around and see you're in my house claiming you just need to talk to me. You can't lie. You want my body more than my conversation."

He sensed her firmness. "I think I did want . . . you know. But now, I'm not really sure. I can't tell you what I want."

"Then let's try it out, see where it takes us. I'm willing. You?"

His hands fumbled to find his wine glass. He gripped it and took a gulp. "I don't believe you said that."

Bianca backed up, giving them at least arm's length distance. Why, Mr. Wright," she purred in a 1-900 voice, "maybe you don't realize where you live. This is the Hoopla Capital of the Midwest. Married. Single. Gay or straight. Doesn't matter. People get together. Stick with your wife, I don't care."

Job had gone off-track in a wave of conflicting thought. He glanced at the magazine and then at her.

She told him, "Let's take our time. Pace the relationship."

"Huh?"

"I can take it slow. There'll come a time when I don't have to ask. I won't have to request. I'm confident enough to know that you'll want to let your wife go and, be with me instead."

"What?" Job set his glass down, shocked that he didn't break it by the stem. "You done lost your mind for sure. How you came to that conclusion is beyond me."

"Easy. In a short time, I've gotten into your head." She drew a descending line from her neck to her navel. "You and I can't help but digest each other."

"Know what? You're probably right. Most any man loves attention. But sorry, Bianca. This is too much too fast. I'm just not interested." Job spoke the antidote to the poison of their 13-month long interaction into existance. He only had to reject her. A weight lifted, and it felt liberating.

Bianca stood slowly, brushing her hip against his shoulder. "Oh. I see." Her eyes appeared to have deepened, heavy and dark. "This is a little too daunting for you."

"L-look, I—"

"Oh no," she said. Her strides to the door were soft, but calculating. The metal latch unfastened like a stonemason striking a dash on a gravestone. A final chapter. "There's nothing else to say. I'll see you tomorrow, Mr. Wright."

Job began biting his lip. Her tone had him worried that she wasn't satisfied by how the afternoon had ended. Her face was radiant, but expressionless. She wasn't giving up any clues or revelations. He rose and walked out the door without another look or word.

The door closed as softly as the steps she made to it. Job's moment to inhale the blistering wind was shortened by the dozen plus cell phone messages he'd missed.

Isabel left at least three marked URGENT. Fontella called. So did Larry. Phoenix EMT? Maricopa County

General. His heart bounced off its connection. Too many messages, much too much to filter through. With reluctance, he decided to call Isabel, queen of nosiness.

"Get to your house as fast as you can," Isabel wailed out before Job greeted her.

Job rushed away from Bianca's house, elated to leave her doorstep, but reluctant to learn what he had missed.

Chapter 18

. . . Your lips have spoken lies; your tongue hath muttered perverseness. Isaiah 59:3

"Mr. Wright, you don't look well."

Job could feel Isabel shaking him, but his tongue wouldn't allow him to respond. He was surprised he had the ability to stand, given the devastation.

The house at 2333 Rong was a smoke-ridden façade. When he took a short stroll around either of its sides, there was a hull, a maze of charred studs and ashen adobe. The roof had caved in. Their furniture had been water baptized or incinerated. Monica's Camry looked fire-bombed. Nothing was salvagable. Their estate had been totaled.

Isabel continued ranting even though Job wasn't prepared to hear anymore. "The fire department's not sure when the blaze started, but they were still fighting it around three o'clock. Around the time you usually get home. Isn't that the time you usually get home?"

Our house, our house. "And Monica's where?"

"County General. Thank goodness . . ."

"What?"

Isabel looked around with her jellybean blue eyes. "I don't know if it's my place to say."

Job had reached his patience-peak. He was aware that half her time was spent in somebody else's business while the other half was not in hers. "If you have some information I need to know, then you need to tell it."

She swallowed. Her cheeks began to flush. "Fortunately, Larry and Fontella were available. They took care of Mrs. Wright. Followed her to the hospital."

He understood Isabel's implication. She was right. He had been MIA.

"I told the Logans to go ahead; they should drive to the hospital. I stayed here in case someone tried to loot your home."

Job raised his arms, slapped them against his side, and shook his head. "Nothing here to take." He picked up a stone and hurled it toward an unbroken window. It shattered. "Now it looks like the front is burned, too." He glanced at Isabel. "I'm sorry. I didn't mean to scare you."

"I—your house is gone—who knows how anyone would act in your situation. I'm fine, but, how are you?"

"I can't concentrate on me right now. Lemme get to the hospital." He opened the car door, getting in. "I guess Monica can clue me in on what happened."

"If she's able to talk. Mrs. Wright inhaled quite a bit of smoke. She was hoarse and semi-conscious when the ambulance left here."

"Don't tell me that." Job slammed the car door and rolled down the window. "This is amazing. Will you watch out for us?"

Isabel assured him that that was one favor he didn't have to ask.

He bet he didn't.

* * *

After the front desk attendant pointed in the direction of Monica's hospital room, he wasted no time getting there.

He peeped inside, where a nurse was adjusting an oxygen mask, while Fontella fluffed a pillow.

Larry, who was bedside, caught Job's eye and swiftly made his way out to the hall, closing the door behind him. "Hey, my friend, take my advice."

Job asked, "What's the matter?"

"Don't go in there, brother." He looked back into the room. Whatever excuse you've got for being unreachable, she isn't hearing it right now."

Job didn't concern himself with what others may have considered reasoning, no matter how sound Larry's advice might have been. "That's my wife in that room," he shouted.

Larry didn't seem agitated by the outburst. He wrapped his arm around Job's shoulder and escorted him from the doorway.

"You can't be any more correct," Larry whispered, "but take my word. Man to man? Let things cool off." His warning had the strictest sincerity.

"I know we're having some troubles, but not wanting to speak to me after a tragedy like this is a bit over the top."

"She's not the only one. Fontella's kinda hot with you right now, too. Of course, the women have one side of the story."

"Of course." *And I can't give my side.*

"They found your wife unconscious on the front landing. Did you get any of your messages?"

Job had listened to one of Isabel's, but had neglected the others. He gave himself a mental kick, figuring he could have pieced the sequence of events together had he taken the time to retrieve all the voicemails. "I was consumed with trying to get home."

Larry's eyes preached suspicion. "Well, thank God Monica's life was spared. Possessions can be replaced. Things are just what they are. But the Lord saw fit to see her out of the house in time."

Job planted his fingers against his eyebrows and squeezed. He sighed and then mumbled, "Yeah. Thank . . . God."

While Monica was laying in the hospital bed, her line of sight was skewed, but that didn't affect her ability to hear Fontella. Although it was just the two of them inside a sparse hospital room, Monica felt a comfort there, and Fontella's calm demeanor was an antidote for her fears. Monica explained to her that responsible, married men can be contacted at any time during emergencies. So she had a question. Where had Job been?

Fontella had taken a seat on the vinyl chair that converted into a bed. She didn't offer any answer to Monica's question. She did say that, in all fairness, Job needed to be heard.

Monica nodded her head to keep from speaking aloud. Her throat had a flaming sensation, and her eyes kept tearing from the prescription drops she had been given.

"He's been here two hours now," Fontella told her. "Larry can't keep him out of this room much longer."

Monica lifted the oxygen mask away from her mouth, even though the elastic strap held it close to her head. "What kind of excuse . . . could he give you?"

Fontella's brow furrowed. "Who, me?"

"If it was Larry." She inhaled through the mask and then swallowed.

"Oh. Well. I don't know." She pulled the bed's cover sheet taut. "But I know that listening to what your husband has to say could help you decide. Hear him out, and then make up your mind."

Monica understood Fontella's point, but she knew that Job's explanation wouldn't give her any satisfaction. She was worn out, irritated, and sick. If Job loved her, he would wait until she could stand his presence.

Fontella rose out of the chair, moved over toward the bed, and began straightening the sheets. "If you love him, Monica, you'll agree to see him."

"If he loves me," Monica paused to take a breath, "he'll respect me, and not come in here." She slanted her head sideways to look across the room.

"That's fine." Fontella took a seat in the reclining chair and crossed her arms. She met Monica's eyes with a forceful gaze. "Now that it seems we're going to have some quiet, no nurses interrupting, I can talk to you."

Monica lifted her free arm, palm up.

"You rest. I'll do the talking. I really want you to listen."

There was a brief silence before Fontella sat back in the chair and continued. "I haven't known you two for very long. Somehow, I knew right off we'd be friends. So I'm gonna speak as a true, honest-to-God friend."

Monica nodded. She was drugged, upset and weary, but curiosity kept her awake.

"I was born in a little place down South. Bunn, North Carolina. My grandmother still lives there, bless her country soul. Had this saying when I was a child. I could attract more bees with honey than vinegar."

When Monica grunted, she fogged the mask, blurring her line of sight.

"I didn't understand it then. She was telling me that sweetness can get more out of a person than driving them to anger."

Monica coughed. She pulled the mask, strap and all, away from her face, off her head. "Job isn't like that all the time. He can be sweet."

"Not talking about Job."

A moment went by. Memories of things Monica had said suddenly rushed to the forefront. "You have no idea what I've been through."

"Maybe not. But if you love him, if you're trying to stay with him, you got to work with the brother. Give him a chance."

"While ago, you were as angry as me."

"I was. But not hearing the reason why you couldn't reach him is eating you. It's better to have his excuse out in the open. I'll pray for forgiveness about being angry. Later."

Monica's eyes began raining the pain that her heart felt. Fontella had informed her that nothing was recoverable from their home. She almost lost her life, had it not been for her strength, her faith. *Thank you, God. You've kept me here for some reason.*

Fontella told her that she should talk to her man. "There must be some good qualities in him. He's been patiently sitting outside. Think about it."

Thinking was all Monica had been doing. Her brain was in a stressful overload and needed a release. At the moment, Job was all she had. She sniffed, wiping water from her face. "He can come in."

"Will do," Fontella said as she rose from the chair. "I'll wait outside."

"Don't leave," Monica told her.

"I'll be out in the hall. We're not going anywhere. Monica, I'm praying for his salvation. But I'm praying for your spirit—that you get the answers you need."

Monica didn't ask Fontella for clarification, but prayer

was the only device that she felt would help her through the ordeal.

Job crept through the door and plastered himself against a far wall. Monica had seen lobsters in a tank more relaxed.

"I'm sorry, honey," he said. "I'm so sorry."

Surely, he wouldn't have thought a simple apology was all he needed to make. Monica did not try to hide her anger, but she strained to keep her frustration from going into overload. If she allowed herself to go over the top, it would show and Job would clam up; their discussion would come to an abrupt end. "Where were you?" she asked.

His lengthy hesitation made her curious. Job started air washing his hands in a taut, circular motion, like an obsessive compulsive. "Huh?" was his response, as though he'd forgotten what she had asked.

She shook her head. "Nobody could find you. Nobody."

"I know, I—"

She raised her hand to cut him off. "Wonder what you needed to do that was so important." Monica grabbed the oxygen mask, inhaled deeply, and then she let it down. "This isn't like forgetting to meet me at a restaurant. And even that would be bad."

Job began to scrub his hands and shift his weight from side to side. "I never would've guessed you were home. I thought you worked all day."

"I came home not long after talking to you."

"I didn't know. Our house burning down was the last thing on my mind."

"Home is a place where anyone would expect to find me," Monica told him. She stopped for a moment because her temples began to throb. She lifted her hand in the air and fanned as vigorously as her strength would allow. It helped her get her thoughts on track. "But you're avoiding the question. Where were you?"

Job dropped his head and whispered, "I was off-campus at an after school meeting."

She didn't believe him, and she didn't care if he could tell that she didn't. All she wanted to do then was prove he was lying. "No one could reach you, Job."

"I-I had silenced my cell phone to keep from being disturbed."

The air smelled thick, hard to breathe. Her heart raced. The moments of her escape from danger replayed in her mind. "Vibrate."

Job bent away from the wall toward her. "What'd you say?"

"You could've put your phone on vibrate."

Job didn't answer back.

"I feel like trouble follows us wherever we go. Now you've brought me out here to Phoenix, and you're doing a sorry job of protecting me. I'm just sick." Monica couldn't hold the tears and hurt any longer. Between sniffling and coughing, she told him, "We're done talking right now."

"There's no way we could anticipate a fire, honey. No way." That was all he said, all he offered as an explanation. That was no explanation.

Monica twisted away from him; she couldn't stand another minute with his presence. "Go do whatever it is you have to do, Job."

Chapter 19

The thief cometh not, but for to steal, and to kill, and to destroy. John 10:10

The next morning, Delvin took a walk in the yard, *The Art of War* under his arm, hoping to enjoy the rays and breathe the stale, concreted air. He propped himself against the corner of a building about ten feet from a guard tower.

He saw a craps game going on where one pale, shaggy redhead was gambling for the leftover belongings of a Middle-Eastern inmate who died from a blanket party some inmates had given him the previous evening. Comrades in the same cell block got word that the poor wretch had been sympathetic to terrorists on American soil. That gang thought it best that the Iranian or Iraqi or whatever he was, needed to be returned to the dirt from whence he came, with his personal remnants distributed among the lucky.

Delvin walked a few feet past the commotion and opened his book, but before he could engross himself in a page or three, Stinson's fresh-like-the-morning voice boomed as an unwelcome diversion.

"Man, you're in the big time now!" He piled the morning edition of the *Scottsdale Tribune* in his face. "Take a look for yourself."

Celebrated Teacher's Home Is Leveled

Delvin scanned the article several times over, and then bunched it in his hand. "Where'd you get this from?"

"Relax man. Murphy gave it to me, and told me to see to it that you get it. The little man had something else to do, personal-like. Otherwise, he'd have given it to you himself. You umm, had something to do with this?" Stinson pointed to the paper.

Delvin folded the article and placed it inside his book. "Coincidence."

"Oooh. Really?" he said with a boorish jest in his voice.

"Yeah, man. Nothing to do with me."

Stinson lowered his voice, his wild and graying brows blazing with rudeness. "Remember . . . I know ya."

Chapter 20

Confess your faults one to another. James 5:16a

At 5:30 A.M., Job awoke with arthritic bones and unco-operative muscles. Yesterday's shirt and pants had matted themselves against his body. With his face still buried in the pillow, he flung an arm across the coarse sheets and panicked. No Monica. Oh yeah, she was still in the hospital. And he had crashed in someone else's bed.

The exact sequence of events was somewhat faint, but he remembered that not too many hours ago, he'd made a trip to CVS Pharmacy for personal essentials and then drove around the corner to the Best Western on Central for overnight reservations.

It occurred to him why he was there.

The Maricopa County register of deeds may have had 2333 Rong Street documented as a four-bedroom, single family residence, but it was currently a quarter-acre va-cant lot. And dilapidated.

That was the moment he allowed all his emotions to overload.

His tears washed themselves through the pillowcases

down to the pillows. He attempted to put a throttle on his outpour of anger, disappointment, and frustration. It was impossible.

We've moved to Phoenix and nothing's changed. After rolling off the side of the bed, he stood with arms at his sides. Memories came at him, but he refused to let them penetrate his soul. He was drained of more than his energy. His spirit had taken a beating. Monica had given all the time, concentration, and love she wanted to give; now it was up to him. He had to spend that day recreating life.

Job went to the bathroom, removed his clothing and turned the shower up as hot as it would go. Wrinkles needed to be removed and freshness needed to be restored to the only set of rags he owned, so he steamed them while he cleaned up. It felt good to watch part of his anguish seep down the drain.

The next order of business was to call Monica. Her tone was gentler than last evening, it even sounded a bit cordial. She told him that Fontella and Isabel had already called that morning to check on her. "The doctor's discharging me around 9:30."

"I'll be there. That gives me time to do a few things before I pick you up."

"Don't be late," she said.

Job didn't take her response as fussing. She just didn't want to spend another minute there if she could help it. He told her, "We'll get through this, I promise." He pulled his face away from the receiver to stifle another set of tears that dropped from nowhere. "Don't worry, baby. I'll be on time."

There was a brief silence on the line until Monica said, "I had a talk with God. He got onto me about some things, things I've been doing wrong in our marriage."

"Oh?"

"For some reason I can't explain, I feel . . . sure that everything's gonna be all right. Today, it's a new day, a better day."

No matter how many times Job swallowed, he couldn't remove the lump in his throat. "I'll pick you up in a few," was all he said before they hung up. Monica's words clenched him. He felt out of the ordinary and somewhat liberated. *Is this how I'm supposed to feel when God's doing His thing?*

He stretched his arms toward the ceiling and took a few short breaths for energy. It was a new day but a day he'd lose if he didn't get a move on.

He made a call to the school district's substitute line to get his classes covered. He decided to use one of his personal days. An explanation to Bianca for his absence would have to wait.

Job checked out of the hotel and drove back to the house under the possibility that something, anything, might be salvageable from the blackened debris. When he got there, he noticed that two sets of tape surrounded the property. He expected the fire department's orange. There were also strips of yellow tape, the kind police officers use to designate crime scenes. His emotions tried to resurface, but he kept them at bay.

He didn't understand the dual quarantine, and there was no one around to give an explanation. It occured to him to call Statewide Insurance to report a claim. Then he scribbled himself a reminder to call the fire department later that day.

There was enough time to withdraw funds from an ATM before picking up Monica.

He arrived at the hospital, took a direct path to the room, and found her sitting in a chair, scanning the pages of a Bible.

Monica gave a quick hello, a passionate kiss, and told

him that she had started getting ready right after he hung up.

"You're on a mission, aren't you?" he asked.

She grinned. "Umm hmm. I'm released. Everything's been signed." Monica grabbed him by the arm. "Let's go."

"Whatever you say."

As they traveled from one end of the city to the next, completing errands, their interactions were delicate, cheery.

Job pondered the meaning behind Monica's behavioral one-eighty and asked, "Are you all right?"

"Yeah." She flipped the sun visor down and looked in the mirror. Her eyes grew wide. "What? You see something wrong?"

He shook his head. "No." he reached over to her, touching her thigh. "It's okay to let it out. We lost our home and everything in it."

"I know that."

"This morning, I did something I haven't done in a long time. Cried."

Monica smiled, giving the impression that she was delighted with what she heard. "I had my cries too. Half the night last night. But God spared my life. I'm alive with no burn marks."

"You credit the way you're acting right now to your faith in God?"

She shook her head. "It's what keeps me going."

Job gripped the wheel tighter and shrugged. *Unbelievable.*

They decided to eat lunch at Miss Wilhelmina's Café on E. Jefferson, a black-owned establishment where only an individual's personality could be pretentious, because the restaurant was as down to earth as they come. Job wanted to eat there, because he needed to satisfy his craving for soul food. "Can you name a place any closer that fixes oxtails?" he asked Monica after she lodged her protest to the driving distance.

It didn't take her long, though, to settle on Wilhelmina's; other than a drive-through, it was the one place Monica didn't mind being seen in the clothing Fontella had loaned her.

The ills of the day were forgotten when she whiffed Friday's special: meatloaf and side orders of what those familiar with cuisine south of the Mason-Dixon Line would call "fixins."

"C'mon, darling, have a seat," the waitress said, pulling out Monica's chair.

Monica looked around, wondering if there was even room to breathe. People were everywhere with many more packing into the place, their attire ranging from worn-out leisure wear with sandals to expensive business suits with stilettos. Steam from the kitchen rose everywhere, fogging up the black and white wall pics of celebrities that had frequented the place. It didn't take long before the aroma and ambience had her craving the hypertension-building grub that reminded her of what Mama used to make. Mmm.

Job wanted a kiss, but she set passion and good graces aside. After taking a few moments for a personal invocation, she began her meal with a fork of fried okra.

Job commenced with a soapbox of all they had left to do before their day could end. She scrutinized every declaration he made; in particular, the statement on how they would make it through their latest dilemma.

To that, she raised her water glass and replied, "Humph. Can't wait to see this," which was her expressed disbelief that he would commandeer each task in a timely fashion and yield results.

Job looked like a man about to knowingly walk into a

restricted area. "You'll be eating that," he said, referring to her words.

Monica noticed Job's head dropping. She asked him, "What's the matter?"

"Oh, nothing."

She could think of a million reasons, but she wanted him to give her specifics. "I can't help if you don't tell me what's on your mind. Whatever it is, it's got you thinking pretty deeply."

Job let out a heaving sigh and seemed to bear a hole through the table with the base of his glass. "It's going to be a huge expense to stay somewhere while our house is being rebuilt."

"Maybe not." She put her fork down. "Matter of fact, I'm sure it won't be. The insurance company will take care of our stay for the first two weeks, and then we can possibly go to temporary housing. We may not have to take that route, though."

"Why not?"

"We should be able to handle somewhere to our liking. We'll just have to squeeze tight on our budget."

He grunted. "Anywhere decent is expensive. The Oak Woods on Fifty-first and Bell are completely furnished; I mean everything's in them. All we have to do is stock it with food. But the rental fee is high as all get-out."

Monica let out a faint laugh. "You're forgetting about where I work."

"Hmm?"

"Think about it. We can stay at the resort free of charge. I can just book one of the suites long term."

Job's face turned wicked. "We can't stay there." He went off into an annoying tangent about his pride and what people would think, and how Monica's co-workers would gossip about them being a charity case.

Monica replayed his account and played it again, keeping her nerves in check. Oh yes, she wanted to reach across the red and white plaid tablecloth and crown him open-handed like a checkers move, but she came to her senses. They were both semi-public figures in a public place, and slapping the taste out of his mouth could be a well-publicized embarrassment to an otherwise gratifying release of irritation. "Joseph Bertram Wright . . . Are you hearing yourself?"

"I don't care if it is free. I don't want to put others in the position of guessing what kind of shape we are in."

Monica ran her nails along her thigh, her patience frazzled thin by his clear insensitivity. "Are you serious? You'd rather pay money—money we can't afford to pay—for a temporary dwelling that couldn't possibly look anything like Nine Iron's suites because of what you think people will say? Nobody pays that much attention to us, Job."

"You got room to talk. Easy for you, Miss My-Salary-Swallows-My-Husband's."

Silence. If anyone else had a conversation in the restaurant, Monica didn't realize it. "I've never brought up money to you. Never. God gave me my job and I don't apologize for it. The money I earn is our money. Our money keeps us above water. Now I believe I'm seeing the real Job."

"You're implying what?" Job's teeth gritted. "Now you're my analyst and I'm the textbook case? You ain't no scientist, and I ain't no experiment."

"Since we've never been in this role before, where the money-making is reversed, I hadn't had the chance to see how you'd react until now. And you're good . . . you've kept it hid from me for over a year. God has His way of showing you things."

"You don't know what you're talking about." His eyes narrowed. "How much green you make don't bother me."

"You're lying!" Monica felt flush. Her outburst was loud enough to make their argument go public. It seemed that everyone within earshot conveyed their thoughts by facial expression. To her amazement, the looks even seemed unique, specific by ethnicity and gender:

Black men's frowns commanded: *Handle your woman, man.*

Black women smirked, telling Monica they wanted her to *set him straight.*

White men's twisted crow's necks cracked a *just like black folk.*

White women's wishing eyebrows said *If only I had the guts.*

Monica really didn't care what any of them thought. Job was her husband and she had a right to argue with him if she wanted to.

It was obvious that Job could feel eyes on him, too. He appeared as though he was surrounded in a room full of uncracked, spoiled eggs waiting to burst at the first incongruent move. He leaned in toward Monica and lowered his voice to a whisper. "Everybody's trying to find out about us right now. Look around you."

"What does that—look—this is crazy. I'm not going back and forth with you on this. This is just—I don't even know what this is." She started sniffling. "With what has happened, we have no idea the kinds of expenses we'll run into. We need to spend our cash wisely. Getting a suite at my job isn't charity. I work to earn that amenity." She turned away from Job.

"Don't cry, Monica."

"Man, please. You don't see any tears." She hadn't stopped the water from welling in her eyes, but she refused to let the drops fall onto her face.

"Okay," he muttered in consolation.

It meant nothing to her. She wasn't surprised that he had taken a stab at her career and salary. Those moments would be ones she would never forget. "You claim you're an upright man. Start thinking and trusting like one. You're failing . . . not as a man . . . necessarily. It's when you come face to face with a predicament. Under your own strength, you fail almost ev'rytime."

"People take hold of their own destinies," he rebutted. By the vein-popping grip he had on his glass, she had pulled on his conscience, even if he was convinced of his own hype.

"I don't know what's up with you. You don't sound like the man I know. When we were in Louisville, I refused to be the wife like the kind you see in some tabloid, yanking on her man's arm like it's a pillar, showing false support while people who know him watch him fall from grace. *I was praying for you*. You needed help only God could provide. And it wasn't your or my intelligence that kept us from falling all the way down."

"Oh. It wasn't?"

"Nope, and you know it."

"Do I?"

"Oooh!" The crash of a waitress's tray of dirty dishes caused Job to throw his leg up, striking his knee on one of the table's supports. "What was she doing?" he asked.

Monica let out a muffled laugh. "That was God's way of letting you know you're thinking like an infidel. Serves you right. You should be glad your knee is all you hurt."

As Job caressed his leg, he had a casual, witless confidence in his look. "You got too much committed to Him. You might think I don't believe in God. I do. I just believe even stronger that God has expectations of us."

Monica grunted, wishing she could snap him out of his

own ridiculousness. "You better open your eyes. Larry and Fontella tried to tell you when we first met them, that your faith in God should be more prevalent. I knew you didn't go along with what they told you."

Job bucked his eyes. "You're right. I didn't."

For a second, Monica asked herself how she could've been fooled into marrying such an infidel. "Walk by faith and not by sight. Seems pretty obvious to me."

"The Bible also says, 'faith without works is dead.' "

"You're trying to make the Word fit your definition. That's twisted. I can't help but thank the Lord for keeping us—as silly as it may sound to you. So, whoever's been yanking your chain, sending you on the crazy path, they got you, brotha."

"How you came to that conclusion's beyond me. In anything we've been through that wasn't in our favor, we came out clean."

"That's what you don't seem to understand," she told him. "We didn't come away from circumstances as clean as we could have if you'd have put your trust—I mean really—put trust in God."

"Whatever you say, Monica."

"You can act arrogant if you want to. I don't care what you say. On Monday, I'm making a long term reservation for us at my job. You'll have to get over your pride." Monica reached for her water, took a swallow, and then slammed it on the table. "And by the way, we need to pick up the rental car that's been reserved for us. I felt like I needed to remind you of that, too."

Job smirked.

And Monica did not care. "You know? For a little bit, you'd be no different than Delvin."

Chapter 21

Then a spirit passed before my face: the hair of my flesh stood up. Job 4:15

As the week spat out its final grains of sand, Delvin began intimidating Murphy with threatening notes and visitations. Demonic stares at mealtimes. Shadowing in the courtyard. He made his presence known.

Murphy appeared jumpy, but contended that he had no update and that he would, "Relay the procured specifics with immediacy."

Procured? That's right. Murphy sparked his memory. Delvin knew that somebody had better deliver results soon. He'd shelled out thirty thousand dollars for that under-the-prison-radar private investigation work.

After he managed his anger, Delvin's sensible side told him to relent and relax under the belief that new information about Job would run him down without his overwrought efforts of coercion. It had to be the right day, the perfect hour.

And that day finally rolled around.

On Friday, September 21, Delvin felt that his role as an oppressor would be tested once again. It was in his spirit.

Not all spirits are holy.

That morning, a fall Kentucky breeze came through and lingered. It was the perfect weather for jogging, which was what he and Stinson decided to do.

On his way out to the yard, he met Shiloh, who had on his fresh-aglow personality. "Coming to service this Sunday, Mr. Storm?"

"Say a prayer for me, Reverend," Delvin sneered.

The courtyard perimeter had passed their shoeprints about three times when Murphy came up, eyes bulging.

Delvin and Stinson stopped exercising.

Stinson greeted Murphy as usual, slamming him on the back as a mockery. "Boy, you look like you could use some fresh air. Exercise."

Delvin felt his face get hot with irritation. "Why'd you come out here and spoil our run? I oughta break your neck."

"Mr. Storm," he panted out. "You must peruse this." He was shaking the section of a newspaper that had been separated from the whole.

"What?" Delvin yanked the paper out of Murphy's hand with a grunt.

It was from the southern region's edition of the *USA Today*. Wednesday's date. Two days ago. An Associated Press wire had news from Orlando:

Walt Disney Teacher of the Year 2001

Hatred stamped on his accelerator. He studied the article from its opening paragraph to the ending period, smoldering with every sentence. *Joseph Bertram Wright*.

"Well, I'll be . . ." Delvin spat out in bitter resentment. He crushed the article between his palms and stomped back to his cell, leaving Stinson and Murphy in the yard.

Two hours later, a guard informed Delvin that the Warden had some work for him, so he washed up and put on a fresh shirt, placed the article in his breast pocket, and decided to go to the office by the path of the cell block floor. He passed by Stinson's cell. He was inside playing solitaire.

"Boy, how you enjoying being a prison go-fer?" Stinson joked.

"It's hard work. Makes me sweat, and you know I don't like that," Delvin replied.

"Whatever you say, boy."

"It's mostly just petty-patty work, nothing special. But it's time away from the usual, and I do get to use his computer sometimes, when his pants ain't in a wad."

Stinson laughed. "Yeah. I know 'bout that." He slapped down a card. "And you get to use the internet too?"

"Yeah. He claims he can tell where I've been. Figures I wouldn't go to a site that adds time to my sentence. I get information for myself, but nothing that would alarm the boss."

"Don't mess up," Stinson warned, keeping his eyes on the cards.

"Don't fret. I won't."

Delvin found himself in the warden's office, filing reports that held no significance to current inmates. It was ancient material that hadn't been touched in at least a decade.

"After you finish, Storm, you can have some time on the computer. Guard Jones will be in your vicinity, but I have rounds to make," Warden said.

Those were easy directions to follow—the kind that gave him eventual freedom. *Being a good boy is paying off.*

He rested at the computer chair, and clicked on the Navigator icon. The machine started talking back; fans whirled, indicator lights flashed. He was in.

Like pulling out a precious stone, the article emerged from his pocket. He unfolded it, studied it, and outlined keywords in yellow. He placed it on the computer desk and left-moused the SEARCH button. He started sweating. It wasn't physical labor. It was a colossal moment, a breaking point. His only trouble was deciding which key word to search first.

He had to blink, clear the celebration in his head. Each word took a life; break-dancing, hip-hopping, vying for his attention, wanting to be the first to be typed in.

Mountain River High School, Bianca Rizzo, Paradise Valley School District, Disney Teacher of the Year—decisions, decisions, et cetera . . .

The search for Mountain River gave him a phone number. There would be no better day to make a long distance connection than on one of Job's workdays. It was the opportune time to reach Phoenix Arizona. Zero. Six, zero, two . . .

"If you accept the responsibility for collect charges, please press one," Delvin heard the computerized operator say.

Silence.

"Bianca Rizzo," the voice said.

Delvin was used to staunch, pretend-like-you-can-control-your-urge female voices through receivers. He'd been around women like that all of his adult playmaking life. In times past, he'd even made bets with acquaintances on how fast he could lure the female behind the voice on her back, begging him for repeats of physical gratification. And he would oblige. "This is Delvin Storm."

As if she wanted to tell him *so what*, she said, "And the purpose of your call?"

"I have some information that I'm sure you would be interested in."

"Excuse me, but am I supposed to recognize who you are?"

"You accepted the phone charges," he said, trying not

to sound defensive, "or do you make it a habit of taking calls from strangers?"

"School district policy. Mr. Storm, is it? We're required to take the call. We never know if it's an emergency. And I know how to reverse the charges if a person is playing a hoax. State your business."

"Don't you have a Joseph Wright teaching at that school?"

"Yes, we do. Business and Technology."

"Well, I was Joseph Wright's realty partner in Kentucky. He never mentioned his previous occupation?"

Momentary pause. "Of course he has, in a roundabout way," Bianca said. "But he's not at work today."

Delvin wondered why, but didn't ask. "I didn't call to speak to him. I needed to talk to you. What do you know about Mr. Wright?"

"What do you know about him?" she shot back.

"Enough to know that he shouldn't be in a classroom."

"Just a moment," she said. There was a silence, but Delvin could tell that the line had not gone dead.

A minute passed before Bianca returned to the phone.

"Look Mrs. Rizzo—"

"Ms."

"Okay, Ms. Rizzo, I only have so much time on this line. Are you ready to hear what I have to say?"

"Mr. Storm, you're on my dime. What's the hurry?"

"Problem is they give us a time limit on our calls. Guess they figure if we were on here too long, we'd plot a prison break or something."

Delvin heard a short beep interrupting his conversation. He presumed the phone to be tapped. "You ready to listen?"

"Go ahead, Mr. Storm."

Delvin went into his abridged, fraudulent version of how Job concocted a scheme to defraud consumers of down payment funds held in Wright & Storm's possession until their transactions closed. Then, he added a spine-tingling touch by telling Bianca how he became the victim, imprisoned for Job's crimes. "His lawyer was slick, better than the fool I had."

"This is some kind of trick, isn't it?"

He had a feeling that if Bianca could've seen his face, she would have been able to pick through his deception. At that moment, he was thankful for the telephone. "Lady, I'm in prison. I'd rather be out, living the life. Do you really think I would've spent the last year locating Mr. Wright just for the fun of it?"

"It wouldn't be beyond some people's comprehension."

"I'm not into games, Ms. Rizzo." He pulled the phone from his mouth, and chuckled. "I'm merely trying to right a wrong."

"That's what lawyers are for."

"If you ever get the opportunity to witness prison adjudication like I have, you'll know that it doesn't work most of the time."

"Assuming that all you say is true; what does your story have to do with me?"

"You're my means to justice."

"I don't understand. True, you must be Mr. Wright's former partner, I can plainly see that."

"So you believe me?" he asked.

"I know for certain that a man named Delvin Storm was Mr. Wright's partner. The reason I know this is because a magazine I have shows the two partners. And it shows me how you look."

Just like a woman. I gotcha. "I'm not quite like that picture anymore."

"Umm. I question whether you're telling the truth about Mr. Wright. It sounds far-fetched."

"Oh it does? So, I see you've fallen for that conniving excuse of a man, huh?"

"I believe I support a gentleman who in a short time has proven himself a worthy educator. This I'm sure of."

Another short beep pierced the receiver. "Well, I have a suggestion for you, Ms. Rizzo."

"I'm all ears."

"You might want to do a little checking on your great educator. One thing I know for certain is that you won't be disappointed with what you find."

"I'll think about it."

"No," he said emphatically. "You've got to promise me, Ms. Rizzo."

Delvin heard Bianca heave a breath. His skin began to itch from excitement. Her snooping from the outside would arouse just enough suspicion to make Job uncomfortable. Since she didn't give an immediate 'no' to his request, there was hope.

"C'mon, Ms. Rizzo, you have nothing to lose. Keep your search quiet at first if you want. Just promise that you will look into it."

"Okay," she relented. "I'll check around."

"Good. You can always call me. I'll have your name added to my contact list."

"I'm not sure we should ever talk again, Mr. Storm. But I'll make the appropriate contacts and do some checking."

That was all he wanted to hear.

Chapter 22

Judge not, and ye shall not be judged: condemn not, and ye shall not be condemned: forgive, and ye shall be forgiven. Luke 6:37

After spending the last two days running errands by car and sleeping in luxurious but unfamiliar surroundings, a spiritual experience at Chapel in the Desert was the buffer Monica needed to get through the next week.

Prior to the beginning of service, a small fellowship of members including her, Job, and the Logans, formed a circle and offered words of prayer. During worship service, the praise team sang a powerful medley of inspirational selections. She was encouraged by all of it. But it didn't satisfy her craving.

The pew wasn't comfortable that Sunday. She had elbowed Job in the ribs and stabbed his ankles with her shoes a couple of times, and he had to be annoyed. Whether he was engrossed in his own concerns or flat out fearful, he declined to ask the meaning behind her constant shifting. It had to be the anticipation of the Word putting her on the edge.

Pastor Harris, wearing a robe for the first time in

months, began his sermon with, "Many of you, I'm sure, have wondered why my comments about the 9/11 attacks have been limited to a single corporate prayer. You will find out today, why I've said so little." He paced a few steps and turned right in Monica's direction.

The murmuring made Monica believe people had actually thought about Pastor Harris's reluctance to speak of the world event. You couldn't pass a TV, radio, or web pop-up without some preacher taking his or her fifteen seconds of fame to downgrade Osama, Bush, or the entire situation.

Monica's personal problems kept her from focusing on 9/11.

"I needed to wait for that opportune moment when this nation, particularly my congregation, wasn't so emotional with the immediacy of the matter." Pastor Harris put on a compassionate smile. "This way, I would have your attention on what I have to say."

He requested that the congregation turn to Luke, the seventh chapter.

"If I had to narrow my sermon down to a subject, it would be one word. One powerful, difficult-to-deal-with, word. Forgiveness." He told the crowd to look at a neighbor and repeat the word. They responded with claps and shouts.

He continued. "Look at what the terrorists did. They killed." Turning in the opposite direction, he said, "But look at what we do. Led by the President, this United States of America goes on a retaliation spree against the enemy while praying for the victims. That's okay, I guess, but that's not what the Bible says we're to do."

Monica listened, anxious to know where his message was going.

"The Bible says to pray, forgive. It doesn't tell us to

seek revenge on the enemy. We are to pray for them, too. You know, we can always tell what a person's thinking, because they can't help but speak it. Doesn't matter whether it's evil or good. Revenge seems to be on the mind of the United States of America, because prayer isn't really on our president's mind. Revenge is."

Monica looked at Fontella and nodded. In her mind, he was telling the truth.

Then Pastor Harris said, "We are not terrorists, but we commit terroristic acts in our very homes." There was buzzing in the crowd. "We do and say things, hurtful things, to each other. Then what does the other person turn right around and do? Retaliate."

On the inside, Monica stopped smiling.

"My people, unless you've become adept at lying, the things you feel are the ways you speak. The Bible doesn't tell you to retaliate anymore than it tells this nation to. For if we could only see fit to forgive a mass murderer after we've been attacked, then we truly have achieved a spiritual greatness. We then have drawn an oppressor under our feet, while God exalts us in the process. When we say we love, then we should truly be able to forgive. Amen?"

And the people said, "Amen." Pastor Harris left the platform as shouts lifted and the praise team sung a song of invitation.

Monica said, "Amen," with a sigh and shame. She kept on a face of contentment for Job, Larry, and Fontella, but inside, she felt a conviction. She couldn't vouch for the other two thousand congregants, but Pastor Harris had struck her with his message. She hadn't committed a terroristic act, but she had trouble forgiving the other half of herself. Considering all she and Job had gone through and had to overcome, speaking favorably to and about her husband was difficult to do.

* * *

At the Logan's insistence, the two couples took the Sunday afternoon to load up in Larry's car and take a trip to the cooler temperature and higher elevation of Sedona. Along the way, they stopped at a local mom and pop Mexican restaurant, where they feasted on garbage burritos and procured some touring information.

Larry suggested that they stop up Highway 179 to Tlaquepaque, the "art of soul of Sedona." It turned out to be a favorite destination for the Hollywood movie industry, with huge sun-touched mountains, and high-walled canyons flanked by towering pines and sycamores. It was sacred to Native Americans going back some ten thousand years. People in contemporary society visited for physical and mental renewal.

Job was appreciative of Larry's and Fontella's thoughtfulness. He was badly in need of renewal.

Monica and Fontella left Job and Larry after they made sure they were connected to a credit card or two.

The men found themselves wandering into the Red Country Center, a reservations office for Jeep Tour Guides of Sedona. After Larry's hefty deposit, cell phone battery checks, and a thirty minute orientation, they were roughing it four-by-four style.

Job wanted to believe that the forty-five hundred feet above sea level was giving him the jitters. Not so. This was an opportune time to confide in Larry who, in the past, gave him advice without judging him.

"God showed His tail, didn't He?" Job trumpeted almost breathless at the panoramic view. "Awesome."

Larry agreed. "Now I see why people come here to relax. The place is lost in time."

Job leaned against the Jeep. "You didn't have to do this, you know. I would have footed the bill."

"No, you wouldn't have, because I wouldn't have let you. This is our treat."

"The last thing—"

Larry interrupted Job before he went into his soliloquy about not wanting to be a charity case. Larry gestured to him, telling him that he didn't think of it as that. "We're friends, so what's a little money spent to take your mind off your predicament? I don't know what kind of mental state I'd be in if our house burned down. Swallow your pride and take in the moments God's nature has provided."

"I've spent the entire day thinking about stuff . . . just stuff. How we came to Phoenix and how things were supposed to be good," Job said.

Larry looked on without a discernible expression, making no comment.

"I've even considered an affair. I mean really, really, considered it." Job sighed in relief. He had admitted it to someone other than himself.

"An extra marital affair?"

"Yeah."

A long, tense silence followed while they were fixated eye to eye.

Job broke the thickness of the air, telling him, "Nothing's come of it, believe me. Nothing drastic."

"How far has this . . . consideration . . . gone?"

"This woman and I talked, that's all. It didn't go all the way."

"You mean," Larry paused, tossing his cell phone into the vehicle seat, "there's been no sex."

"No."

"Okay. So, does your wife know about this?"

"I'm standing here living, ain't I?" He tried to lighten the conversation, but Larry didn't follow the humor. "I can't tell Monica. This almost-affair was with my boss."

"Aww, man. You let that nature thing get in the way of

your common sense." He nodded, making Job concentrate on his slip in judgment. "What was it? Looks? She can't possibly be better-looking than Monica. God help you for whatever your reason is."

"No. She was just there for me in ways that Monica isn't. It was her . . . I can't really explain it. The woman had a way of making me feel good. Like a man."

"I'm speaking from personal experience, you understand; any woman has the capacity to make you feel like that. But believe me when I tell you that it's a false sense of security. This woman that's after you has nothing to lose. She's not trying to marry you."

"I imagine you're right."

"I know I am. And they don't want to be married to you. They remember that you could do the same to them that you did to an ex-wife. Cheat." Larry shook his head. "If you haven't done it already, do yourself a favor, drop it, cut it off."

"I have. Promise you'll keep this to yourself, especially away from Fontella and . . . my wife," Job pleaded.

"The fact that you realize what you've done should be punishment enough. I don't have to say a word. Anyway, that's not my place. You have to make the decision whether you'll admit it to your wife."

"It'll make our marriage go down the drain."

"If it does, your marriage was never meant to be. Only the Lord holds that knowledge. You know what I mean? He knows what will happen and what won't."

Job had to admit that Larry's advice stung, but he appreciated it. Driving that Jeep off one of the cliffs would have been easier than accepting what he said, though.

The fact that it was Sunday didn't slow the Sedona Starbuck's one bit. Monica witnessed shouts of latte, mocha and, espresso from the corners of the shop while inviting aromas occupied the gaps. People were lined up like eternal life could be ordered by the cupful.

She and Fontella moseyed around the room as two inconspicuous listeners, deciphering the central buzz as theocratic dialogue. How the Methodist compared to Baptist. Whether praise and worship was more effective than hymns. Charismatic versus high-church. The usual denominational debating that never comes to a resolution.

Monica wanted to get some things off her chest, and she assessed that inside the coffee shop was the wrong place for an in-depth discussion of her life.

They took a seat outside under the shade of a broad, teal colored table umbrella. The afternoon was pleasant; the closing stages of monsoon season had kept the desert heat at bay.

Fontella took a sip of her mocha frappuccino. "Have you found out how the blaze started?"

"We don't have a clue. Our insurance adjuster should be getting back to us the early part of this week." Monica had taken great pains to avoid thoughts of all she and Job had lost. She didn't blame Fontella for bringing the subject to the forefront, but a frantic struggle to get life back to some decent order had kept her from pondering the source of the fire.

"You should know by now that if you need anything, all you have to do is say so," Fontella told her.

"I know." She sniffed her caramel apple cider, hoping the aroma would settle the explosion mounting inside her. "Girl, I-I want you to help me."

"What's the matter?"

Monica lowered her cup into her lap. "I've been thinking about leaving Job."

"You're not serious. Why?"

"It's not on my mind as strong as it had been, but the thought hasn't completely left me."

Fontella's concern escalated. "For some reason, I was sure you all were working together through this gigantic mess."

"It's just appearances. We can't seem to agree on anything." She held up her hand and spread out her fingers to count. "How we live life. Should we have a baby? Will we run out of money? Is our spirituality on the right track?" She dropped her hand. "Nothing's working for our well-being."

"Girl . . ."

"Every topic turns into an argument. Now, I have to admit there were a couple instances lately where our talks were really nice; but overall, we're constantly at each other."

"Think about it, Monica," Fontella said. "What you've had to go through is stressful, at the least. It's the kind of stuff that can break even the strongest marriages apart."

"That fire wasn't the beginning of our problems. We haven't been right for a long time."

"Oh."

Monica took another sip of her cider, which was getting cold and losing its flavor. "Pastor made me uncomfortable today. It was like we had talked and he used that message to get my business out in the open. You know what I mean?"

Fontella chuckled. "Girl, that's discernment. Pastor Harris knew that message was needed for someone. You happened to be one of the ones."

"I know. I felt it. Now, I don't know what to do. Pastor got me really confused."

Fontella disagreed, telling Monica that she was in

more of a state of conviction than confusion. "Neither one of you is probably thinking straight. You should call the church and get a marriage counseling session."

"I know my husband. He'll think counseling is ridiculous."

"Pray about it. I mean really pray about. Fight for the sanctity of your marriage, girl. I know you love him."

"Sure I do, there's no doubt about that. But I want more. I want to be able to admire my man."

Later on that evening, Job and Monica were cooped up in the hotel room exchanging glances. It was the two of them, alone, without Larry and Fontella there to mediate.

Job was tossing between two opinions. *Should I tell her about Bianca? No. What good would it do?*

Monica crossed her legs Indian-style in the bed and lifted her head out of her Bible. "Hey, honey?"

Job felt salvation in not being the first to break the silence. "Yeah, babe?"

"Oh, nothing," she said. Monica dove back into her book.

Job sighed. The silence felt better right then. Tomorrow promised to be hectic day, so raising an all-night conversation on a complicated topic wouldn't have been wise. He decided that maybe a few hours of sleep would give him the answer he needed on whether to reveal his secret.

Chapter 23

... Cause me to understand wherein I have erred. Job 6:24

Job and Monica got an early start on Monday morning. They packed what few possessions they had and checked out of the hotel. Before he dropped her off at work, she reminded him of her promise to reserve a suite at Nine Iron, and that they would have to rent her a car.

"What about watching our budget?" Job asked, recalling her sermon most of last week.

Her eyes widened. "You've got today to decide who'll keep our only personal vehicle and who gets a rental."

"Why is that important right now?"

Monica adjusted the latch of her earring. "Just like today, Job. I have a post-op appointment with my doctor. I'll take a company car to the clinic, but just for today. There is such a thing as taking too many privileges." She didn't step out of the Yukon until it was clear that she wouldn't be a slave to the only working auto and his work schedule.

Monica rolled out of the front seat and opened a rear door to retrieve her briefcase when Job grasped her by the arm. "Honey, I love you." He meant it in every way possible. He wanted that week to start with a fresh perspective, and he didn't want her to go inside without seeing and feeling his sincerity. "I know a lot has happened, but we're going to be fine, I promise."

She kissed him on the lips. In a breathless phrase, she said, "I love you, too, now you know that love feels better when we have some money in our pocket, now go off to work because I've got to get in here myself. Bye." She patted Job on the arm, closed the door, and hurried off toward the administrative entrance. It wasn't quite the cordial send-off he'd planned.

No one else but Bianca could have met him at the side entrance of the school once he arrived, with a stack of papers as usual.

"You take the strangest avenues to avoid seeing me, Mr. Wright," she stated.

"Believe me. What has happened in the last several days was by no means intentional."

"Umm hmm." She held the door open for Job. Her eyes were planted on him for what seemed to be eternity. "Some interesting things have taken place since you been off the scene. I don't have time to really go into it though."

"Any hints?"

"Oh, no. It's nothing you have to worry about."

Why did she say that? Now, I'll worry.

"Everything . . . everyone, all right with you?" she asked.

"Oh yes, Monica and I are fine. Couldn't be better." He thought back on the very last interaction with his wife. He remembered that the situation could, indeed, be better. "I hope I still have a job," he joked.

"Is there any reason why you would think otherwise?" she asked. "I mean, nothing has come up that would make you think you were about to lose your job. Or is there something I need to know?"

Job wasn't sure how to take Bianca's questions; therefore, he decided to take a safe road in his answer. "Well, you know, I had no control over a fire. The district can't fault me for an absence because of that."

Bianca cocked her head to one side and twitched an eyebrow. "No. I don't guess they can." After Job cleared the doorway, she twisted past him and began to barrel down the hall. "Be sure to sign off on the substitute approval form. It's on your desk. Get it to me ASAP. That's the only way she can get paid." Within seconds, she became a shadow.

To Job, that exchange was awkward, but he didn't have the time to concern himself with it because his pride and joy waited.

He entered his classroom to a crowd of anxious and inquisitive students who wanted to know all of the smoky details of his absence.

"I don't have anything to tell you," he found himself speaking in a high-pitched tone, "because by the time I got to my house, the fire was already out."

"Jesus!" came from a corner of the classroom, "how did you manage to miss that?"

Job felt the past push forward to the present and settle in his throat. "Okay, okay, students. Enough of my boring drama. We've got a lot of work to catch up on." For the moment, he avoided unpleasant thoughts.

The routine of lesson plans, grading papers, and after-school extracurricular assignments had all come back by noon. Playing catch-up was easier than he had anticipated. During his lunch break, several colleagues approached him with assurances that if he needed their help, all he had to do was ask and he could consider it done. Near the end of the break, he was paged with a message that he had a visitor, waiting for him in the counselor's office.

"I'll be right down," he said to the secretary.

He was met by a tall, robust, Caucasian gentleman who seemed to be straight-jacketed in a six-button, double-breasted suit coat, and a cloth badge where a pocket square would usually rest.

"Mr. Wright?" He didn't wait for a response. "My name is Jeffrey East. I represent the SIU for the Valley."

"I don't understand."

"The Special Investigations Unit for the Fire department." Mr. East smiled. "I'm sorry to arrive unannounced and speaking with the acronym. It's a force of habit."

SIU? Fire Department? "Oh," Job said, trying not to sound puzzled.

"Obviously, I could not call your home, and your recent absence from work kept me from talking to you here. So, I drove in from Mesa this morning with the intention of chatting with you, getting some information, today."

Mr. East's explanation signaled Job to put his guard up until he had a few more details as to the purpose of the investigator's visit. "I'm forgetting my manners. Have a seat," Job told him. "Pardon me, but why a fire investigator?"

"Well, Mr. Wright, every house fire is investigated, and each examination can reveal things—making them not as cut and dry as you might think." Mr. East had a burdened glaze across his face. "We're called in by insurance companies when there's a need for clearance and further warrantee on a critical or poor risk."

"My insurance company?" Job asked.

"Yes. Mr. Wright, this is standard procedure by insurance companies—"

"For what?"

"Arson."

Job laughed. "Come on."

"The evidence collected from your home gives us reason to believe the fire was set intentionally."

Job's humor curled up, giving him an empty feeling. "I haven't done a thing. I assure you."

Mr. East leaned back. "We have no current suspicion that you did. Again, this is standard procedure. And part of our investigation involves talking to the homeowner."

"You're going to talk to my wife also?"

"She was questioned the day of, shortly after she was pulled from the house and stabilized. No need to bother her anymore." He flipped through some documents attached to a clipboard. "We have her statement."

"Oh."

"You'd be surprised, Mr. Wright, how many people, no matter what their social or economic status, would attempt to defraud an insurer with a carefully concocted scheme." Mr. East leaned in. "By the way . . . where were you on that day?"

Job swallowed. "But I thought I'm not a suspect."

"You're not; at least, not right now. But even you have to admit, Mr. Wright, your background and financials would give us reason to put up a red flag."

Job felt an instant rush of anxiety. He looked around to see if anyone, other than the two of them, heard Mr. East's comments. He asked in a whisper, "You checked up on me?"

"We check everything. Insurance investigations are serious business. Our work helps to keep one of the most powerful U.S. industries afloat."

There was a brief silence.

"I was thinking maybe you had seen suspicious activity around your home without realizing someone could be stalking the property for criminal activity," Mr. East explained. "Anything would help."

"I was at a school-related meeting." Job didn't feel

much guilt in that account, but he still had a queasy feeling from knowing his background had been checked. "You can confirm my whereabouts with Ms. Rizzo."

"Oh yes, the principal," Mr. East took some notes.

"Exactly."

"Any enemies or someone you've had a recent quarrel with?"

"An enemy?" Job looked around the room, which seemed to close in on him. "I've had arguments with people before . . . but my last one was years ago."

"With whom?" Mr. East asked.

Job hesitated, but he finally told him, "A Delvin Storm, my former business partner. But that was quite some time ago, in a totally different part of the country." He scratched his head. *Delvin? Nah. He's still in prison.* "Other than him, there's no one else I can think of."

Mr. East scribbled a few more notes and mumbled Delvin's full name under his breath. "Okay. This just about wraps it up here." Mr. East twisted his wrist to glance at his watch. "I have a couple more visits to make before I head back to Mesa."

Reality set in. "My home was *set* on fire," he said, although he didn't intend to say it aloud.

"By all indications, yes sir. And, if I were you, anything that can help me . . . well, don't hold back. Right now we have no leads. Since you're not a suspect, and how professional this job apparently was, leaves me to question why would somebody want to do this? And if their motive wasn't for monetary gain, then what?" He held out a business card for Job.

After Mr. East left, Job returned to class with a relief that the interrogation was over, but with fear and confusion over who would want to do him harm. Could the arson suspicion be true? By the time he closed his classroom door and continued with Marketing II, he was busy trying to convince himself that the competent Mr. East was on a fishing expedition with no real accusation, no real facts, and no real evidence.

After the last bell, Bianca wormed her way into Job's room, asking about his eventful lunch break.

Job, who was seated at his desk, rose up to face her. "Did Mr. East get an opportunity to talk to you?" he asked.

"He did." She peered at him with laughing eyes. "You know where you were that day."

"I'd just as soon forget it, too."

She pursed her lips. "And I know where you were that day."

Job didn't want to question her behavior. He'd had enough peculiarity for the next twenty-four hours. "We both know where we were. And nothing happened."

"That's right. Nothing." She paused. "You tell Monica?"

"No. I haven't."

Bianca turned around and headed out of the door. "Oh, . . . okay."

Chapter 24

Be kindly affectionate one to another with brotherly love . . . Romans 12:10

Monica gathered up her work and briefcase, kissed Job, and walked away from their Yukon that morning. She hoped that what her husband said he would do and what he actually did would line up by the end of the day. *Just take care of me*, she thought.

No sooner had she unlocked her office door and dropped her belongings on the desk than Nami met her with a cappuccino and crème cheese Danish. "Hey, stranger. You finally decided to rejoin the rat race, eh?"

"If I stayed out any longer, Cory would be putting your nameplate on the door." Monica smiled and accepted Nami's offering. "The company Intranet kept me abreast of the business you've been taking care of. You don't know how much I appreciate it."

"You know you're welcome. I was just doing my job."

Monica took a sip of her drink. "So what else has been going on that's been kept under the radar?"

"Girl, let me tell you," Nami said in a heavy Creole accent. She took a seat and began to unload the business behind the business, the interoffice gossip, and other cheeky goings-on at the Nine Iron. Her eyes were lit like French Quarter night life.

They giggled at the who, what, and where, and then made a pact to keep it all to themselves. "Well, I know I'm behind on everything. I guess we'd better get to work," Monica said.

Nami opened her schedule book. "Don't forget. You have an afternoon post-op with your OB-GYN."

"Oh, yes. That's at—"

"Two o'clock. A little after lunch."

"Right." Monica searched the top of her desk for her Palm Pilot, and then remembered that she hadn't taken it out of her purse that day. She found it, pulled out the stylus and scrolled to the contacts screen. "Before we get too bogged down, I've got to secure the executive hotel suite for an indefinite amount of time."

"For when?" Nami asked.

"How about, starting immediately?"

"Can't do. It's taken for two weeks."

Monica refused to be frustrated. "The hotel we were in was nice, very nice in fact. But it's become like a rodent's maze for me and Job. I've got to get something here, if at all possible. The Lee Trevino Suite?"

"It's available now, but you'd have to clear out in about ten days. Then it will be occupied for two and a half weeks. What about the Pitching Wedge Suite? It's spacious and available 'til kingdom come."

Monica knew it was much larger than where they had been staying. And it was much more reasonable—along the order of free. "Book it."

" 'Til when?"

"Kingdom come."

Dr. Najib was a mere ten minutes off schedule when Monica was escorted to an exam room and told to slip into a gown. She hadn't had time to turn past the front cover of *Woman's World* before the doctor entered.

After Monica felt the grip of a blood pressure monitor and the icy bond of a stethoscope, Dr. Najib gave her the prognosis on her out-patient procedure. "It's baby-making time now," she said.

Monica considered all that had happened in the recent days and weeks. "You know, doctor, I'm not exactly sure having a baby is a priority right now."

"I don't see a problem, Mrs. Wright. Everything is great. You are in great condition, I assure."

Monica did a quiet chuckle at how pronounced Dr. Najib's accent became when she got keyed up. "Oh, no, I don't mean medically. I meant my mind, whether I'm psychologically ready for it."

Dr. Najib brushed back her silky black strands. "You'd be surprised at the power the mind has. Powerful organ."

"Yeah, but you have to be up to it."

"This is true, true. I know personally that many people don't heal if they're mind had not willed it. You strong woman."

"How do you know this?" Monica asked, doubting that Dr. Najib would come up with a satisfying answer.

"You got man's job, eh? That means you can do what you want. *If* you want."

"I'll have to see." Monica knew she would have to draw on her Godly belief for the right and true answer, not just one she could be satisfied with. Right then, the satisfying answer might have her living by herself.

Later that evening, Monica entered the Pitching Wedge Suite. A mound of luggage and boxes stared at her and a drowsy husband lay along the edge of the king-sized bed. She had asked Nami to call Job earlier that day to tell him where their temporary/permanent residence was. It was his job to have their belongings not meet, but beat them there. By the looks of things, the task had been completed.

In a lethargic voice, Job told her about the visit from the SIU fire inspector. "We should be getting a settlement check soon."

Monica yawned. "Okay." She wasn't disinterested. She was exhausted and a one word sentence was all she could put together. He would just have to understand.

He rolled off the edge of the bed and landed on his feet. "Did you hear what I said, honey?"

"Yes." She wondered if he heard her the first time. For a moment, it made her think that he was up to something; something deceptive.

Job maneuvered between the boxes and suitcases, leaned into her chest, wrapped his arms around her, and pecked her on the cheek. His face broke into a smile. "How was your day?"

Job seemed to be making a valiant attempt at being the loving, caring, willing-to-listen-despite-my-own-fatigue type of husband. Monica could see this, but she voted her convictions in spite of his pressure to do otherwise. "Fine," she mumbled.

"And, um, the results from the doctor?"

She yawned. "Just fine." Her faith in God was weary just then. And her faith in Job definitely had to wait. "Good night, Job."

Chapter 25

. . . put away the evil of your doings from before mine eyes; cease to do evil. Isaiah 1:16

On Tuesday morning, Attorney Edward Kirkpatrick made one of his rare visits to the prison. He gave Delvin the latest quarterly spreadsheet with balances of off-shore accounts, and personal mail that had come to his law office instead of to the Ashland Prison mailroom.

While Delvin pondered how to handle each of the documents, Kirkpatrick found interest in a mahogany and gold Mont Blanc he had pulled from a breast pocket.

Kirkpatrick told him, "Word in the rumor mill is that you may have something to do with that fire. Wright mentioned your name when he was questioned. The SIU is onto the fact that the fire is suspect, but they're far fetched for concrete evidence or eyewitnesses."

Delvin remained expressionless. He strongly believed that some pieces of information shouldn't even be privy to one's attorney, so he decided to keep his version of the truth behind Job's misfortune to himself. "That rat'll do anything to get me in trouble. How did this tale get to you?"

"It's my job. You pay me to stave off problems but, like

I said, there's no evidence supporting any accusation that you were involved. As your attorney, I advise you to remain silent on this issue—"

"Hush up, man. Cut all the lawyer talk."

"Look. We're not talking about money laundering or racketeering. Arson is a crime of violence. Real prison time."

"Relax." Delvin felt an air of confidence. He decided to play the mental game to the end. "Wait a minute. You think I had something to do with that?"

"Did you?"

"Oh, yeah," he declared with sarcasm. "Warden gave me a four or five day furlough. I flew out west, set fire to Job's home and flew back here in time for a weekend meal. Yeah, I did it."

"Don't be a wise guy. Lucky for you, the authorities thought that your involvement was far-fetched."

"No, you wise up. Of course I didn't have anything to do with it."

"I hope you're telling the truth."

"Truthfully, it's impossible for me to have set that man's house on fire. That's the truth." He called the guard to let him out of the room, which he hoped was Kirkpatrick's sign that the visit was ending on that declaration.

The meeting with his attorney was a flesh-wound compared to the rest of Delvin's day.

Murphy had crept his way up to Warden's office, where Delvin had busied himself with what could not have been more than an hour's worth of filing and dusting.

He noticed Murphy's left hand, bandaged in thick gauze and hanging in an improvised sling.

"You break something?" Delvin inquired.

Murphy, without invitation, sat down in Warden's office chair with his neck held straight and chest in a regal position. "Occasionally, Mr. Storm, battles that utilize verbal wits just don't work with the unschooled. I didn't win the slight altercation I was involved in, but I do recollect holding my own."

Delvin couldn't help but laugh. "You got your butt whipped, huh?"

"I cannot allow minor injuries to be a prohibitory cause . . . Mr. Storm. Pressing issues await."

Delvin slapped a dusty rag against Warden's desk, sending debris into the atmosphere. "I knew your day would come. That crafty mouth of yours finally took someone to the edge. Well? What've you in mind today?"

"Well, you see, Deliverer and I were in a series of discussions. Actually, I did the talking and he did the agreeing."

"I'm sure that's exactly how it went."

"We've seen the latest incident—the fire—to fruition. Now it is time to heap the ultimate misfortune his way. Don't you agree?"

"Come again?"

"We do not see another avenue, aside from following through with the ultimate step." Murphy's brows ran across his dark, slick face; straight and assertive.

They began an exchange of stares that lasted a while. They were busy telling by eyeing, not by saying.

Then, Delvin understood what Murphy was implying. "Oh, no sir, oh, no! Nobody is going to die. Not now, not ever. I'm not going to have that guilt on my hands."

"You paid for this game, Mr. Storm. It must be carried out until there's a winner."

"You don't have to remind me who paid for what. And this is *my* game." Delvin remembered that another phase of his scheme had already been set in motion, courtesy of Bianca Rizzo. Why kill Job when humiliation would last longer?

"It is true that your financial contribution initialized this scheme, however, you are a fraction of this pie. There are others who rely on their reputations of dependability by what they say they will deliver. This forward motion cannot be stopped."

The amount of apprehension Delvin felt could not be defined. He felt a force pinning him to a wall, an energy compelling him to come out fighting. "I know how to stop the money. No one will want to follow anything through when they see their dollars have been cut off." He began thinking then how to be rid of Murphy's presence so he could make contact with Nadia.

"Money's not everything to everybody, Mr. Storm. Some men's adrenaline is fueled by pride. Some get a charge in their capability to take matters to higher levels. I can pretty much say that, yes, this is the crowd that your money has commissioned."

Delvin reached over and put a tight grip on Murphy's decrepit limb. "I'm not asking you, I'm *telling* you, stop this." He let go, watching the co-conspirator grimace in pain.

After a long period of silence, Murphy, with a nervous glance, stood up and told him, "I refuse to promise anything, Mr. Storm. It's not completely in my hands. I will do my best, if you really want your man to be left alone."

Delvin leaned against the desk. He found it difficult to stand under the pressure. His ability to maintain control over countless situations had weakened under this maze of concrete and steel. "I want the craziness to stop. Leave him alone."

Chapter 26

Oh that I were as in months past, as in the days when God preserved me. Job 29:1

"Good grief, Job. Leave it up to you. You can defi-nitely find a way to have a good time and spend some money."

That was Monica's reaction to Job's request for a night out on the town. To say that their last few days were or-dinary would not have been too high an assessment. He called Monica around lunch and found out her day was dragging along as well. TGIF. Life needed to get better.

"We need an opportunity to get our minds off things. That's all I'm trying to do."

She laid it all out on the line, reminding him of their current condition. She was driving a rented car. Thanks to her high-end job with benefits, they had an above av-erage place to stay. What little savings they had was being sifted into necessities they wouldn't have needed if their house had not been leveled. There were no foresee-able prospects on who burned their home, if arson was even the real reason behind it.

"And you want me to be so elated about going out this

evening? You've got to be joking. We probably need to save our money for this Florida trip coming up."

Job had pulled the phone away from his ear about halfway into her ranting. When he realized the airway was clear and he could get in a word, he asked, "Don't worry about the Disney trip. It will take care of itself. Where's that faith you're always talking about?"

"You leave my spirituality out of this. This is a mess you created."

Job seethed underneath, and tried with all his power to stay composed. He looked around to see if anyone had crept into his presence. He was in the parking lot of the school. The headlights of automobiles were the only eyes watching him.

"You know what? I'm sick of you constantly laying all the blame on me. Try supporting me on one suggestion I make in this marriage. I'm doing the best I can. Now shut up. Figure out what you'll wear. Appreciate the fact that through our list of dilemmas, we can enjoy each other and life; if we allow ourselves to."

It was a while before there was a response. A long while.

Monica huffed through the receiver. "Where'd you have in mind?"

Job, trying his best to sound upbeat, said to her, "I'll call Larry and Fontella. Think about it. You know what the deal is."

Western Arizona had long been a cherry dipped in the fondue pot of culture. Until recent events kept them from their usual routine, Job and Monica had explored into the social scene over time, particularly Last Fridays Phoenix, a monthly engagement geared specifically for African-Americans who enjoyed social interaction and professional networking. The party would always start around six and last well into the night.

It was uncertain whether the September affair would take place because it was so close to 9/11. But the organizers of the activity, a couple of real estate developers, felt that Phoenix's 20 to 40ish business men and women of color needed that time, if nothing else, to vent. Cancellation was not an option.

It was common knowledge that dress code was "to impress", and everyone in attendance followed that decree. The Wrights carpooled in the Logans' Navigator to the Sheraton Crescent, the usual venue.

There were business announcements, complimentary hors d'oeuvres and door prizes. For those who arrived early enough, there were dollar chances for Brian McKnight and Tyrese concert tickets in Sedona. And the brothers and sisters? The ballroom served it up—deep chocolate to olive to mulatto, with everyone looking like the main event.

Job stood back to admire Monica—Nine Iron's power exec—and the way she commanded her presence. Confident, poised. *Fine.* She was networking like a pro. And to top it all, she had relented under his suggestion to attend tonight's party, without much discussion.

Meanwhile, two brothers decked in Sean John approached him.

The first gentleman was of medium height, athletic build with Ben Franklin glasses resting high on the bridge of his nose. "You're the umm, brother . . . man," he said in disgust. His memory had taken a rest. "Your name. It won't come to me."

"Me either," said the second gentleman, a much taller man with sullen eyes that seemed to never get enough rest. "But I know one thing. This brother's in real estate. I *know* he's the one."

Job listened, standing in suspicion, as the two pondered his identity and past career. They weren't carrying around a *Black Enterprise* for reference. They didn't need it. Their recollection was doing just fine.

"Don't leave us hanging," the first man said. "You're in big business, aren't you?"

It was the first time since the court case that forced Wright & Storm's dissipation into the heavens that Job admitted his identity. He tested their acumen by tossing a few complicated industry terms around.

"Real estate, that's it. That's why we know you," the second man replied with a gratified smile. "Listen, we are involved in residential and commercial realty here in the Phoenix area. I'm Vincent Fuquay," he said while beckoning with his hand. "My partner, Donald Terry."

Job gave them his full name.

"Joseph Wright, yeah. Wright and Storm, am I right?" Vincent asked. He didn't wait for a response. "I know you're doing well. It would be an insult to ask."

A couple of moments passed and the silence marinated.

Vincent and Donald informed him that the monthly soirée was their brain-child. Job pointed Monica out. She was across the room chatting with a couple of execs from the hotel and resort industry. The men asked how long the Wrights had been in Phoenix and what company, if any, handled their residential sales transaction.

"Because I know we didn't," Donald declared with humor in his voice.

Job told them it was Vonson & Hickell and apologized that he didn't know of Fuquay & Terry at the time.

"I'm shocked they didn't grab you up," Donald said.

"The man's got his own company," Vincent said, "and judging from what the mags said, Vonson & Hickell should be applying to work for him.

"Well, truthfully," Job said, "We're out of business."

Vincent and Donald gazed at each other. Job imagined

that they wanted to fade off the scene. He wished he could go out ahead of them. He looked around, hoping Monica was nearby to prop him up, but she was hemmed up by a small group of people, chatting and grinning away. Job chuckled to himself, thinking she was being cornered for free spa memberships. He then remembered that he was busy in his own zone, with admirers who may walk away in sorrow.

After the awkward moment had time to apologize for itself, Vincent asked whether Job had done any commercial realty lately.

"I'm in the education field now. Haven't done any real estate for a couple years."

Donald said, "With a little practice, it would come back to you."

"Maybe the two of you didn't hear me," Job said more in protest than reprimand. "I haven't fleshed out a deal in—it's felt like ages."

Vincent and Donald had turned a deaf ear. They were following their own train of thought, and refused to be thrown off.

Donald said, "We got some ideas coming around the bend that could use your expertise."

"But—"

"Look, Mr. Wright," Vincent interrupted. "You are . . ."

Job shook his head. "Not any longer."

"Okay . . . you *were*—the king of the raw land deal."

"In Kentucky."

"Dirt's dirt." Vincent's lips curled into "what's the difference?" "With your knowledge, we could broker some really big deals."

"You're forgetting an important piece. I don't have a license."

Vincent told him, "Not an obstacle at all. We only deal in commercial, not res. And you wouldn't need a license, not in the manner in which we'd use your expertise. Listen . . . think about it. You and your wife are here with some of your friends. You don't come here just to socialize, do you?"

Well, yes. "Well, no, I don't guess."

"I wouldn't think so."

"Vincent, come to think of it, we could use Joseph in that deal we're trying to close in on going up toward Sedona. It's about four, five months away, but it'll take us that long for the research, to secure the proper financing," Donald said.

The two men sparked Job's real estate savvy all over again. But he thought, in all fairness, that he should give them all the details of his exit from the business.

"Listen, whatever it is, let's get together and discuss it at another time. We won't put a downer on tonight's festivities," Vincent said. He held up his glass.

Job looked around for Monica. He hoped that she could help him process what he thought he'd just heard, but fortune didn't have it that way. He looked at Vincent and Donald, and smiled. *Maybe it really is God working things out.* He lifted his glass in a toast.

Late, late that evening, after parting from the Logans, Job and Monica were cuddled up on the loveseat in their suite. He told her about the possibility of entering real estate again with Vincent and Donald. She responded with passionate, stirring embraces. Seconds turned into minutes, and minutes warmed by as the two talked and caught up on each other's magnetism. That time seemed to take on an air of perfection, and Job felt that he could enter a zone of honesty and truth.

"I want to take a chance at something, something I've wanted to let you know for a little while," he said. It seemed any subject could be discussed, but Job consciously unclenched his jaw to keep from developing a headache.

Monica's silky tone calmed him, making him feel wanted, loved. "What is it?" she asked.

He took a breath and then unloaded with every detail of his contact with Bianca, including the day of the fire. "But nothing ever happened, honey. Believe me. There's nothing between us. I made sure of that."

Monica's chin hit her chest. "So I haven't been enough for you, huh?"

"No. That's not true."

"What then?"

"Monica, you've got to admit that sometimes it's hard to talk to you. Tonight is wonderful. I mean, we're into each other. But we haven't had a night like this in . . . I don't remember the last time."

Her eyes began to water over and turn pink. "I see. You found someone to talk to."

"Yes." He paused, thankful that he could make a sincere statement. "Larry."

Monica raised her head and swabbed a tear. "Who?"

"When it was impossible to get a loving discussion out of you, I would talk to Larry. You should've known I was talking to someone."

"No, Job. That wouldn't have been easy to figure out. You didn't talk to me, and I'm your wife. But you found time to talk to another woman." Monica curled her lips. "Then, what will be the future with you and your boss?"

Job cleared his throat. "We have no future. Not from the angle you're thinking. Nothing ever got started. Ms. Rizzo's not the type you can talk to. And, even if she is, it's always been my desire to be able to talk to you, not any other woman. And I apologize. I should've never considered talking—to another woman—about our issues."

"What stops us from talking?"

"We both play a part, honey. I know that in the past I've been a know-it-all. My stubbornness keeps us from communicating."

Tears began to drop from Monica's face. There was no whimpering or stuttering. Only the tears. "And me? What do I do?"

"The way you talk to me. It makes me feel like you hate me." In the silence that followed, Job regretted initiating the subject, especially since the rest of the evening had been so . . . perfect. Yet, despite the subject, Monica did not present her usual icy gazes, thoughtless comebacks, or seething demands. And Job didn't know how to take her.

"I love you." Monica wiped away a lone tear. In a supple voice, she told him, "But I need to think about what you've done and your explanation."

"Do you forgive me?"

She nodded her head in directions that didn't point to the negative or the positive. "In a matter of days, we're supposed to travel to Florida so that you can receive an award based, among other things, on a recommendation from the same woman you *almost* had an affair with? We're displaced from our home by what may have been arson." Monica's bloodshot eyes drew together. "With all that, you could see justification in us celebrating tonight. You know what? I need time to think."

Chapter 27

The following day, Nami tried to go over the day's schedule of meetings and priority correspondence, but she was constantly interrupted as Monica discussed the previous evening's events, including Job's admission. Monica opened her mail. Among the letters was a legal-sized envelope from Statewide Insurance. She and Job had agreed to have homeowner's insurance information forwarded to Monica's business address to insure prompt receipt.

"All right, I understand. You're saying hubby's a liability and you can do bad by yourself. Did I sum it up pretty well?" asked Nami.

Monica sat up in her desk chair and chuckled at Nami's accent. "It's amazing that you deduced all of that from what I said. But you're wrong."

Nami raised an eyebrow. "Am I?"

"I didn't say all of that."

"Oh, okay . . ." Nami paused, "Can I be real with you?"

"Now you know that you're more than just my AA;

you're a friend. By all means, be frank." Monica gave a sassy laugh. "Not that it's ever stopped you before."

"Let's see. Who makes more money?"

"I do."

"Hmm. Have *you* ever cheated on Job?"

"See, you took that all wrong. I didn't say he cheated. He didn't even say he cheated."

"But the stage was set, right? He had the opportunity and almost took it."

"And?"

"And, as a man thinketh in his heart, so is he. The Bible says that you know."

"But I don't know that he was thinking about cheating. He says he needed someone to talk to. Someone who would talk and not fuss."

Nami gave that "I'm-not-convinced look." "And you believe this?"

"He hasn't given me a reason not to."

"Okay," Nami said in Creole drawl, "did he have a reason to believe that he couldn't talk to you?"

Nami's statement halted Monica's every thought, emotion, and response. Nami had put a finger on the pulse of a problem. Job did have a valid reason for needing a confidant without an attitude; one with an open ear. And since Monica knew Job, his poor judgment in selecting a confidant should not have been a surprise.

"But why did he have to talk to another woman?" Nami asked sternly.

"The issues he needed to talk about are between him and a woman. Most people would think that reasonable. I'm not saying that I agree or disagree; I'm just saying that most would find that reasonable."

And then, Monica sat back in her chair and gasped. "Nami! You tricked me."

"What are you saying?"

"I'm saying you used that slick Louisiana backwoods wisdom to help me see things as they really are."

"Call it what you want. Mother wit, backwoods wisdom. I don't know what the label would be. I know you have to ask yourself if you truly believe he's done something wrong."

"He's not completely cleared . . . in my mind."

"Okay. Then go with that. But I've been around you long enough to know you can fuss that man out. Not such a bad thing, considering most men need a good fussing now and then. It has a way of keeping them on their toes. But you have to love a man into doing right."

Monica purposely stopped eye contact with Nami. "I can respect that."

"I'm asking you for your benefit and the benefit of your marriage . . . have you prayed for your answers?"

If Monica could count praying hard to fight off the urge not to leave Job, or praying not to stir her rough exterior as she knew she could . . . then, yes; she had prayed for answers.

Monica felt a heat rush her body. "I admit. No. I haven't prayed like I should."

"Pardon me for saying so," Nami said, "but you know better. You have to do spiritual things if you want your hubby to be spiritual."

"That's what I get for soliciting an honest opinion." Monica picked up her letter opener and ripped the edge of the insurance letter. "You take honesty to another level and—" She read the first few sentences, and the letter began shaking in her hand uncontrollably.

"What's wrong?"

"Nothing, actually." Monica straightened the folds in the letter and placed it on her desk. "We'll receive our claim money under separate cover. Soon." *Thank you, Lord.*

Nami applauded. "See? Good things are coming around the corner. The insurance claim will be met, and you have a trip to look forward to. It's nothing but God at work."

Thoughts rushed through Monica's mind. "I guess you're right."

Monica had already dropped onto the bed in their suite when she realized she wasn't alone.

Job was seated at the bureau desk in a corner of the room. His head seemed to be one with the computer screen.

"You startled me," she said.

"Umm. I figured one of two things. Either you weren't speaking to me, or you didn't see me in here."

"What're you doing?"

He tapped a few keys. "I'm on the internet, pulling up the requirements for an Arizona broker's license."

Disgust overtook her. "For what, Job?"

He reminded her of his acquaintance with Fuquay & Terry the previous evening, and the possibilities of future realty work. Job turned to her and smiled. "I want to be prepared so that if the opportunity presents itself, I'll have the necessary paperwork out of the way."

Monica hadn't heard enough explanation for enthusiasm. "I thought you were a teacher. I thought teaching was what you enjoyed."

"Oh, believe me; it is. But I can have more than one stream of income, right?"

She shook her head. "Real estate is one of the things that got us in this trouble."

Job's face crinkled. "Real estate had nothing to do with our trouble. Having the wrong business partner had a part to play in it, or other things, but not the line of work

I was in." He redirected his attention to the computer screen. "You gotta stop trippin'."

Monica crunched her hands together as self-punishment for initiating a ridiculous argument. "Hey. I'm sorry."

Job nodded.

"We got some good news today." She explained the letter from their homeowner's insurance company. "I guess we can start making plans to rebuild."

"Great news," was all he said. His tone was less than jubilant.

Monica lay on the bed, thinking that maybe Fontella and Nami were right. Her stretches of moodiness, no doubt, made Job's life miserable. But before she could gather any strength to resist, she asked him, "Did you ever think that I have a right to be angry with you?"

Job stopped tapping away at the keyboard and turned in a look of confusion. "Huh?"

She was ashamed at her outburst, but she couldn't think of a way to humbly bow out of what she said. "You have the nerve to be angry at me? Job, you don't have a right to question if I'm not speaking to you . . . although you're wrong. I came through the door tonight with every intention to settle what's going on between us. But now, I'm not so sure."

Job sighed. "You mean we're not going to lay our feelings out on the table?"

She rubbed her eyes to get a clear picture of Job's dark complexion, but it was overshadowed by memories of fighting through a fire while he and Bianca were together. "I've made a decision about something," she said.

"What?"

"I can't go with you to Florida. I need some time away from you. I have to assess where we are and where I feel we're going. And I have to do it alone."

Chapter 28

. . . and thou shalt be called, the repairer of the breach, the restorer of paths to dwell in. Isaiah 58:12b

Two weeks had gone by at the prison without a major incident. All the inmates had occupied themselves by marking walls and counting time. It was the one month anniversary of 9/11 when Delvin indulged Stinson in a friendly game of chess after breakfast.

Delvin was the victor, with his muscle-clad cohort admitting that brains, not brawn, won strategy games.

"Next time we challenge each other, the game is arm wrestling." Stinson laughed like thunder and walked away in defeat.

Delvin smiled, realizing that he wouldn't be as lucky in physical combat. "You're on."

No sooner had Delvin reset the board when Murphy thrust his head into the cell. "Care to allow a worthy opponent an opportunity to reign triumphant?" he asked.

"Sure," Delvin said, "if you think you can."

Murphy positioned himself on Delvin's bunk as Stinson moved away from the mirror and sink toward the cell opening. "I'm gonna let you all have at it. I've got a Sprite with my name on it and—"

"You might try some water," Murphy interrupted. "That carbonated beverage may be a tad warm."

"How in the world would you know?" Stinson asked. A brief silence went by before he said, "Never mind. It's no telling with you. I guess I'll go nap on my own bunk." He left.

Ten minutes in, Delvin and Murphy's match was a dead heat between the opponents.

"Why chess, Mr. Storm? Why do you engage in such an activity?"

Delvin wished Murphy hadn't spoken his riddles, particularly while he was concentrating on his next move. "Why do you ask?"

"Ahh, chess. A game created so that finance and real estate criminals like ourselves can keep our negotiation and battle-like reflexes up to par. It's the ultimate game of strategy. Don't you agree?" Murphy sneered in the oddest way. "Check," he called out.

It annoyed Delvin that Murphy sounded like a commercial for Milton-Bradley. He could see no way around it; he was soon to be defeated. What aggravated him most was Murphy's saucer-eyed expression, his lip twitches and clamped teeth. It was more than just a friendly game, more than one about to check-mate a rival. But Delvin didn't know what was really happening.

Murphy made his final move, shouting. "Shall we go?"

"Where?"

He pursed his lips. "Oh . . . nowhere." Murphy continued to speak in clipped and vague sentences.

Thirty, maybe forty minutes into a second game, the prison sirens went off. Either someone had died or a new batch of inmates had made their way to Ashland.

It didn't take long at all for Delvin to get his answer. Questioning.

It was the word that became the theme of Delvin's life that day.

The questioning began about 2:45 P.M., two hours after Stinson was scraped up from his cell, mottled shirt and all. Delvin was stupefied. He had lost someone he trusted.

Delvin had been escorted to an empty isolation ward often reserved for inmates known to go crazy. The walls were bland, with tears in the padding at the creases. Correctional officers grilled him for two hours. He knew nothing, so he told nothing.

Then, he was marched up to the warden. On the way, he reminisced about when Shiloh had introduced himself as the chaplain and given him a Gideon Bible. One of the Biblical passages spoke of a man claiming to be the Savior being trotted through judgment halls. Jesus was eventually found innocent. Delvin desired a similar outcome.

Warden's personal hellhole had just received a fresh scrubbing; Delvin was sure of it by the way his nostril hair stung from the piney clean stench.

"This is a tremendous disappointment," he scolded, "a farce." Warden was an antithesis of his usual calm self; throwing books, fussing at the guards standing watch. "A man dies while I'm in charge, under my watch?" His eyes stuck to the ceiling. "Please tell me, somebody . . . that I'm dreaming."

Delvin, the guards, the wind; nobody dared mumble a word.

It was clear by the frustration on Warden's face, that the perpetrator had not been identified. The prison administration's noses hadn't even sniffed up a cold trail.

Oh, but there was going to be a fall guy. Delvin looked around in dismay. No one else seemed to be sharing that cliff with him.

Warden picked up a Sprite can that was similar in description but not the actual criminal evidence. "A hypo needle punctured through the top of the can. The poison was inserted that way." Warden demonstrated how the person must have done it. Then, he put the can down, picked up a nearby book and shoved it into Delvin's chest. "Come out and fess up, Storm. Whatdya know?"

The routine was quickly becoming old. But Delvin remained calm. What the admin couldn't see was that he really didn't have any light to shed on the subject.

Since they had nothing, no witness or real evidence, Delvin was returned to his cell, his trustee privileges suspended, pending further investigation.

"Stinson's dead, Murphy." Delvin decided, for once, to visit his cell unannounced.

"I'm fully aware of that," Murphy said, as though Stinson's death had been in the history books for years.

"He's not just dead, he was murdered. Poisoned." Delvin could feel his heart rate and breathing increase. He bowed his head, almost too choked to speak. "I think it was a message meant for me."

"How do you come to that conclusion?"

"You think I wasn't listening to the things you said a while ago? I didn't understand then, but I do now." He grabbed Murphy by the neck. "You had something to do with it."

Murphy shrugged. "You could be waning on the edge of correctness. I'm not at liberty to say, however."

Delvin scowled, hoping to scare Murphy. "I told you I don't like killing. I could kill you right now, though." He let Murphy's neck go with a jerk.

Murphy seemed undaunted except he needed a moment to catch his breath. "The conclusion that I can safely make is that somebody must be angry and somebody has caused somebody to be angry." He paused, pressing a fingertip against his lips. "Oh, and another conclusion . . . I'm sure that the drink was not delivered from the *bottling plant* with that caustic solution inside. Arsenic, was it?"

"It's amazing how you know things I didn't tell you." Delvin stepped back from him to avoid the urge to grab his neck, this time to choke him to death. "Yeah, you know what's going on."

Murphy face froze. Delvin had never seen a black man flush before. "Okay. I see someone has a noose around your butt. Well, then fine, you peon. Say nothing."

"I'm befuddled, Mr. Storm. Your accusations are tremendously unfounded."

"I'll bet they are." Delvin slapped Murphy's bunk, knocking the linens out of place. "Since you insist on being their crony, give them this message. I'll fix everything, *everything* I've fouled up before they get to me. You be sure to tell them that. Got it?"

Murphy slowly nodded. "And I have a line of advice for you as well, Mr. Storm."

"What?"

"Look out, listen up, *for the law of my name.*"

After Delvin left Murphy's cell, he went to get permission for a guard to escort him from the cellblock, beyond the dormitories, and down a long hallway that held a dozen pay telephones. He plugged one ear with his finger while looking gruesomely at a loudmouth on the phone next to him.

The operator received an acceptance on the other end. "I'm happy that you took my call, Ms. Rizzo," Delvin said.

"I thought we agreed that we wouldn't contact each other unless the need arose," Bianca said to him.

"That need has arisen; otherwise, I wouldn't bother

you." Delvin inspected his surroundings. The hallway was still noisy, but the phones adjacent to him were unoccupied. "Let me get right down to why I needed to speak to you. I've made a terrible mistake."

"Oh? How?"

"You see . . ." Delvin gave Bianca the actual chain of events that led to his imprisonment, the downfall of Wright & Storm, and the truth of Job's involvement.

Yes, Job benefited from a few of Delvin's schemes. And, according to law, his punishment would've been minute. But he was due a punishment.

And, no, Job's hands were never directly involved in a single deed to steal, deceive, or otherwise pilfer for his personal gain.

"You see, Ms. Rizzo, if Job Wright is guilty of anything, basically, it's just stupidity."

At that point, Delvin realized his icy core had melted somewhat, and that he had found himself capable of panic. He was also capable of empathy, grief, and any other human emotion that he had previously attributed to weakness. The phone trembled in his hand; he realized that he was also able to forgive.

Yes, for months, he had wanted to punish Job in any way possible. Destroy his reputation. Burn his house down. But he didn't want him killed. He never wanted that.

After his explanation, Bianca said, "What you're telling me is commendable, Mr. Storm. However, this new story is futile. I've long passed your previous account to the proper school authorities."

Delvin leaned his head against the wall. He was being stalked by his own fears. "Then, you've got to convince them that you made a mistake, that your sources were incorrect," he demanded.

Bianca gave off a heaving sigh. "Which part of the story is true? Is it all a lie? Are you a lie?"

"Listen to me, Ms. Rizzo—"

"No, you listen to me, Mr. Storm. I'm a principal in one school in a huge school district. Allegations such as the ones you told to me are always investigated by a district official. As soon as it was in my hands, it was out of my hands. You and I are just going to have to let this Mr. Wright situation play out."

Delvin hadn't been that desperate in his life. His anxiety even surpassed the day he was sent to prison. He had initiated a seemingly unstoppable catastrophic chain of events on Job's life, and neither he nor Monica deserved it. "So there is nothing you can do, huh?"

Bianca was huffing into the receiver. "I can't help. Honestly, I don't want the investigation to cease."

"I don't understand. Why?"

"Because I have my own reasons," she said.

Chapter 29

The preparation of the heart in man, and the answer of the tongue, is from the Lord. Proverbs 16:1

In the first week of October, Vincent Fuquay and Donald Terry listened to Job's story of losing his firm and Delvin Storm's role. They told Job that they wanted time to "mull over their thoughts." Those body-numbing thirty seconds went by without a hitch. Since that time, early mornings and late evenings were devoted to analyzing commercial prospects on their behalf. Job told them that their confidence in him was a blessing from God.

A couple of weeks later, just three days before his trip, Job found it difficult to ignore the adulation he received from the students, colleagues, and well-wishers. It seemed as though everyone he knew, and many he didn't, wanted to make some presentation in the form of a phone call, card or gift.

At a special assembly in Job's honor, Bianca presented him with a plaque for which Mountain River's students, faculty, and staff had pooled their dollars and pennies. She handed it to him, shook his hand, hugged him, and then gave him the most disease-ridden stare he'd ever seen. Job eventually dismissed it.

Job was troubled, however, over Monica's refusal to accompany him to Florida. Up to the night before he was to leave, she had not changed her mind.

She switched on a happy mood when they attended Monday night's Couple's Class. It seemed deceptive, especially since they hadn't held a healthy conversation in almost two weeks.

Pastor Harris's message spoke to Job in a special way. He stroked his silver-streaked goatee, which contrasted his cocoa brown complexion. "The Bible says, in John the fourth chapter, that a man is without honor in his own country. Amen?"

The group chorused their acknowledgement.

"Now I'm paraphrasing," he continued, "because the scripture actually uses the term prophet. To my knowledge, none of you here claim to be a prophet. But I'm sure, if each of us peered into our lives, we would see that we have some knowledge of the future, if we simply do one thing: obey God."

Someone in the group, who Job didn't recognize, said, "Amen."

"Now, we as Christians can say that we see physical evidence, that if we live right, we can reap benefits beyond our needs. We can have pleasant times."

The group's responses ranged from low moans to joyous shouts. Job reached over and touched Monica's arm. There was no reaction.

Pastor Harris raised his voice. "We can have a good time in the Lord *before* we reach heaven—this is a good testament."

Job smiled and nodded.

"In the case of each couple here tonight, your helpmate is right here with you. Each of you, individually, carries a half-life; only together can you live true life to the fullest. God's blessing. God is good."

Monica was quietly shedding tears. Job wrapped his arm around her. He thought of their struggles and he fought back his own tears.

But that calm, unified feeling lasted a short while.

After class, Job was up late packing for the trip, alone. Monica had dropped him off at the suite and gone grocery shopping. Meanwhile, Larry called to wish him good luck and Godspeed.

"I don't understand. This has got to be the longest Monica has held a grudge in the history of our marriage." Job didn't want to unload his unhappiness, but it seemed inevitable.

"You've gotta be patient. She didn't say she was leaving. She told you she needed time to think, right?" Larry asked.

"Yeah. But think about *what*? That's what I don't know."

"Let me ask you something, Job. Did you make the attempt to be honest in her sight?"

"It's all I've been trying to do."

There was a brief moment of quiet before Larry asked, "You remember when we first met, how you attributed your future and fortune to your hard work? How you claimed it was your efforts that made things happen?"

Job was humbled by his forward comments. "Well, yeah."

"Okay, now, you recognize that your future is not relegated by you. You're a lump of clay, you're just sand. Your problems and solutions should be left to a rock that's higher than you."

"But the problems are so great." Job couldn't help it. He could feel the inner fight to regain confidence, and it seemed to be overtaking him. "But as Pastor Harris says, I'm trying to let go and let God."

"Then, let Him work for you. Put it in God's hands. You're just learning how to make a turn around for the best. Now you've got to trust the only one who can be trusted to make it right."

"I know that this trip won't be the same without Monica."

"We all know that. But I tell you what—take the time to really seek God. Orlando's got some wonderful places where you can get away by yourself."

"I won't have that kind of time. The awards ceremonies, interviews, banquets, and everything will keep me busy."

"Listen, man, you better make the time. Take some time with Him. He made this trip possible."

Job studied Larry's words. "By myself, huh?"

"Nobody but you. Uninterrupted time. He can talk to you that way. And you can praise Him in return."

"And Monica?"

"God will deal with her, whether she believes it or not."

Five-thirty the following morning, Monica was at the breakfast table, reading the *Arizona Informant* and sipping on hot green tea when Job came through the hallway with his suitcase.

"You're still staying?" he asked.

"Umm hmm. Give me a kiss." It was mere physical recognition of his departure, no passion. "I'll see you when you get back."

"At the airport?"

"I'll pick you up at the airport, yes," she said. That gave him a bit of assurance that she planned on being there when he returned from his trip.

"I'll miss you," he said.

She gave no response.

The front desk called to inform him that the shuttle was downstairs waiting to transport him to Sky Harbor International. Job pulled his luggage into the hallway, and peered down at his cell phone. "I wonder will I need this," he said, hoping that Monica would have a change of heart and call. Since it seemed that he might get a ring, he shoved the phone down in his pocket. As he closed the door to their suite, he hoped that it wasn't a sign that he was closing a door to his life, his and Monica's life together.

He rode to the airport in constant prayer for his personal safety and for God to protect Monica while he was away. While he prayed, Job focused on Pastor Harris's words and Larry's advice for comfort for the trip.

Job understood why they called Disney a land of enchantment. Between the events that took place for the honorees, he took advantage of some Universal Studio tours, the Disneyland theme park, and the Hard Rock Café. But he couldn't shake the feeling that the trip would be better with Monica.

Prior to the award banquet that Thursday evening, he had all afternoon free. He left his room, took the elevator down to the hotel lobby and asked the concierge to hail a cab.

"Where to, my friend?" the driver asked. Job was fond of the gentleman's obviously British accent.

"Orlando have any mountains?"

"Oh, no. The city is made up of lowlands. Is there any reason you asked?"

"I need a quiet place where I can do some thinking."

"No mountains. Sorry, chap. Looking for a high place, eh?"

"Yeah, I guess," Job answered.

"The building with the highest elevation is the down-town SunTrust Bank building. Rather impersonal, though. Would you like to go there?"

The bank building didn't interest him. "Where else is there?"

The driver looked up at Job through the rear view mir-ror. "Pretty amazing, with all the theme parks and the like, you want something different. Well, I guess when I contemplate—the people could be rather distracting."

Job told him, "I don't want too many people. I need a calm place."

"Yes, yes, someplace calm." The driver signaled a left turn. "I know just the place. You're not frightened of water, are you?"

"Oh, no," Job said.

After a twenty minute drive, they arrived at a rather large, but serene, body of water with Orlando's sky-scrapers at a distance.

"You want me to wait?" the driver asked, implying that Job wouldn't be long.

"I'm going to be a while, but yes." He handed the driver a fifty-dollar bill. "Please wait."

The driver tilted his herringbone Kangol forward and shut the engine off. "At your service, sir."

Job got out of the cab and walked along the shoreline of what the driver called the centerpiece of Orlando, Lake Eola. Lush greenery formed the backdrop of the body of water and, except for a couple riding a gondola, the lake was isolated; perfect for a serious talk.

He didn't care about the stain that would come if he sat on the grass with his feet in the water. He didn't look around to see who might be watching him as they tried to determine if he'd lost his mind. People couldn't offer him a solution. Job needed, wanted, to hear from the Lord.

You told me to prepare my heart, and I'd hear from you. My life is a seesaw. One thing will go right, then another will go wrong. I can't go on living like this. I NEED YOU.

I went with my own thoughts and ways. It hasn't worked. Now, Lord, I'm doing all I know. I want your help.

Protect Monica. Help her see that I truly love her. When I think about it, maybe she hasn't let me in because I haven't let you in. I'm trying to take that time now.

Job felt his shoulders shake. It wasn't the chill blowing off the lake. Tears began to fall. He brought his hands up to his face. He peered between his fingers. His vision was starry, like the reflection of the water. He strained to contain the message God was giving him.

I know that I shouldn't expect life to be easy, but please, help me understand how to place my cares in you. No matter what happens. No matter where I—we—reside, help me to live right even when . . . wrong occurs.

It seemed as though eternity went by when it had only been minutes. But a bag full of burdens was lifted. Job felt like he could go on. He would make it another day. *Thank you, God.*

He received the Teacher of the Year award that evening with an unusual humility, and a thankfulness that only the One he depended on could deserve.

He went through the remainder of the trip in a fog that only a return to Phoenix could lift.

Chapter 30

And I said unto my master, peradventure the woman will not follow me. Genesis 24:39

"Good morning," Monica said.

Nami was in Monica's office tidying files that needed attention. When she flung her head around, her seasonal hairstyle, shoulder-length micro braids, fanned the air. "Aren't you back a day early?"

Monica wasn't going to say. Not right away.

"Oh. My. God. I cannot believe it," Nami exclaimed.

"What?"

"You really did it, didn't cha?"

"What?"

Nami's eyes widened. "You taken leave of your senses, true?"

"I might be able to help you—if I knew specifically why you believe I've lost my senses."

"I know what you did." She shook her finger at Monica as though she were giving a warning. "I know what you did."

Monica rested her purse, adjusted the jacket of her burgundy two-piece, and sat on the edge of her desk. "Thrill me with your knowledge."

Nami had a "you can make fun of me if you want" look on her face. "You let that dark, fine man of yours fly off to the Land of Enchantment to enjoy that expense-free vacation . . . by himself. I tell ya. You should be horse-whipped! I'd do it myself, but I just got my nails done."

"What? You would've gone with him?"

"Yes, ma'am. If he were my man. Any disagreement we had could wait 'till after the trip was over! You need to take lessons from me on how to do; if I may say so." Nami's voice dipped and rose like she was singing ca-lypso.

Monica couldn't help but burst into laughter. "I told you that I had considered staying here."

"Yes, but I would have wagered a paycheck that you were at Universal Studios with a pair of 3-D glasses for Jurassic Park or some other crazy flick."

"Instead, I was here, huh?"

Nami displayed her judgmental furrow. "You made the decision, boss. Hope you can live wit' it."

"I assure you, I can. I'm glad I didn't go."

"So the trip ends tomorrow, and Mr. Wright comes back?"

"Yes."

There was a brief silence before Nami asked, "Then I'm perplexed. You had vacation time, and you took it. That's no secret. So, if you didn't accompany your husband on the trip, where've you been for the last five days?"

That sequence of events was vivid in Monica's heart.

She had every intention to hold Job as he prepared to leave for Florida. Just hold him close, close against her breast so that she could feel the tension of his body and whiff the remnants of his cologne. That way, her senses would've been able to retain his being until he returned from the trip.

The Satan in her kept her from doing what she desired.

But the God in her softened her hardened heart right at the moment Job closed the suite's entrance door. All of her emotions, all of her thoughts and all forms of her resistance, met at a central point and broke her into the deepest sob and strain she had ever known. Not just seconds, or even minutes—hours of crying then a period of rest, only to start crying all over again. She couldn't control it. She had reason to believe a spirit of sadness had possessed her.

When her melancholy died somewhere around noon that day, Monica wanted to demonstrate her stern exterior by and showing up to work the latter half of that day. She got dressed and everything. But stronger forces wouldn't let her make that journey.

There she sat, looking like a catalogue model between jobs. Sometime that afternoon, she fielded a call from the Fuquay & Terry firm, who, thinking they were calling the day before the trip, to wish her and Job Godspeed. She let them give their congratulations, but she didn't bother to correct their mistake.

She spent the early part of the second day automobile shopping. She thought that sampling Beemers, Benzes, and Jags would be satisfying, but when she considered the current state of her and Job's finances, that futile exercise made her feel foolish.

Fontella, the only person who knew Monica's true whereabouts, had taken the liberty of arranging a meeting for her with Pastor Harris, who graciously accomodated her.

"I'm not trying to leave him," Monica stressed to her spiritual leader. "I want correction. I need God in a real way."

"Truthfully," Pastor Harris said, "God hasn't gone anywhere. He's not lost."

Monica felt her heart being pricked. "I just don't know what to do. I think sometimes that my prayers aren't being heard."

That's when Pastor Harris told her, "Some directions don't come to you when you pray only. Some things only come when you fast and pray."

"Fasting?"

"Along with prayer. You would be amazed. That form of seeking God yields powerful results. His spirit sneaks up on you when you least expect it. Take some time while your husband is away to deny yourself."

For the next seventy-two hours, Monica's sustenance was four small V-8 juices, water, a package of Bisca Organic Water Crackers, the Bible, and prayer.

She ate and drank just enough to survive. Between her sparse meals, she devoted herself to prayer and reading the Bible.

Pastor Harris was right.

While her body was empty, her spirit took time to listen to His spirit. God made Himself known, and, through prayer, He answered her most intriguing questions.

She didn't feel like she came out of the fast perfect, but she did come away perfected. She came away ready to love her Job.

"So, what you got to say for yourself, boss? Where were you?" Nami asked.

Thank you, God, for your revelation. "A few days ago, I went into a hole because I was under attack. A few days later, I came out of the hole, fighting. That's all I can really tell you."

Chapter 31

But and if she departs, let her remain unmarried or be reconciled to her husband. I Corinthians 7:11a

Job returned from Florida that Sunday as a household name in the Paradise Valley School District. He had ten thousand dollars worth of blessings in his pocket, courtesy of the Award Selection Committee. Above it all, he had spent invaluable time with God.

He ran through the airport concourse, scooped up his luggage and went outside of the terminal so that Monica would be able to see him.

Minutes went by. He patted his pants and belt, but had forgotten that he'd left his cell phone uncharged. *Is she coming?*

He let out a sigh of relief when Monica pulled up to the curve. When she got out of the car, he grabbed her and swirled her around. "I missed you," he said.

"I missed you too." She breathed short, intermittent pants that left her with a polished, rosy appearance. "Guess all the activity was overwhelming."

"It's much more than you can imagine. I had a tremendous time in Florida—"

"Fun?"

"It was nice, but the award and the city's attractions are not what I'm talking about." He paused to keep his emotions at bay. "I got what I needed while I was there. From God."

"What happened, Job? You all right?"

"Oh, I'm fine. Couldn't be better. I want you to know that I'll never keep anything from you or lie to you again. Let's make a fresh start."

Monica's expression seemed pleasant, but was indefinable.

"Let's just say I got what I needed. I don't know any other way to put it, other than . . . I want our marriage to work," Job said.

"I've done a bunch of thinking," she told him, "and we've got a lot of catching up to do. This time, I'll listen more and criticize less."

"Me too, Monica."

The drive to their suite was emotional, stimulating. Neither of them gave a look that brought back the dreadful years of their marriage.

"We're going to get through this time," Monica said. "You've been right all along." She pulled out an envelope with the return address of their insurance company. "Let's get our house built. I'm ready to start living on Rong Street again."

"Me too." Job couldn't help but look over at her and see the glow that shined through her expressions. He didn't want to spoil the moment with questions, but he needed to know. "Honey, umm, what *did* you do while I was gone?"

"Seek answers, that's all." It was evident she did not want to elaborate. He didn't care, because at that moment, all that was dear to him was the hope for delightful times ahead.

"Me too." Job planted his attention on the highway.

They arrived at their suite and, after emptying luggage, sat at the dining room table, replayed the voicemail messages, and began rummaging through the thirty-some-odd offers for summer property, complimentary carpet cleaning, or lowering their house payment overnight.

There was a detailed message from Assistant School Superintendent Buddy McManus, requesting to see him on Monday morning in his office. "Your classes at the high school will be covered," was the last sentence.

"Sounds like Mr. McManus is planning to give you an extended vacation. Paradise Valley's really made this Disney Award thing a big deal. Well . . . I guess it is," she said.

"You oughta be proud of me." He pulled the award envelope out of this pocket and began to shake it in the air. "We got some much needed cash out of it."

Monica walked around and grabbed it from him, looking inside the envelope. She appeared to lose her balance, her eyes sparked with laughter. "Oh, my . . . I am proud. You had to ask?"

"It's good to hear you say it." Job stood up and approached her.

Monica shrugged, eyeing him with a blink in her eye. "I'm saying it, satisfied?"

Job felt his desire ignite, and he slid his arms around her waist. "You know the last lie that I need to correct?"

"What's that?"

"When I said I got what I needed in Florida?"

"Yes?"

"I got the spiritual part. This other part I need only you can provide."

She nuzzled her head against his abdomen. "Oh."

The next day, Job wore a suit and tie for his visit with Buddy McManus, figuring it would be fitting for his meeting with the always-animated head of personnel. He felt like high-stepping into the opulent surroundings. Once inside though, he became unpleasant.

The custom paintings and exotic fish seemed to have taken a battle stance, closing in on Job as the draftee who had left as war a hero and returned as an enemy.

Buddy sat behind his desk, twirling a monogrammed letter-opener with his fingers. He was crammed into his chair, unsmiling; his countenance, a contradiction to the personality Job had known at every other meeting.

"Mr. Wright," was his terse greeting.

Job wanted to be jovial, but he was too busy surveying the unknown. "You wanted to meet with me?" he asked.

"For the last few days, I've been hoping—dern near at the point of praying—that the information Ms. Rizzo had given me is wrong. It can't be right."

"Huh?"

"I've been saying to myself that maybe so much Phoenix sun's been beating down on the people here that they have a bad case of the sunstroke. But then, what I've been told didn't come from out of Phoenix."

Didn't come from out of Phoenix? Job's fear grew larger than reason, and he didn't know why. "Mr. McManus, what're you talking about?"

Buddy's mouth turned under. He had the look of keen mental insight, about to impart hidden knowledge. If his intention was to make Job's seat tighten in on him, it was working.

"I don't know what all I could be talking about. But there's one thing that seems to be evident. You had a heap bit of trouble back in the little town of Louisville. Am I right?"

Louisville. Trouble. A heap bit. Job thought words like those had been buried in the deepest recesses of his memory. Out of the reach of other's discovery.

"This is just . . . *man.*" Buddy tossed the letter opener in the air. Wood and metal landed against Plexiglas and wood. "I don't know what to call this."

"Listen, I can—"

"I'll call it a sheer disappointment, that's what I'll call it," Buddy interrupted. "When you first came here, I told you about our image. I know I did." He slammed his fist on the desk. "Never would I have dreamed in a thousand lifetimes that in one week the most celebrated teacher in America would deface our district image. Never."

Lord help. "Whatever it is that you think you know, I guarantee you, there's an explanation."

"For all our sakes, Mr. Wright, I hope you have a believable one. Believable enough for the school board."

"The board?"

"Yes. Anything, anything questionable has to be investigated by the school board. In the meantime, I have to follow policy and—suspend you."

"Aw, no. C'mon. Please. You're making a mistake."

"I wonder. Just how much of a mistake have I made?" He pulled out an 8½ x 11, mauve piece of paper. It had the Paradise Valley letterhead and was entitled FORM 1195. "I need you to fill this out for my office. I need a complete explanation as to the alleged falsification of questions relative to your criminal and civil discretions that a background check could divulge." Buddy gave the form to Job.

He refused to pick it up. "Please, Mr. McManus."

"Policy, Mr. Wright. I follow policy. Fortunately, this suspension isn't because of acts in the classroom. And, because of your recent notoriety, it's easy for me to justify suspending you with pay. Pending the outcome of the investigation, though, you may be dismissed. You can't know how sorry—no—extremely disappointed—I am."

Job picked up the form. "I cannot believe this is happening."

"If the truth doesn't incriminate you, Mr. Wright, then you have nothing to worry about. Nothing."

This is exactly what Monica told me would come to haunt me. Lord, you're gonna have to guide me on this one.

Job sat in Paradise Valley's parking lot under a canopy with his car off and the windows down.

"Well, it's too late for 'I told you so.' But I did," Monica said when he had gathered up enough nerve to call and break the news to her.

"It just ain't right, it ain't."

"You're dealing with people. The same ones that praise you one minute will kill you the next."

"But what they may find out about me, what they will find out, is nothing."

"Honey, I hate to be the one to tell you this, but I'm saying this in love. What they will find out is that you didn't tell the absolute truth on your employment application. You didn't know when or how, but you should've known they were eventually going to find out about Louisville."

"I know. You said it from the very beginning. What's puzzling me is—how?"

Monica told him, "It doesn't matter how they found out. Fact is, they didn't find out from you. But I'm not going to fret over it. We're in this together, no matter what."

She spoke with an assurance, which was far from the chastising style she had used in the past. "You mean, that's how you really feel?" he asked.

"I'm not backing out now, Job. We said we would take our marriage to a new level. With the Lord's help, that's what I intend to do."

"Okay, honey. I'm with you."

"We have to get past the troublesome points in our history. This go 'round, we'll get past it in truth, in Jesus' name. Then our future will come out right."

Job started his ignition and flipped the air conditioner to 'cool.' "In a few minutes, I'm going to write my explanation on this form and turn it in. I'll go home. Then I'm going to pray and continue to put my trust in God. Whatever He allows, although we may not see it, will be for the good."

Chapter 32

The last enemy that shall be destroyed is death. I Corinthians 15:26

The following morning, Delvin bypassed breakfast to meet Shiloh under determined circumstances.

"You've had very little sleep. I can tell," Shiloh observed. Inside the chapel area, a small space had been partitioned off, studded in concrete, as a designated office. He reached into the drawer of his desk and handed a couple of granola bars to Delvin. "I always keep several of these handy for those times when I don't want the prison food. I'm sure you can relate to that."

Delvin took one of the granola bars and opened the package. He said nothing. He didn't realize how famished he was.

Shiloh walked over to a compact fridge, the type parents send with their college freshman children, and pulled out a small carton of orange juice. "You'll scratch your throat without something to wash that down. Here."

Delvin took a couple of sips, and yanked the carton away from his lips. He couldn't recollect having had any orange juice without some Grey Goose or Armadale mixed in. He got used to the initial taste shock and gulped it down. After resting for a moment, he said, "I need you to do a favor for me."

Shiloh's eyes widened. "Me?"

"Yeah. And for your eyes only."

"But you're a trustee, Mr. Storm. I'm positive Warden would do you a favor—"

Storm waved his hand. "Not this." He pulled out the mishmash stack of papers he'd spent the better part of last evening writing. "You have stamps, envelopes?"

After a brief hesitance, Shiloh took the stack of papers. "May I?" he asked.

Delvin assumed he wanted to read the contents. "Yeah."

Minutes passed. Then, an hour. Shiloh politely put off a couple of inmates who wanted to speak with him and kept his attention on Delvin and the letters.

Shiloh read each one, then reread. Delvin kept silent, allowing the chaplain as much uninterrupted time as he needed to ingest the chronology he had documented in one evening.

"This is . . . humph," was Shiloh's response. "You don't need copies of these lying around."

"Do you see why I didn't want anyone else to see these? Why a head guard wouldn't allow this to pass mail inspection?"

"I do." Shiloh rubbed his bald head until it turned pink. "Why now, though? What're you hoping to accomplish?"

Delvin remembered the troubles he was sure he'd caused Job. They could only be a glint of what his former partner must've endured. "Maybe it's not too late."

"I'll mail them for you, Mr. Storm. It's probably best that I allow your letters to be on the inside of the envelopes, but mail them with my signature and my return address. But your work is what the recipient will get, I guarantee." He straightened the stack of letters. "Are you positive that these addresses are correct?"

Delvin told him, "One hundred percent."

Shiloh put the stack in a center drawer and locked it with a key from his vest pocket. "Then they will go out in today's afternoon mail. But I'm curious. What do you mean by, 'maybe it's not too late'?"

"You know . . . to set the record straight."

"Redemption."

"Yeah."

Throughout Saturday night, a monstrous mid-May storm swept the entire state of Kentucky—tossing brush and drowning greenery.

Ashland remained a mighty fortress, withstanding the thunder, wind, and rain. Although the building itself was left intact, the weather kept the inmates stirring for one reason or another. Including Delvin.

He retired before the routine call for lights out; usually half past ten. He awakened at midnight, shaved by feeling his way in the dark. Back to bed around 1:00 A.M. Awakened by earthquake-like thunder. Must've been around 3:00 A.M. Thinking that it was better to give in rather than fight the insomnia, he sat up, and read the Bible by pen-light.

There was no sensible progression to the passages Delvin chose to read. He wasn't trying to find one. The hours until daylight were waning. He didn't want to be discovered by fellow inmates with his head still buried in scriptures around the time bacon and eggs were being served.

For him, it wasn't to critique the book's validity. Or to see if the King's English had a flaw. He was reading for a single motive: Inspiration.

Four A.M. He'd forgotten there was a storm, and he

briefly disregarded the fact he was imprisoned. He'd run across a story that held his interest.

Delvin read and reread until he almost had it committed to memory: A particular man, who couldn't make children, had a large amount of the financial power in Egypt. The same man had a problem understanding God's Word.

He met some guy named Philip, who showed him how to get an understanding of the Word. He eventually asked if the man believed in Jesus. The man said he did. The Philip guy told the man, "That's all there is to it." Just believe that a guy called the Christ died on the behalf of others who do wrong but willing to do right. *Make a change. Believe.*

For Delvin, the comforting words lifted off the pages of the cheaply produced Bible, clung to him, seeped through his skin, and plowed through the hardened ground of his heart.

Six A.M. Delvin had ruined those few pages of Acts with the uncontrollable water from his eyes. The black ink on the flimsy pages had turned blue, then pink.

Delvin's heart was washed white. It was evident. He had taken the Lord, the Christ, as his Savior.

The Catholic mass that morning had a late start; it began at 9:20. Delvin observed the men filing into the chapel area from his cell. For the next hour, he listened for music, a loud cry, anything. Not a thing. The men filed out.

The Protestant service followed at 11:00 A.M. Delvin joined the other inmates for that service. In fact, he *beat* them there.

He sat on the first row of chairs; it was three chairs wide. He didn't care. He had been told, and he later learned, that spirituality wasn't about the aesthetics of the building. The men were unfamiliar to him. No Saks, of course. No Stinson, no Murphy. Yet, at the same time, he could see the familiarity in each of their eyes. A kindred desire. A sincere yearning to be better men. A wonderful feeling to have.

Shiloh entered from the back, making his way down the short, narrow aisle to the rostrum. Delvin saw Shiloh glance his way, but he neglected to make his recognition obvious.

"God is good. The way that I know He's good is that I look around and see that each of you in attendance have made it through another week, unharmed, in good health."

Delvin heard murmurs. He didn't turn to see the physical activity behind him.

"I want to talk to you about the pain and suffering Jesus Christ endured on your behalf. Actually, it was known that He would have to endure torment before He was born. Years before He was born." Shiloh asked the inmates, those who had their Bibles, to turn to Isaiah, the fifty-third chapter. He paced the room, shaking hands with the inmates as he delivered his ten-minute sermon.

Delvin listened to Shiloh's every word with intensity. He even took out a ballpoint pen and made notes in the margins of his Bible.

Shiloh had worked the entire room, making his way back to the front. "For our music today, I found this tape by an African-American brother named . . ." Shiloh paused and glanced at the face of the audio cassette, ". . . Ronald Winans."

Delvin chuckled at the way Shiloh twanged out the "African-American brother."

Shiloh continued. "It conveys the message with such lyric, such a clarity; I would have had to practice preaching for years to compete. Listen," he instructed.

Shiloh slipped the cassette into the player. Although the tape was scratchy, Delvin agreed; the song said it all:

> Come on let us reason together
> I already know what you've done.

"So, if any of you are ready to come home," Shiloh chimed in as the song faded, "home is ready for you. Won't you accept Him?" He stretched his arm up and out.

Delvin turned and looked behind him. Never had he witnessed a gang of men, regarded on the outside as financial wizards gone bad, making such sensitive cries for someone he had learned was born two millennia ago. He was now in that gang of men. He stood, approached Shiloh, and reached out his hand.

Shiloh grasped his hand and embraced him. He whispered in Delvin's ear, "Your letters were your repentance. Welcome."

Delvin felt a season-changing comfort, unlike anything he'd experienced before. It choked him up, made him overflow—without any thought of who might be observing. *It doesn't matter.* "Thank you, *Reverend*," he replied. "I accept Him as my Savior."

"I knew this day would come," Shiloh said with an air of confidence. "I'll come by to see you late, late this evening to talk. Only if you want."

"Please."

After dinner, Warden had sent word through the cell block supervisor for the evening shift that he had some papers that he wanted Delvin to file. "The usual stuff," were his exact words, according to the guard.

"Yeah, okay," Delvin replied. He was busy with an important task. At least it was important to him. Pulling, ripping, exposing his cell wall shred by shred. Tearing down mischievous representations of his past. He wanted to be rid of his personal shrine to Joseph Bertram Wright's destruction before nightfall.

The guard escorted him to the showers, where he finally washed Saturday, and now most of Sunday, away. With fresh clothes and a hygienic feeling, he made his way to the administrative wing of the prison.

Warden greeted him in what Delvin felt was a reserved form of cordiality. He paid it no mind. It was likely that Warden still had doubts about his innocence; Stinson's killer was yet unidentified.

But he still seemed to possess enough confidence to leave his office in Delvin's hands; a guard posted, of course.

"You know what I need, Storm. This stack of papers should have you in a sweat over the next couple hours, so take your time. No hurry."

"I'll get right on it." Delvin wasted no time sorting through the various documents. Again, it was old stuff, left unfiled from years of neglect.

An hour later, he was inserting the last document and slamming the file door shut.

He reached into his back pocket, the one normally reserved for a wallet. For an inmate, the least worn part of his slacks. What purpose would a wallet serve?

Delvin reached in; he hadn't forgotten. His trusted Gideon Bible, the pages of Acts chapter eight now dried and discernible.

He went behind Warden's desk and slumped into the battered leather executive chair. So many scriptures to read. He was a new Christian, and there was too much knowledge to gain. Much too much for one evening. He was happy to be able to start somewhere.

Shiloh had told him about how the Old Testament, the first part of the Bible, gave hints that Jesus was coming. "Where was that passage?" he asked out loud. The half-asleep guard grunted and asked Delvin if he was talking to him.

Delvin told him, "No."

Shiloh said Isaiah. Yeah. He thumbed through the pages, found the fifty-third chapter. After the first few verses, his eyelids began to weigh on him. He shook himself to restart his body.

He read: . . . *wounded for our transgressions, he was bruised for our iniquities, the chastisement of our peace was upon Him; and with . . . his stripes . . . we are—*

Sleep.

It was a bad dream. No, it wasn't.

Delvin tried to pinch himself into complete consciousness, but he was constrained. What he felt was reality.

He could feel his eyes popping, his wind blocked. It wasn't a rolling desk chair under him anymore. It was a sturdy, prison issue, metal one.

One, two . . . three men, all of them huge or at least, from his vantage point, they had excessive girths. They had him by surprise.

He couldn't make out anything they said, with the exception of one comment about *cut off our loot*, or something to that effect.

Oh Lord. Delvin knew he was seconds, at the most, a couple of minutes—away from death. The truth came to light at the eleventh hour. What he didn't know was how painful his termination was going to be.

They had rendered him helpless, fixed his arms and legs like a quadriplegic.

Delvin shook his head, trying to ward off punches

while at the same time, get a view of the three men who had caught him by surprise.

The rag they used to gag his mouth tasted of Dial soap, the same kind an old school teacher had given him in the fifth grade for cussing at another student. Tasted like Dial. Smelled like Exxon.

They wanted to be cruel, and had planned it well. They kept his eyes uncovered so he could see his own paced, animated torture.

Help! Delvin tried to scream, but it was shrill, muffled. Where was the guard? Paid off, lurking in a remote corner, eyes in another direction. Everybody has a price. How well Delvin knew.

One leg broke away from their grips, punted one of his attacker's private parts. "Ohh! Got me!" the guy shouted. His face contorted in pain.

That made them more aggravated. One of them landed his hammer fist across Delvin's jaw. One cracked mandible.

What happened next had him counting down to a finish line. One of the men, tall, several days of gray stubble against his ashy brown skin, and a build more stocky and intense than Stinson's, jammed a homemade shank into his chest cavity. Below the rib cage. Left-hand side. The red stuff spewed in every direction. Oozing on Delvin. Splattering on the other three.

The trio left Warden's office cracking jokes, cussing. Not dead yet, but fading.

Seconds later, a shadowy figure passed by. A man with a drooped body. Recognizable. Barely.

It was Deliverer, his eyes lit like halogen.

Fine, Deliverer. This is how you do it. But I've made my peace with the Lord. I haven't known Him long. But I've taken the opportunity to know Him. He knows me.

It was finished.

Chapter 33

Therefore, my beloved brethren, be ye steadfast, unmovable, always abounding in the work of the Lord, forasmuch as ye know that your labor is not in vain in the Lord. I Corinthians 15:58

Job experienced what he believed to be the most punishing two and a half weeks of his entire life. He was careful to obey the school board policy which forbade him from corresponding with school colleagues or students or their parents, and prohibited him from being present on Mountain River's campus. Paradise School District had been hush-mouthed about their assessment or any action they were considering. He hadn't heard a word from Bianca, which he thought was peculiar. But then, when he thought about it, resisting contact with her was a blessing in disguise.

But he needed to do *something*.

Monica had shown her spiritual and emotional support. On her suggestion, he consulted Wendy Axford, their attorney and friend from Louisville, who advised him on case law and precedent. When Wendy broke down her legal-speak to laymen's terms, Job viewed realism face-to-face, and considered the fact he may not have a job to go back to once the district published their decision.

There was just too much going in the right direction to have a set-back based on long term unemployment.

But he was realistic. The majority of their ten thousand dollar award helped them play catch up and take care of responsibilities not covered by homeowner's insurance; but those funds were waning. And the district's decision to keep him on paid leave proved beneficial during his forced hiatus, but keeping that job was, at best, a fifty-fifty chance.

On that Thursday morning, November 1, he peeked at the clock and darted out of bed with a rush. He was sure he had told Monica not to let him oversleep because what lay ahead was a busy day. He and Larry had made last evening their time, but it wasn't bogged down with their usual physical activities—bowling, pool, or sometimes weight training. Their time was consumed feasting on ribeyes at Ruth Chris's and talking. He didn't understand his exhaustion, but in the future he would reconsider having a boy's night out with Larry within hours before he would have a loaded schedule.

The last comment Job remembered came from Larry, who had asked how he was holding out with a new-found destiny in the Lord, particularly with his most recent school district problems.

Larry continued to be a source of encouragement. "Demons have a way of making your issues compound, especially when you claim an undying faith in God. Your problems stack up so they seem unbearable. It means the victory line is staring you in the face. Hold on, bro'."

After that, whatever was said and how Job made it home safe remained a mystery.

Job trounced over to the bathroom door and found it locked. To his astonishment, Monica had not yet gone to work. And his banging didn't make her move any swifter.

"I'll be out in a bit," she scolded. After that, either time did a virtual frost over or her showering, eyebrow tweezing, and make-up application really was exorbitant.

Job was thankful to whoever invented the shower massage on that day. It proved a brisk revival for his mind and body.

When he left the bedroom for the kitchen and found Monica still in the suite grappling a glass of water, he knew something was irregular, but she didn't elaborate and he didn't immediately question.

Job poured a glass of orange juice and took a seat beside her. "I've decided to make the district aware of Ms. Rizzo's sexual advances," he declared.

Monica took a sip of water and met Job eye-for-eye, with an understanding expression on her face. "You think it will help your situation?"

"I don't know and don't care. I only have one reason for wanting to make it known."

"That is . . ."

Job said, "If the record is going to be revealed about me, then the whole record needs to be revealed. The only discomfort I endured as a teacher involved her, whether she agrees or not."

"You don't see it as an act of desperation on your part?"

"With nothing hidden and everything out in the open, I can move on in a clear conscience."

She nodded. "If that's what you think you should do, then do it."

All right baby. Your support makes me want to put a rush on it.

"I'll have a conversation with McManus today." He snapped his fingers. "I better change that. I'll send him a detailed e-mail. He'll get the message, and that's proof I sent it."

"You think Mr. McManus will act upon your accusation?" she asked.

"Shoot naw. But I'll know I did my part."

"And seeing him in person wouldn't be better?"

"With all I need to do today, I can't be pulled in two totally different directions. It's been a long time coming so I'm going to see how our home is coming along."

He was correct. Between extensive periods of rain, Apex Construction had come from Mesa to remove the heap of charred remains and commence with what would soon become the new 2333 Rong Street. According to contract, topsoil had been graded, foundation had been poured, and the frame was pieced together. Job planned a visit to the construction site as sub-contractors ran plumbing and wiring through the studs.

Monica sipped the last drops of water from her glass. "Some people might see checking on home construction and defending personal reputation as equally important."

Her train of thought was unmistakable, but his relentlessness overshadowed her line of thinking. "I only have so much time today. I'm giving each issue the amount of attention they deserve."

When they talked about why Monica was in no rush to get to work, she made an inaudible but evidently sarcastic statement, dropped her jaw, and twisted her neck.

Job didn't pursue the matter any further. Anyway, he didn't feel he had a right. He, after all, was the one suspended from a job. He did what he believed was the clever thing. He bowed out and left.

It was effortless to picture each room of their home as Job stepped along the sub-flooring, examining the workmanship while he joked with the construction workers.

As far as he could tell, he and Monica would be moving in by Christmas if Apex Company kept its pace.

"I hope the weather holds up for a week without a torrential downpour," the supervising contractor said.

"Really?" asked Job.

"Aw, man, yeah," he said. "This isn't like nailing planks or even laying brick for the exterior. When we spread this adobe, we need time when the stuff can dry."

Lord, please. I'm thankful for the suite. But I'm ready to move on. And move on was what Job decided to do. He had spent more time there than he'd planned. He needed to hurry to an appointment with Donald and Vincent.

It was a working lunch date at, of all the unconventional places to meet millionaires, McDonald's. Job arrived before them, so he went ahead and ordered a quarter-pounder meal. Job had to do a double-take when the two partners arrived. They looked more like a hip-hop musical duo than high-stakes real estate dealmakers. Donald was bespoke in ENYCE® and Vincent in Rocawear®. Their outfits bursted with tint and twinkle.

Job stood up and bowed to them as a joke. "You'll need to explain yourselves," he said, referring to their dress.

"There's nothing to explain," Vincent told him. "It's what we like to wear. Surely you don't think a brother has to always wear a stuffy gray suit, do you?"

"Your point's well taken," Job said.

After they ordered their lunch, they proceeded with the business at hand.

It was Job's responsibility to create a profit and loss projection based on a three-year period and usable square footage of the commercial property that the Fuquay & Terry firm managed.

"This one's in the hopper. If these numbers are, in fact,

lining up, and they seem to be according to my calculations, then we can take this to the client. They'll be pleased. Great work, Joseph," Donald said.

As they flipped through the proposal, Job wondered if there were any new commercial deals in need of consultation. He had caught wind of a Sedona mall project that their firm had won the bid on. "Hey, when do you plan on doing this presentation?" Job asked.

Vincent and Donald exchanged glances, as if waiting for the other to speak.

After Vincent jerked his eyes and raised a cheekbone, Donald came forth as the one tapped out to act on their behalf. "Hey, man, you know? It's not our style to beat around the bush. It's about this current client."

Job danced his eyes from Vincent to Donald to get some kind of take on where they were going. "Oh?"

"Yeah, well," Donald said, "your work with us on this project is pretty much completed."

Job took a moment. "Why?"

"Well . . . it's not *us*, understand, but our client."

Job could not believe what he was hearing. "Yes?"

"The guy heard about your trouble, especially the school district and all. Doesn't want you involved in this undertaking. Personally, I don't see how you're able to stand upright. I couldn't bear the pressure."

"Why? How did someone find out about that?" Job felt his skin gripping. He dropped his arm for a moment so the blood could circulate before he resumed the inquiry. "I'm doing the work, right?"

"Oh, yeah, it's not that. But hey, you know how word gets around. And the client is boss," Vincent chimed in. "It's not your work. The guy's kinda paranoid. He thinks that if a school district will want to fire you, they'll get crazy and not grant any building contracts to anyone you're involved with."

Job checked his voice and frustration level to keep from drawing attention. "So what do you all say you want me to do? And who is this client?"

"The client was generous; and, wants to remain anonymous with you. But the good news is that he wants you to get paid according to agreement. He just doesn't want you physically on the scene, especially making presentations," Donald said.

"And you're saying?"

Vincent replied, "Hey, man, it is a trip. But we've got to honor his request. You understand how it is when you work on commission. The client is king."

"Yeah, I see your point. What about other jobs?"

Donald assured Job that they would be using him in the future, that that set-back wouldn't affect their relationship in the least.

"I'm praying that this isn't the end. Aside from enjoying what I do, I could use the work—and the money," Job pleaded.

"You'll hear from us, no problem," Vincent said.

Job held no confidence in their promise, especially when he caught the two of them bouncing sly looks at each other.

When Job had a moment to breathe and assess the day to that point, he found himself sitting on a couch in the foyer of Nine Iron. Whatever else needed to be done would have to wait. He had reached his finish line.

"You know, when you don't know what to do," he told Monica when she made it home, "all that's left is to pray." He informed her in a brief synopsis about all he had witnessed. His lack of rest had caught up and overtaken him. He made an early evening of it.

Job awakened, believing he would be able to match the efficiency of the previous day. The sleep left him refreshed, unlike the morning before. He thought about spending the day at Chapel in the Desert. The mission work there was a neverending cycle and the assistance of men during the daytime was always welcome.

Job made up in his mind that whatever his activity was, it wouldn't involve stress—like, worrying about money.

He saw that Monica was already up and dressed when he made way into the kitchen for his daily shot of orange juice.

She was seated before a half-eaten turkey, bacon, and mayo on wheat as the mini-television yelled the day's temperatures according to the Weather Channel. Her ambivalence to the noise was understandable, since she was engrossed in the front page of the *Arizona Republic*.

Job took his juice and decided to stand near her at the counter top. "You don't have to hang so tightly to the sports section. Who's playing who this Sunday?" He was referring to the NFL.

It was apparent that Monica didn't hear or comprehend a word he said. By the flush color of her skin, she was astonished by his presence.

She separated the front page from the rest of the paper and handed it to Job. "Read this," she demanded.

With a cautious eye, he removed one boldly printed heading and the subsequent story from the rest of the newsprint on the page. That's when his anger took height:

AWARD-WINNING TEACHER DISMISSED
FROM PARADISE

"What a poor way to treat an employee. I'm sorry you had to find out about your job this way, honey," Monica told him. The empathy in her voice was buried by the seemingly ever-present emotional turmoil. Job felt it.

"They advertised it. Like . . . you're nothing," Monica said in a low tone.

Job heard her but wasn't going to waste time responding. He gulped the OJ in a swallow. He tossed the cup into the sink and cringed for a moment. *Oh, Lord. Oh. It's plastic.*

He felt Monica's eyes on him as he darted toward the bathroom.

"What do you have in mind, Job?" she asked.

"The last thing anybody should do is make a black man mad."

"Well, you need to hold on," she said, breaking the energy of the moment. She blew a kiss as she pranced by him.

He let out a boisterous laugh, praying she wouldn't take as long in the bathroom today as she had the previous morning.

Job was angry but determined not to commit a sin. But he didn't take the time to follow protocol when he arrived at the district administration building. If anyone asked him to—and one, maybe two people did—they were wasting their wind. Paradise District could call Job whatever they wanted that morning, but he was going to be heard.

Job failed to check whether he took the door of Buddy's office off the hinges. *I'm sorry. But that door was in the way.*

"Mr. Wright!" Buddy was enjoying the benefits of the Phoenix horizon when Job stopped in the threshold. "Now, this is a surprise."

"Man, don't play me. I didn't come to listen to your

okey-doke chatter. An e-mail, a phone call, a voicemail. I didn't get nothing! You need to explain yourself!"

Buddy appeared as though he could've died instantly. He cast his eye down onto the desk and began to scramble through a set of documents. "Why, Mr. Wright, I swear to you—"

"What?"

"You received—"

"What?"

"Lemme get a word in. Please . . ."

Job moved in closer and slammed the door. "Man, you better make up a good lie, 'cause I'm not leaving *this* office without an explanation I can live with."

Buddy brushed his hair and began to move quicker as he continued to look for whatever it was he was searching for. "You know I received your e-mail yesterday. Matter of fact, Ms. Rizzo—"

"You didn't bother to respond to that either."

"Well, I'm pretty sure I did—"

"Stop lying, Mr. McManus. I know you didn't. I've checked, more than once." Job was making the room taut on purpose. He'd let one man run him over in the past, but today would not be Buddy McManus's day."

Job could discern that, as the wall clock ticked off the seconds, Buddy was escalating in fear. The item he was looking for could not be found.

Job closed in until he stood against the desk. He was close enough that, if he desired, he could feel Buddy's panting.

"I, umm . . ."

"What's your problem?" Job asked.

"You talk like you didn't get our letter." Buddy's hands began to tremble and his details sounded nervous and chatty.

"Letter?"

"Why yes. A letter specifying the board's decision to terminate your employment."

"When was I supposed to get a letter, Mr. McManus?" Job wore a tight athletic top that day on purpose. When he drew his arms toward his chest, his biceps and triceps flexed, giving a menacing look.

It was effective enough to make Buddy's eyes bulge. "On yesterday. By certified mail."

When Job gave thought to the explanation, it torched him to the core. "I blame you, man. And I wonder if you were responsible for some consultant work that I was denied."

Buddy's face wrinkled up, which led Job to believe he might've been mistaken about Buddy's involvement in the real estate work.

"Please," Buddy said, "It wasn't my decision."

"I'm talking about you had to be the one who planned to have a news feature published about me right on the same day that I find out . . . by a letter. That's the mark of a big, fat coward."

"I didn't—"

"Stop lying. Every person in this district knows you give strict instructions about news interviews. You only want to be the one who gives them; for the district's image."

Job was sure that any moment, Buddy would fly off into tears. His face was flush like death and he had ceased his endless search for the missing item.

"Mr. Wright," he croaked, "we are truly grateful for the service you rendered. But my hands are tied and the decision's been made."

"The way this district handled this was sorry. I'd feel better if I punched you out. The Christian in me keeps me from doing it, though."

"I would be remiss if I didn't tell you that even though

we've terminated you, you're free to apply with another district."

Job shook his head. "That's the stupidest thing I've ever heard. He walked to the door, the exact opposite of what Buddy and his secretary, no doubt, thought he would do.

He closed the door with the graciousness of a happy man.

With that ordeal behind him, the day had to be downhill from there.

Or, so he thought.

On the way out of the front entrance of the district's building, he met a woman hiding behind large, dark sunglasses. She was quickly striding to the door in a gait as strong as a man's. He took a closer look, and her face met his.

"It wasn't enough, was it?" Bianca asked in an angry, yet deceptively soft, tone.

"To do what?"

"What's this you're trying to pull? This revenge tactic isn't going to work. I'll be able to keep my job."

Job was confused. "Revenge tactic?"

Bianca tensed her lips and backed up a few inches as though she'd misspoken. "We shouldn't be having this conversation anyway."

"Why not? I've nothing to hide."

"Like I do," she interjected.

"My situation is over, Ms. Rizzo. I'm not an employee of these schools, so I'm not governed by their rules. Not now."

"That's unfortunate, really, Mr. Wright. Maybe if you'd been a little more cooperative, we wouldn't have had to take this path."

"Humph. Maybe so. But I'll credit the Lord for keeping me from getting into that trap too deep. You have a great day, Ms. Rizzo."

While he was still in the parking lot, he phoned Monica and told her that that chapter of his life was over. "Time to start working on another permanent job," he said.

"And yours is on the way for you," Monica told him. No doubt, she had fed from His blessed assurance tree.

"Actually, I'm not too worried." He jabbed his fist into the upholstery. "But I loved that job."

He returned home after a day of emotional turmoil and closed the door to all that was behind him. And sure enough, there it was.

Paradise Valley School District's letter, which had taken two full days to reach him since it made a stop at Rong Street before being forwarded on to Nine Iron.

The letter, which was complete with a royal blue U.S.P.S. acknowledgement of receipt sticker, rested on the carpet just below the mail slot in the door.

He sneered at it and picked it up, refusing to even break its seal.

Chapter 34

For the weapons of our warfare are not carnal, but mighty through God to the pulling down of strong holds. II Corinthians 10:4

Monica couldn't take another bite out of her breakfast sandwich. She was positive that Job didn't notice her stuffing the leftovers into the garbage and covering it with a sheet of Bounty. She didn't want Job to see it, and think that his getting fired had given her indigestion; that wouldn't have been true.

She could identify with Job's neglect of her, but more than an uneaten sandwich had slipped under his senses.

Her extended stays in the bathroom each morning were for a far greater reason than a physical reaction to external issues. To be certain, though, she made a stop at Walgreen's for a Clearblue Easy, which confirmed her suspicion.

She continued to keep Job at bay during lunch when he called to check on her. Monica grunted loud enough to resound in the receiver.

"What's wrong with you?" Job asked.

"Still have an awful case of indigestion. Got to call Dr. Najib to find out what I'm allowed to take. I'm all right."

"Girl, all that burping and stuff sounds crazy over this cellular."

There was only so much holding off she could do.

As she conducted the scheduled safety inspections, she walked the halls of the administrative wing and caressed her midsection; the painful part, she was confident, was now blossoming.

In addition to its physical benefits, walking allowed her to release tension. She was still broiling over the Paradise Schools uncouth exploit that made Job's dismissal public.

She kept Job's ill-gotten notoriety in the forefront of her mind, staying prepared for any idle comment she may hear. She didn't question if the news had reached her office. Her wonderment was over who would have the bravery to mention it to her. Nine Iron's employees and patrons were avid periodical readers during cocktail hour, lounging, or a break between golf rounds.

The only time when there appeared to be some insolence came from Cory, which was out of character.

She was in the lobby with reps from E-Golf Corporation discussing a discrepancy in reservation dates for a workshop. Cory meandered toward the group and tapped Monica on the shoulder.

"I guess we're going to have to link you with an image consultant, huh?"

There was no mistake that comment was a stab at her, whether his intentions were good-natured or not.

Monica responded with a proud, cold look.

The one person she could always depend on was Nami, who hit her straight when it came to the buzz around work. Monica soon realized that day was no different.

"And, oh, my. They had the mitigated gall to print the story on the front page," Nami exclaimed.

"Please don't remind me. I'm trying to see the benefit of making it public. It was somebody's morbid way of humiliating my husband."

"Well, boss, I have nothing to report. No one has seen the story, they're not dimwitted enough to relate it to you, or they are talking outside of our presence. But I haven't heard a word."

"I don't know what to think, if no gossip has passed by your ears," Monica joked. Anyway, I'll consider it a good thing. Maybe it will blow over."

"It made you mad didn't it?"

"You know it did."

Nami lowered her voice to a whisper. "Mad enough to want to kick somebody's . . ."

"Girl, what has gotten into you?" She wasn't surprised at Nami's comment.

"I'm sorry. But I would've set my Christianity on the shelf just long enough to whip me some tail. This is one of those times when you have to remove your earrings." Nami ran across the middle of the office and demonstrated how she could remove her stilettos without breaking stride. She held her shoes and declared, "Hey. It's how I do."

Monica cracked up. "I wonder sometimes why I hired you."

"Because I'm good at dis job."

There was no argument there.

Nami headed for the door but stopped to pick up a file that was propped against the water cooler. "I'll bring you a coffee in about ten minutes when I have the new contracts printed off."

"Uh, I don't think I better have any today, thank you.

But can you get catering to cut up a pomegranate? For some reason, I have a taste for one."

"No caffeine, eh? Fruit?" Nami turned toward her and narrowed her eyes. Monica could feel her examining her soul. "We'll expect a girl . . . hope you've started taking some pre-natal vitamins," she said.

That's the strangest woman. "How? Who? That's . . . how do you pick up on that—"

"Call it a sixth sense. Have you told the hubby?"

Monica was stunned. "No."

"Maybe you should."

"No, please. Don't act like you know anything when you get around him, Nami. I'm begging."

"I won't. I'll give you ample time to tell the news. Don't keep it a secret. Hubby has a right to know."

"I want to be sure first."

Nami smacked her lips. "Fair enough. But I won't hold out too long."

Just to keep Nami from following through on her threat, Monica called Dr. Najib's triage nurse to give a brief report of her overall state, her temperature, and the results of the home pregnancy test. The nurse would, in turn, set an appointment date.

That evening, Job suggested a light dinner and a play at the Helen Mason Performing Arts Center.

Monica wasn't feeling up to going out that evening. Her stomach churned with anxiety. And her womb was churning with a fetus.

She couldn't make up her mind whether to tell Job the wonderful news that evening, or to wait. She offered the alternative of home-cooked blackened chicken salad, with *Survivor* for entertainment.

"Tomorrow is the weekend." *Tomorrow is the day that*

I'll give you this glorious news. "Can I have a rain check until then?"

He shrugged his shoulders and frowned. "Sure, honey," he said. There was no excitement in his voice.

Monica thought that he would be fine. He would be elated with what she had to tell him.

Chapter 35

Also the Lord gave Job twice as much as he had before. Job 42:10b

Their plans changed overnight. At least Monica's did. Job was in the middle of the master bedroom floor, watching *This Old House,* and pretending to do aerobic exercises. He knew that Monica was watching him, but she never made a comment.

When the phone rung, she answered it, and carried on a five minute conversation. By the time she finished, Job had completed ten or eleven knee bends, moved over to the edge of the bed, and was sprawled across the pillows, out of breath.

"That was Cory calling," Monica told him. "I've got to go in and correct a few problems that've come up in the reservations department."

Job jumped off the bed, stepped back, and put all his weight on one stiff leg. "You've forgotten today is *Saturday?*"

"I'm not on an hourly wage, honey. I'm salaried. And clients do play golf on Saturday. Whether we like it or not, I'm on call."

"You can't call Nami to take care of whatever it is you gotta do?"

She flipped open her cellular and held it out for Job to take. "You think you're brave enough to tell Nami that she needs to show up for work today?"

The apple of Job's throat rose and fell with an audible thump. "Okay," he whispered, "I think you need to go do your job."

Cory instructed Monica to meet him at his office before she did anything.

When she arrived, he invited her to have a seat so they could talk. He took a seat near her, but away from his desk.

"This is informal," he said. "I started to wait until Monday to tell you this, but I couldn't wait. The excitement of it all, I guess."

Monica listened as Cory rambled on in such a robust style, but she couldn't make out what he was referring to. "Excitement?" she asked.

Cory grin diluted to a pleasant smile. "I'm sorry about yesterday, about my comments. I can get carried away at times."

Monica didn't think anything else of it. Cory was decent, in her eyes, but she knew that comfort with him should be carried only so far. "It's all right."

His complexion gave him a hung-dog appearance. "Well, regardless, I felt bad. I shouldn't have said that to you, especially in the presence of clients."

"Cory . . ." *Let's move on, boss.*

"Anyway, I'd like to make it up to you. I had an idea. More than an idea. I took the liberty to act on it and bare the consequences if anything went wrong."

Monica knew that with Cory, she'd have to wait until he gave all the details of his actions. He was an astute businessman and the biggest prankster she'd ever met. She leaned toward him, ready to hear the rest of the story.

He shifted his weight and crossed his legs, exposing his cashmere socks and Kenneth Cole loafers. "You know I have a few connections out here."

"Umm hmm." She'd seen that for herself.

He leaned back into his chair with an "impart-the-knowledge pose." "After bumping into you yesterday, well, after reading yesterday's news, I thought that you could use a boost."

"What kind of boost?"

"The boost is actually for that wonderful husband of yours."

"Oh, Lord. What have you concocted?" she asked. "I think I should be afraid. Very afraid."

"It's not bad, really. I talked to an acquaintance of mine in the educational field."

"Hmm."

"He's a Nine Iron member who frequents when he or that fancy wife can." He laughed.

"A teacher?"

"Let me tell this," he chimed in, "but since you asked, no. He's higher up than that. I said he's a member *of this particular club*."

She knew what that meant. Cory's White, Anglo-Saxon, Protestant persona was seeping out of his mouth. Like a public school teacher can't afford a membership.

"Anyway, the guy's a friend of a friend. I scratch your back, you scratch mine type a thing. You know how the white boys do it."

"Umm hmm," she mumbled. Working at Nine Iron had taught her all too well.

"Don't be like that," Cory said. "I'm not expecting anything in return. Like I said. I felt bad."

"Go on."

Cory had a pitiful look of appeal. "I thought, you know, Mr. Wright needs to be hooked up with someone that cares less about whatever his situation is."

"He did love to teach. He hasn't said a lot about it, but I'm sure he misses his students."

"Then if he loves it, he needs to teach. So if he had someone who would look at his teaching record as a criterion, then he stands a chance at getting back into the classroom. Am I making any sense?"

Monica sat dumbfounded by what Cory had done on Job's behalf. "Probably, for the first time in your life, you're making good sense."

Cory reached over to his desk and picked up a small stack of papers that had a handwritten note attached. "Take these. The gentleman is a higher-up in the Deer Valley School District. This is the application. This is if he's interested. The door's open."

"I'm sure he'll be."

"Well, hey. There you go. Now let me warn you. They're already privy to some of the stuff that news article divulged. They'll check things out for procedure's sake. But that inroad should be okay."

Monica took the package.

"I know, I know. You're speechless." He grabbed a cigar that was labeled Don Juan or something, and a cutter. "But seriously. You're an excellent VP. I thought that as efficient as you are, you couldn't have made a terrible choice in husbands."

"Thanks, Cory. Really"

"Don't mention it. What I've known about the two of you and what that news article said, well, it just didn't match up. What da he—, heck. I should do my part."

"I'd never figured . . ."

"What? That a white-bred like me had a heart?" He waved. "C'mon! You should know me better than that."

"Thanks isn't sufficient."

"Yes it is." He repositioned his legs. "You have the hard part yet to do anyway. Convincing him to fight for a job might be work. But I'd think that they'd love to have a celebrity teaching in their district. Gotta get your husband to Deer Valley with the application."

"Deer Valley, huh?"

"Not far from your subdivision. West of Paradise Schools," he said.

If only Cory could see her inner smile. She then remembered other matters needing her attention. "I've got to get to my office."

"No, you don't. That was my scheme to get you here."

Her jaw dropped. "You're a rascal."

"If I told you that I needed to talk to you, you would've said it could wait until Monday."

She couldn't argue with that rationale. Cory took a phone call from someone who, she was certain, was inviting him for a few hands of poker. She thought, *Joseph Bertram Wright. Even the devil can bring you a blessing! Now that's two things I've got to tell you.*

Chapter 36

Observe and hear all these words which I command thee, that it may go well with thee, and with thy children after thee for ever, when thou doest that which is good and right in the sight of the Lord thy God. Deuteronomy 12:28

Job couldn't help but feel apprehension while he waited for his interview with Deer Valley School district to commence. He had to set his completed application on the floor to keep from wrinkling it up and making it appear worn. At least the ambience of their headquarters didn't give him as much of a sense of inferiority.

Monica told him that he would be meeting a Dr. Knight, the director of employment.

Through a bit of research, Job learned that this set of schools was not as large as Paradise, which could turn out to be a great asset. They may be more personable.

"Dr. Knight will see you now," the receptionist told Job.

He entered into a meager, yet well-organized office. It was far from the over indulgence of Buddy McManus, but was well suited for its purpose.

"Hello. I'm Dr. Knight." He smiled and reached for Job's hand

Job shook hands and introduced himself to the slim

gentleman of average height with a Middle-Eastern shaped beard. He was impeccably attired. Job's excitement burst open when his memory caught up with his eyesight. "You're a jazzman. A *big time* jazz musician. Umm, Zachary Knight, the alto saxophonist. I saw you months ago at the Rhythm Room."

He expressed sophisticated amusement. "That's my hobby. At my day job, they call me Dr. Knight. You call me Zachary."

Dr. Knight took the application and examined it with precision. "I have been briefed, more like drilled, on recent discoveries about you."

Job's leg swung once before he grabbed his knee. "My application," he murmured.

Dr. Knight fanned the pages of the application, and placed it in a folder labeled with Job's full name: Joseph Bertram Wright. He looked straight at Job.

Job looked nowhere. He was determined to do what he should've done when he applied to Paradise Schools; apply with total honesty.

"I've considered your coming to Deer Valley Schools very carefully," Dr. Knight told him.

"Yes sir, but I want you to know—"

"Let me finish, Mr. Wright." Dr. Knight sat back and relaxed in his chair. "The findings are most unfortunate. They were unfortunate from the standpoint that Mr. McManus was dumb enough to let his board dictate to him who to keep and who to let go."

Job couldn't believe that he was hearing someone downgrade the Paradise School's superintendent. His attention was diverted, in part, because the gist of the meeting was yet mystery.

And, though he vowed never to admit it, his anxiety about the meeting had stirred his physical senses; he needed to use the restroom. "Excuse me?"

"We don't have an available, permanent business and technology position in any of our schools right now."

Job was disappointed.

"We would like you to sign on as a part-time instructor with full-time pay until a permanent position opens. Will you consider that?"

Job was elated. Halfway in was better than not in at all. "I just considered the position. The answer is yes."

"Great." Dr. Knight gave him directions for completing his employment forms, security passes, and other details. "By the way," he said, "your references were impeccable, and the certified copy of the letter from Paradise Schools gave us a detailed explanation of your misfortunes."

"Letter? From Paradise Schools?"

"Well, the copy came from McManus, but it was written by a Mr. Delvin Storm." Dr. Knight had a look of amazement. "What? Don't you know him?"

Then, he really had to use the restroom. But it would've been to vomit. "Yes . . . I know him. But I didn't use him as a character or career reference." *Now this I don't believe.*

"Sometimes in life, Mr. Wright, circumstances present themselves in a positive fashion, without our interference. Sometimes, things are just meant to be . . . you are now leaving it alone," Dr. Knight joked.

"Yeah, I agree. Blessings in life will come." Job wondered how that blessing came about. "But Delvin Storm?"

Times had improved. Things were healthier. At least, that was what Monica believed.

Improved times and healthier things were in the forecast; God's blessings made her want to celebrate. The rain check she promised for Job had now been forty-eight hours later, but it wasn't too late. Tacos, various chilies, and Mexican cheese dishes formed a culinary bouquet that seemed to stick to the adobe walls, breathe, and sing in chorus, *Hallelujah.*

And it was all for her man.

She was ready for the positive outcome from his meeting at Deer Valley. Her faith told her that it would be so.

And when he got home, he stopped in the foyer.

Monica laughed because she knew the aroma was paralyzing him. The last time she cooked Southwestern cuisine, they were merely planning a move to Phoenix. Now, they had become a fixture.

Job stepped toward the kitchen, and, as he began to speak, the phone rang, and he answered.

Job started doing silly things: rolling his eyes, pulling the receiver from his ear and holding it in the air, or making faces with his tongue. He was definitely out of character.

"Fontella?" Monica asked.

He nodded in the positive.

Fontella must've gone into a stream of indeterminable sentences. He acknowledged her with happy sounding grunts. "Listen." He covered the phone with his palm and tried to make Monica take the phone.

Monica twisted her mouth at him.

Job told Fontella, "We're gonna have to call you back. Probably tomorrow. Or the next day." He laughed aloud.

"Short, sweet, to the point," Monica chimed.

Job said, "See ya," and hung up. And then they both laughed.

Job had to lay out the details of his interview with Dr. Knight twice. The first time came out in warp speed. The repeat was understandable. "I look back, thinking about how I most likely could have bypassed some problems if I had confronted them in the onset."

Monica responded, "It wasn't supposed to happen that way."

"Yeah," Job agreed, "We were destined to go through it and make us better. I know I'm a better man for it. How do you feel?"

Instead of answering his request for an explanation, she moved toward the sink and lowered a skillet she had emptied into it. "Since I've been married to you, it's been one thing after another." She moved a strand of hair. "I'm tired now. Really tired."

Job looked as though he had contracted shingles. "I've really put God in my life," he pleaded.

Oh my God, he doesn't get it. I'm tired. Monica knew she had his psyche off-centered. If he'd only known that the fatigue was a result of her pregnancy.

While they were hand in hand, Job led Monica out to the suite's balcony that evening. The lights of the Phoenix suburbs were twinkling out in the distance where crowds of city dwellers were rushing about to late night restaurants and bars, doing whatever they did on Mondays when they were restless and not ready to go to their homes and destinations.

Keep me in your care, Lord. Monica was glowing in a tide of joy and security. She stared into Job's eyes. "I love you, man."

He responded with a smooth, sultry, "I love you, too."

They sat down in a couple patio chairs, looking into each other's eyes. Job poured himself an Arnold Palmer from a pitcher on the patio table. "God is good."

"He is."

"Ahh. Isn't this great?" He didn't wait for an answer. "I just want to take a moment to feel the warmth against my face, view the peaks of the mountains, and listen as the wind work its way between buildings across the city's industrialized desert."

"Boy, you so stupid," Monica said. She couldn't contain the giggle that had been welling inside her ever since Job came home.

Job said, "I know I'm being silly. I just feel, God, I feel blessed, you know?"

"Blessed. That's the right word for now," Monica said lightheartedly. Then she paused, batted her eyes, and then she planted an intentional look of solemnity on her face. "But I want you to know that you've gotten me into some trouble." But she kept grinning; she couldn't help it.

Job wasn't picking up on her childish behavior. He sighed as though he was preparing himself. He reached over, took her hand, and said, "Okay, baby. Tell me about it."

Baby. Mmm, he's almost right. "Honey, it's the kind of trouble that makes me have to decide on a blue room or a pink." She pursed her lips and waited for Job's next response.

Job's speech started drifting off on some subject, and then he said, "Blue? Pink?" He tried to rise out of his chair, but he lost balance and fell forward, landing on his knees. Job looked over at Monica, who was then laughing uncontrollably. "Oh, my God," he said, "are you serious?"

Between pants of laughter, Monica said to him, "Yes, honey. I want to introduce to you baby boy, or baby girl, Wright."

Job gave up on getting back in his chair, and sat down on the concrete balcony floor. "Monica," he whimpered. Tears welled in his eyes, and then they dropped. He touched her belly. "You're beautiful, this is beautiful. Now this is living well."

Monica planted her legs across his thighs and looked into his eyes. "We're not living well. People that live their lives without God can do that. We're living *right*."

READER'S GUIDE QUESTIONS

1. What story parallels do you see between Joseph Bertram Wright and the Old Testament, Biblical Job?
2. In what way did Delvin Storm refuse to harm Job? Compare this to God's refusal in allowing Satan to harm Job in a particular way.
3. Should a person receive prison time for ignoring an acquaintance's committal of a crime?
4. Which caused Job more complications: Delvin's plots against him, or the poor decisions Job made for himself?
5. Can you recall a time when a spiritual revelation or enlightenment helped you see the error of your ways?
6. Which scripture (at the beginning of each chapter) gave you the best insight to the plot of the story?
7. Consider the steps Job took to avoid Bianca Rizzo's sexual advances. Could he have done more to avoid the temptation? Is it really possible for a twentieth century male to avoid or not yield to a woman's devices?
8. There wasn't an opportunity for Delvin to be baptized by Shiloh. Do you consider him to be saved? Are deathbed repentances possible?
9. In the story, do you believe God reserved blessings for Job and Monica until a certain point in their lives? Why were blessings eventually showered on them?
10. Do you see any justification in Job answering 'no' on the Paradise School's application? What would you do if a false answer stood between you and a good job?

ABOUT THE AUTHOR

Titus David Pollard was born in Michigan, raised in Tennessee, and currently resides with his wife in North Carolina. He's multitasking as a residential and commercial realtor, award winning music instructor, actor, composer and author. *Living Right On Wrong Street* is his breakout novel. He is currently anticipating the completion of his second novel.

Titus Pollard loves to talk to people! You may contact him for questions, comments or engagements at *learn gospelmusic@nc.rr.com*. Visit him at *www.tituspollardpublishing.com*

Urban Christian His Glory Book Club!

Established January 2007, *UC His Glory Book Club* is another way by which to introduce to the literary world, Urban Book's much-anticipated new imprint, **Urban Christian** and its authors. We are an online book club supporting Urban Christian authors by purchasing, reading and providing written reviews of the authors' books that are read. *UC His Glory* welcomes both men and women of the literary world who have a passion for reading Christian based fiction.

UC His Glory is the brainchild of Joylynn Jossel, Author and Executive Editor of Urban Christian and Kendra Norman-Bellamy, Author and Director of Talent & Operations for Urban Christian. The book club will provide support, positive feedback, encouragement and a forum whereby members can openly discuss and review the literary works of Urban Christian authors. In the future, we anticipate broadening our spectrum of services to include: online author chats, author spotlights, interviews with your favorite Urban Christian author(s), special online groups for *UC Book Club* members, ability to post reviews on the website and amazon.com, membership ID cards, *UC His Glory* Yahoo Group and much more.

Even though there will be no membership fees attached to becoming a member of *UC His Glory Book Club*, we do expect our members to be active, committed and to follow the guidelines of the Book Club.

UC His Glory **members pledge to:**

- Follow the guidelines of *UC His Glory Book Club*.
- Provide input, opinions, and reviews that build up, rather than tear down.
- Commit to purchasing, reading and discussing featured book(s) of the month.
- Agree not to miss more than three consecutive online monthly meetings.
- Respect the Christian beliefs of *UC His Glory Book Club*.
- Believe that Jesus is the Christ, Son of the Living God

We look forward to the online fellowship.

Many Blessings to You!

Shelia E Lipsey
President
UC His Glory Book Club

**Visit the official Urban Christian Book Club website at *www.uchisglorybookclub.net*